'Charles L. Harness is a weaver of spells – descriptions swirl, take shape and flow out to catch the reader in a web . . . you suspend disbelief immediately and marvel in enjoyment.'

– *Books & Bookmen*

'The odd thing is that fantasy on such a scale becomes almost hypnotic.' – *Sunday Times*

A novel of complex incident with a wealth of imagery; on one level a thoroughly enjoyable galactic mystery, on another a satisfying exploration of the themes of cyclical recurrence, time, identity, chance and determination.

Also by Charles L. Harness in Panther Books

*The Rose*

Charles L. Harness

# The Ring of Ritornel

Panther

Granada Publishing Limited
Published in 1974 by Panther Books Ltd
Frogmore, St Albans, Herts AL2 2NF

First published in Great Britain
by Victor Gollancz Ltd 1968
Copyright © Charles L. Harness 1968
Made and printed in Great Britain by
Richard Clay (The Chaucer Press) Ltd
Bungay, Suffolk
Set in Linotype Plantin

This book is sold subject to the condition that it
shall not, by way of trade or otherwise, be lent,
re-sold, hired out or otherwise circulated without
the publisher's prior consent in any form of binding
or cover other than that in which it is published
and without a similar condition including this
condition being imposed on the subsequent
purchaser.
This book is published at a net price and is
supplied subject to the Publishers Association
Standard Conditions of Sale registered under the
Restrictive Trade Practices Act, 1956.

# The Ring of Ritornel

## The Cycles of the Ring

# 1: The Die Is First Cast

'Magister,' said the Captain deferentially but firmly, 'I will take you no further. We are now well beyond the danger point, and we have yet to close the quarry.'

The young man in the simple blue tunic smiled. 'Your jaw is set hard, Captain, and your face is pale. Are you afraid?'

Captain Andrek studied his guest with blunt honesty. He found such chill hauteur vaguely disquieting in one who had barely attained his majority. This, he presumed, was the consequence of centuries of ancestors accustomed to command. The young man's dark, humourless eyes held a striking presence; he wore no ornament of rank, or badge of authority, nor had he need of any.

The Captain thought briefly of his own background, and knew there was no comparison. For generations the Andreks had given their share of professional men to the advancement of their corner of civilization: military men, physicians, advocates, artists, even theologians for the temples. The Captain had a tremendous respect for the non-violent professions, but he loved space and – some said – danger, and was happiest in action and combat. He had long ago reconciled himself to the probability that he would be killed in service. Yet, now, when the moment seemed clearly upon him, he was shaken. It was all wrong. This was not a proper way to die. Furthermore, he was totally unaccustomed to this brute clash of wills. He did not know how to deal with it. Still, a direct question had been put to him, and he had to try to answer it.

'Afraid, sire? I served with your father in the Terror mop-ups. After he died, I served your uncle, the Regent. Next week, after your coronation, I hope I will be privileged to serve you, as I have them. Until now, sire, no Delfieri has asked me whether I was afraid. And until now, I have not been afraid. But now ... Yes, sire, I am afraid – that you may not return from this hunting trip. And it is a great fear.'

'I have given you a direct order, Captain.'

The officer stood mute.

It was suddenly becoming clear to the other officers and crew that in this conflict between two personalities, the irresistible force, whose very whim was the law of the Home Galaxy, had finally met an immovable object – their captain. And it was equally clear that this kind of thing had never before happened to the young man in blue. At first, he was too astonished to be angry. Even when he got over his surprise, he was still not angry; only logical.

'Captain, you are right on one point. We *are* running out of time. But the trail is hot. It is now or never, for I can never come here again. You will proceed as ordered, or I will have you shot for mutiny.' His voice was almost casual.

Captain Andrek, not commonly given to the use of adjectives in his thinking, now found himself indulging in strange imagery, and he considered his own mental processes with mingled fascination and amazement.

Throughout his long career in the League navy, Death had been a very personal and intimate companion. His wife (whom he had adored while she lived) had wryly named Death his mistress. This had puzzled him. He had always accepted Death as a condition of his life, but had never (he thought) actively sought her. There were rules about Death in the service. All his life he had followed the rules. He had been faithful to his contract with Death, and it had never occurred to him that finally Death would be unfaithful. She was sometimes cruel (he'd often wondered whether he would die screaming), but at least his own Death ought to be a phenomenon directed exclusively at him, and in which he would play a vital role. And now this. Death by default. Death was bored by him – if it noticed him at all. It was a farce, a silly playlet without merit or point, a chance encounter between strangers. Death was not scintillating; Death was a mindless oaf.

He thought of his sons. Omere the poet – the strange one. And Jamie, the logical one, not yet in his teens. From here on they would have to take care of each other.

He looked around calmly at the shocked faces of the under-officers, then spoke to the Lieutenant. 'If I am killed, it is nothing. But get the ship out of here, quickly.'

The young man in the blue tunic nodded to his aide. 'Huntyr, kill him.'

Huntyr was a big man, yet quick and nervous in his movements. He had none of the ponderous gentleness that often accompanies a big frame. His face held more cunning than intelligence. And it was a subservient face, which frankly drew its substance from the young Magister, thereby being pleasantly released from personal judgments, and choices between moral

8

values. Captain Andrek wondered where Oberon had picked him up. The association seemed to reflect some subterranean malignancy in Oberon's own mentality, and augured ill for his approaching reign.

Huntyr started to draw his biem.

The young man frowned. 'Not the biem, you fool. It will not fire in the Node area.'

'Sorry.' Huntyr replaced the biem, drew his slug-gun in a smooth motion, and fired. Captain Andrek staggered against the wardroom wall, clutching his chest. There, he floated up slowly in a weightless heap. Blood circled a neat hole in his shirt over his heart.

Oberon sighed. 'Get rid of him.'

Two ratings finally clacked on magnetic shoes over to the corpse and shoved the body ahead of them into the pilot room.

'Lieutenant,' said the young man to the nearest stricken face, 'will you accept my orders?'

Just at this moment, parts of the Lieutenant's cerebral processes were jammed, awry, and other parts were whirring senselessly. Nothing inside his head seemed to mesh, grab, or take hold. Nothing like this had ever come up in the classrooms at the academy. However, his ultimate reaction, while not textbook, nevertheless promised survival.

'Yes, sire,' he whispered.

'Good. What is the latest on the quake?'

'Time is still oh seven hundred.'

'Probability?'

'Oh point eight nine. Up two-tenths, sire.'

'Have you ever been in a quake, Lieutenant?'

'No, sire.'

'Do you know anyone who was ever in a quake?'

'Yes, sire. That is, I knew them before . . .'

'Before they were killed in the quake, you mean.'

'Yes, sire.'

'*Xerol* is a very strong little ship, Lieutenant, specially built. It's supposed to resonate with the wave-length of the quake.'

'Yes, sire.'

'But you don't really believe it, do you?'

'I believe *Xerol* is strong and specially built, sire. And it might even resonate. But a space quake is like a living thing, sire, contrary and capricious. It might not vibrate at the predicted frequency. Or it might start out at the right frequency and then change to another one. Those physicists at the Node

9

Station are sometimes wrong. And if I may make a point, sire, *they* left the Station two days ago.'

Oberon laughed.

'If I am concerned,' said the Lieutenant, 'it is not for the ship, or myself, or the crew.'

Oberon frowned. 'Let's not go into *that* again. Now, if you would help me into this suit.'

'Of course, sire. Yet —' He hesitated. 'May I speak freely?'

'Please do.'

'The Magister is proving a thing that does not need to be proved.'

'You are oversimplifying, Lieutenant. You perceive only limited sets. After my coronation, there shall be no more hunting. The last of the Delfieri will belong to the state, body and soul. So, in this last hour I must get enough hunting to last the rest of my life, for I shall never enter the Node again. When I grow old sitting at the Twelve-Table in the Great House, I want this to remember, and to think back on.' He paused, musing. 'Did you know the son of the late Captain Andrek, Omere, the Laureate?'

'Only by reputation, sire.'

'Omere has written an epic for my coronation. He will soon programme it into the great computer, for delivery with full orchestration at the proper time in the ceremonies.'

'It is known, sire,' said the officer cautiously.

'How can an epic be written for a man who has reached his majority and done nothing?'

'Omere writes for your *being* the crown, sire. Not for *doing* anything. It is not necessary to do anything.'

Oberon brushed that aside. 'It may be something of an advantage never to have done anything,' he said dryly, 'and there may be even a degree of notoriety in this. Yet it can be carried too far. I would like to justify that epic. Omere is the greatest poet in all the Thousand Suns. I have heard a pre-run of the tape. It makes my skin tingle. I think to myself, am I this Oberon of whom he sings? Oh, to own a brain like that! I would rather have written the epic than slay the krith. When I am crowned, I think I shall attach him permanently to the Great House, whether he will or no.'

He turned to the raman at the scope. 'Report,' he said softly.

'Eighteen kilometres. Course steady. Closing, one kilometre per minute.' The raman's voice took on an uneasy edge. 'Sire, the mass confirms at twenty-one hundred kilos. It is probably a krith.'

'Of course it is a krith,' murmured Oberon. 'The most vicious of the cryotheres.'

The Lieutenant broke in. 'Shall I load the bow guns, sire?'

'Certainly not.' Oberon picked up his helmet.

'May I assemble a rifle party to accompany you?' said the Lieutenant unhappily.

'No.' Oberon pulled his helmet down over his chest and locked his visor. 'Cut engines in five minutes.' His voice took on a mocking metallic quality through the inter-com. 'And stop sweating. It makes me nervous.'

'Sire, we have to be out of the Node within the hour. . . .'

'I know. Now cease this concern with trivialities and attend to business. As soon as I leave, activate the tractor beam and stand by to focus out a line on the meanest creature ever hauled out of the Node.'

The Lieutenant gave up. 'Yes, sire.' He opened the inner door of the space lock, helped Oberon into the cramped chamber, and spun the hatch shut behind him.

A few seconds later Oberon floated free of the little ship, and the exhaust of his suit-jet twinkled in an ever-lengthening trail ahead of the ship. He gave himself twenty minutes to find and slay the krith, ten minutes to rendezvous with the ship, and lock the tractor beam, and a final thirty minutes to get *Xerol* out of the quake area.

The ship disappeared behind him into the black depths of the Node.

Oberon looked about him into dark nothingness and felt a sudden awe. He was at the centre of creation. He pondered this. The universe expands. Hydrogen is continuously created. Yet the density of matter remains a constant – about one proton per cubic metre. Which means that space must also be continuously created. Where does this new space and new matter first greet the universe? As far away from existing matter – which is to say – the galaxies, as possible. The locus is the central area between the galaxies. And where the galaxies appear as groups or clusters, this locus is at their centre, their Node. So space is born out of the womb of the Deep, and begins life at the Node.

How strange, the Node! Here, at the geometric centre of the Twelve Galaxies, the expanding universe gives birth to new space, amid titanic birth pangs, vast quakes in space that release unimaginable energies. And strange life-forms come to feed on those energies, and stranger life preys on that life. At the bottom of the life cycle are the ursecta, minute creatures like the plankton in the great seas of his home planet, Goris-Kard. The ursecta in turn are the staple diet of larger creatures, and these in turn are eaten by still larger. And at the top of this pyramid of cryotheres are the great carnivores, and of these the most dangerous is the winged spider, the krith, fast, cunning, terrible.

He looked about him. The darkness was total. This was not surprising. The Node was the point in space farthest from matter in this part of the universe: the central point of the vast hypothetical dodecahedron formed by the twelve faces of the local cluster of galaxies.

From here, the individual galaxies – each over three million light years distant – were barely visible as hazy points of light. He turned over slowly and looked about him. One by one he picked out the twelve. 'Overhead' was a pinpoint of light, the Home Galaxy – at this distance, not detectably different from its spiral neighbour, Andromeda. By twisting his head he found the others. In all, three spirals, six ellipsoids, and three irregulars. Actually there were four irregulars, if both of the Magellanics were counted. But everyone – including the Magellanics themselves – considered the twin clouds as one. Twelve in all. Alea completed.

Even as he stared, something blotted out the points of light ahead of him. And then something long and sticky struck his side and coiled like a whip around his waist, where it clung. The great arachnid was trying to truss him up in a web before closing in. But he was prepared for this, and cut the strand ends immediately. And then another filament hit him, and another. For a few seconds he was very busy with the knife.

Finally free, he checked his scope hurriedly.

The krith filled the plate. It was charging.

Despite his thermals, Oberon suddenly felt cold.

He lined up the cross hairs of the slug-gun. The creature had to be hit in the body. A wing shot was worse than useless. When the metal pellets penetrated the chitinous shell of the body, they provided nuclei that immediately crystallized the beast's already super-cooled body fluids. The horrid creature would be converted instantly to a frozen statue, and could then be hauled back to Goris-Kard for dissection and mounting.

He fired. Even as the recoil turned him head over heels, he knew the shot had hit a wing.

And then something gashed him painfully in the leg. Frozen spatters of his own blood clattered against his helmet. He turned wildly to fire again. But his port body jet had been hit. He spun in a crazy arc. The cross hairs wouldn't line up. He was hit again – in the back – hard. A filament coiled around his gun and jerked it loose from his hands. The krith was trying to kill him so that *he* would freeze. After that he could be hauled away to some distant webby lair and there be eaten at leisure.

But just as he had resigned himself to death, he heard urgent voices on his phones, and sensed that guns were firing all around him. Huntyr and the Lieutenant had followed him, and had witnessed his humiliation. Before he blacked out, he cursed.

They revived him on board. He glared up at Huntyr's white face and managed a harsh whisper. 'I told you not to follow me.'

The aide gestured helplessly. 'Sire, we *had* to come after you. Just after you left, the Lieutenant received a revised estimate of the quake from the computer-broadcaster at the Node Station.'

'Really?' His eyes shifted to the Lieutenant. 'Well?'

The Lieutenant licked his lips and looked at his watch. He spoke with difficulty. 'It's due in two minutes, plus or minus thirty seconds.'

Oberon looked over at him curiously. 'What are you doing about it?'

'I've called the Group. They're sending two flights – one to come into the quake zone. The other will stand outside. After the quake, the second flight will come in, also.'

'I see. You don't think either flight can do anything?'

'Not really, sire. We're still very close to epicentre. If we get out, we won't need either flight. If we don't get out, the first flight will get hit the same as us. In that case, the second flight will come in afterwards for what is left of us.' The young officer knew he was not saying it properly, but he rushed on. 'And now, sire, if I might make a suggestion, we want to get you inside this special emergency suit, with foam sealant.'

'I suppose so. Pass the word, suits for all hands.' Oberon sighed. 'A frustrating day.' He reached into the blue folds of his tunic and drew out his necklace with its pendant, the golden dodecahedral die of Alea. Each face bore a number, from one to twelve, and each number was a sign from Alea. He unfastened it and held it in his palm a moment.

'Perhaps Alea will say, how it shall be with us.'

Huntyr's face was ashen. 'It is sacrilege to call idly on the goddess!'

'Whether I call idly is entirely up to Alea,' said Oberon

calmly. He let the die float away and took the foam suit from the Lieutenant. 'When the quake comes, *Xerol* will be her die cup.'

'It's *Xerol*, all right,' said the Rescue Commodore softly. Not being given to superfluities, he added only mentally, 'Or what's left of her.'

The search beam from the patrol launch stroked the stricken ship from stem to stern. There was no movement.

The Commodore barked into the communicator. 'Lock on, midship, by that break in the plates. I want four men with torches to slice out a hole big enough for a stretcher party. On the double. They'll save time if they work next to the crack in the hull. When you get inside, spread out. I'm coming in with you, and I'll start with the pilot-room. Call me there if you find anything.'

He was not surprised at what he found inside *Xerol*. The portable searchlights showed havoc everywhere. The quake must have continued for some time after it had broken the spine of the ship and let in the awesome cold of space. Men had been quick-frozen and their bodies cracked like whips. As he worked his way up to the pilot-room an occasional arm or leg floated past him, and his stomach began to writhe.

The door was jammed, and they had to burn it off its hinges. Inside, he saw Captain Andrek not even suited, and slumped queerly on the wall. The whole thing was incomprehensible. The Captain was a splendid officer, with an impeccable record. It had been his duty to protect the Magister, but he obviously had failed in his duty. Perhaps the Captain was lucky. Had he lived, he would face a summary court martial and certain death.

Just then he got an urgent call on the communicator. 'Commodore! Calling from sick-bay!'

He didn't get it at first. 'Sick-bay?'

'*Xerol* sick-bay, sir. Looks like we've found the Magister. His chest is crushed, but he may be alive. And another chap, a big fellow, with his head banged up. Sealant still oozing out of their suits, no pulse, but body temperatures within permissible limits.'

'Stretcher them out of there. I'll alert our own sick-bay to get ready. Anybody else?'

'No, sir. Everybody else was killed. We'll need a fair-sized burial detail.'

'No time for that, Sergeant. We'll send a tug out later for

*Xerol*. You get the Magister on board within three minutes or you will never see Goris-Kard again.'

'Yes, *sir*.'

The Commodore met them on the cat-walk. It was indeed the Magister. The other one, the big man, he did not recognize. And the Magister's chest, as reported, was indeed crushed. Jagged red pieces of rib-bone had punctured the suit. Foam had evidently covered some of the protruding pieces and had then broken away. The Commodore's stomach was bothering him again. As the sergeant hurried past, he held out his hand and gave the Commodore something. 'What is this, Sergeant?'

'An Alean die, sir. It's gold. Must belong to the Magister.'

'What number was showing?'

'Number one, sir.'

The Commodore, a practising Alean, felt his flesh crawl. One, the sign of the false god Ritornel, and disaster at the Node. It had to be. 'Carry on, Sergeant,' he growled.

## 2 : Jimmie and Omere

For a long time the vibrations and the flashing lights seemed only a part of Jimmie's dream. In the dream, he was at the Node, the cross-roads of the universe, and the gods were dicing for his life. At each roll of the die, a great space quake would crash through his body, and in his head the lights would go on and off.

Jimmie finally woke up, and when he did, he was awake all over. He didn't have to stretch and cough and groan the way Omere did. He turned off the alarm button on his night table. The bed ceased its rhythmic insistent shaking, and the ceiling lights stopped flashing and came on full. Jimmie didn't even have to look at the clock face. He knew that it was four in the morning, and that Omere wasn't home. Because if Omere were in bed, Jimmie's alarm would automatically have been deactivated. Therefore Omere wasn't home.

Jimmie found his robe and slippers and hurried into the phone room. He sat down in front of the multiceptor, fished the little black book out of the top drawer, and began dialling the long series of numbers that would connect his inquiry tapes simultaneously with nearly two hundred restaurants, bars, and sundry strange places strewn all over the night side of Goris-Kard.

He found the right place within minutes. 'The Winged Kentaur', an odd place, a bar with reading and music rooms, haunted by bearded, thin-faced men and the strangely-dressed articulate women they brought with them. Painters, writers, singers, poets, scientists, priests. Omere was often there. Jimmie thanked the receptionist, turned off the ceptor, then ran back to his room to get dressed. He checked his money. It was important to have the right change for the capsules. Nobody liked exchanging big bills this time of night – or morning, and sometimes they'd look you over, making sure you were just a ten-year-old kid all alone, and then they'd try to steal it from you. But he had to take *some* money. He calculated. He'd need, say, five gamma for the regular doorman, ten for that mean-looking substitute. He counted out fifteen and put it in his top jacket pocket.

He boarded the feeder tube in the corridor outside the apart-

16

ment, punched the computer co-ordinates inside the capsule, put the coins in the slots, and waited. The feeling of motion pressed at his stomach, then went away, and then there were turns, right, left, up, down. It was impossible to keep a sense of direction. And then it was over. The capsule rolled out to an exit tube, and he was on the brightly lit street. It was in the theatre district, and the drama-houses seemed to alternate with all-night bars.

The 'Winged Kentaur' was just ahead. In the luminous tridi sign over the doorway, he could see the kentaur's wings moving in slow majestic arcs. Omere had once tried to explain how the proprietor had selected the strange symbol. It was all mixed up in ancient fables that had come down from their Terrovian ancestors, centuries ago, and Jimmie doubted that he understood it all. The winged horse was the symbol of music, poetry, and the creative arts; and the kentaur was the symbol of the sciences, so a winged kentaur was the symbol of the best in the arts and sciences – the final step in the evolutionary process. But of course no such creature had ever really existed.

The doorman smiled wryly at him and took his money with a nod. 'Second room back.' Jimmie thanked him, braced himself, and walked in.

Inside it was a strange blurry mixture of sound, smells, smoke, and laughter.

A little group, mostly women, was watching the visi-screen. Even without the narrator's explanation, Jimmie knew instantly what it was. Terror burning. It was all being broadcast from Terror's single moon, complete with sound. You could hear the low eerie moaning of the flames, and the hiss of steam rising in hideous clouds from the boiling seas. All life was of course long vanished. The narrator was talking: 'The mills of justice grind slowly, but they grind exceeding fine. And what will be the fate of this terrible world? When the fires die down sufficiently, the great shaft will be drilled to the iron core, the explosives placed, and Terror will be towed far inward to the Node, and there be blown to bits – an eternal lesson to tyranny. . . .'

Jimmie walked over. Sure enough, there was Omere, right in the middle. Jimmie frowned. Sometimes it was hard to get Omere away from women. Jimmie didn't like the women. He had a very vague recollection of his mother, who had died when he was very small, but he was certain she had nothing in common with these creatures.

And now one of them happened to spot him. She tapped

17

Omere on the shoulder and called out harshly, 'Hey, it's the kid! Join the party, kid!'

His brother turned on his swivel stool and looked full at him.

'Hello, Jim-boy.' The secret grin, known but to Jimmie, was spreading across the youthful face. Whenever Omere did that, the boy's heart pounded. It didn't matter that the face was prematurely lined and furrowed and glowed ghoulishly under the dim blue ceiling radiants. It was the handsomest face in the world.

But now to business. Jimmie said flatly: 'You have dress rehearsals for the Coronation recitals this afternoon, at the Great House.'

Omere sighed. 'Another night slain, by the icy edge of innocence. Yes; the Coronation.' He took a sip from his glass, then put it down clumsily on the 'chord', where it nearly overturned. 'Logic. When all else fails, he retreats into logic. Logic makes no sense. If you keep this up, dear little brother, we'll turn you over to the advocates. Rehearsals? Why should I worry about rehearsals? While I'm here, working my fingers to the bone, where is the distinguished subject of my new epic? I'll tell you. Oberon is on a hunting trip, having the time of his life. Is *he* worried about rehearsals?'

Jimmie bored in closer and took Omere by the sleeve. 'What's that got to do with you? Oberon is the Magister. He can do anything he likes.' His voice was becoming anxious. 'But you have got to get some rest before rehearsal.'

Omere appeared to consider the matter briefly. He began to chant:

> 'If you make me go to bed,
> I'll put a bullet in my head.
> Maybe two, if you are rough.
> Three should surely be enough.'

Jimmie grinned. This meant his brother would come peacefully.

He was about to help Omere down from the bar chair when someone spoke just behind him.

'Who is your young friend, Mr. Andrek?'

Jimmie turned and looked up curiously at the speaker. The man – if he could be called that – was clearly not a native of Goris-Kard. Jimmie had never seen anyone like him before in his life. He wore the pale blue robes of the Great House, and on each lapel were the eight-armed spider-like insignia that indi-

18

cated his profession. He was a physician. On each hand was a white glove. His head and neck were draped in a blue hood. Jimmie thought for a moment that the hood covered even his eyes, until the eyes blinked. Then he noticed that there were actually two holes in the hood for the eyes. And such eyes! They seemed to flicker with a strange blue radiation, as though lighted from within the skull. Jimmie shivered.

But Omere just laughed. 'Doc,' he said, 'this is my brother James.'

The doctor's gloved hands grasped each other to form a circle, in the manner of the Ritornellians, and he bowed gravely. 'We are one in Ritornel,' he murmured.

'With Ritornel we return,' replied Jimmie politely.

All this seemed to amuse Omere greatly. 'You have to be careful with Doc. He *really* believes in Ritornel. You'd think he invented the whole thing.'

The blue lights in the doctor's eyes seemed to vibrate. 'It's the duty of every man to formulate his own gods,' he said sombrely. 'And then, while he lives, to follow through to the end. Only then can he accept the grey robes of the pilgrim, for the last journey, for his reward and his release. Only then can he accept death.'

'Don't be alarmed, Jim-boy,' said Omere, with faint malice. 'The good doctor isn't quite ready to die. He's waiting for the Sign.'

' "Sign"?' said Jimmie, puzzled.

'The Laureate cloaks the truth with humour,' said the doctor. '"Yet, by my beard, it is the truth. I await the Sign. The Twelve Galaxies will be brought to an end by the omega of Ritornel. Yet, Ritornel decrees that the end is but the beginning of a new life. For that new life, a pair must be saved – male and female – the cream of creation. And a planet must be saved for them, to be their home, for them and their descendants. These things shall come to pass when we see the Sign.'

'And what *is* the Sign?' asked Jimmie curiously.

'A woman,' said the doctor. 'It is written. A virgin, born from a man. A motherless child.' The pale blue lights seemed to burn into Jimmie's head. Jimmie felt the hair on the nape of his neck stand up. He didn't like this. And certainly he didn't understand it. He took a step backwards.

Omere came to the rescue. He yawned elaborately and arose unsteadily. 'So much for Ritornel. Let's get out of this den of religion before we run into an Alean.'

Jimmie stepped over to help him, but the doctor was already there.

'Allow me.'

Jimmie hesitated, but he was helpless. Together they helped Omere down from the chair, and then the three of them bumped their way through crowded rooms and out into the street.

Here, Omere had a bad coughing fit. Jimmie cleaned up the sputum from his brother's blouse. It was blood-flecked. The doctor stood by silently. Omere seemed to read his thoughts. 'Let's get home, Jim-boy. It's not really bad.' The doctor helped Jimmie get Omere down to the tube entrance. It took both of them to put him inside the capsule and seated upright. Jimmie closed the door and, just before the capsule dropped into the subterranean entrails of the city, he stole a last covert look at the blue-robed figure behind them. All he could see in the semi-darkness were two points of blue light. They seemed to be studying him intently. He turned back quickly.

Back in the apartment, Jimmie put his groaning brother to bed. One sandal had somehow got lost; he removed the other, loosened the belt, and pulled the coverlet up gently.

Omere spoke out sleepily in the semi-darkness. 'Don't go just yet. Sit on the bed.'

Jimmie sat down. 'You should get some sleep.'

'I know. Dress rehearsal. What'll I wear?'

'Your clothes are all laid out. Your new black synthetics, black hose, ivory lace collar and cuffs.'

Omere was silent for a moment. Finally he said: 'The Commodore left *you* in *my* care, Jim-boy, and now you've got it all mixed up. One of these days he'll come blasting in from outer space, and we'll both be court-martialled.' He turned over and coughed hollowly into his pillow. 'I haven't done a very good job on you, have I?'

'Don't talk like that,' said Jimmie uneasily.

But Omere continued in sombre vein. 'If anything should happen to me before Dad gets home, you are to go to the dons in the prep school at the Academy of Justice. The papers are in my desk. The papers will tell you whom to see ... everything. There's plenty of money.'

Jimmie was shaken. 'Is your cough worse? I'll call the doctor right away.'

'No, no, don't do that. Doctors don't know anything. He'd

try to get me to cancel the rehearsal. He might even try to cut me out of the coronation. Imagine, the Laureate not reciting his epic at a coronation! And what a coronation ... the pomp and pageantry, music, priests chanting. Both temples, Ritornel and Alea, will be saying all kinds of words over Oberon.'

'Which temple do we believe in?'

'We burn incense in both temples,' said Omere blandly. 'We believe in everything. It takes twice as much faith, but it's safer. We stand still with Ritornel, while randomly advancing with Alea.'

Jimmie knew his brother was teasing him. They hadn't been inside a temple since he was seven. 'You're' – he sought for a word – 'cynical.'

Omere laughed silently. 'Such a big word from such a little boy. Yes, the dons will get you. Words are their business, their weapons in fighting the quarrels of other men.'

They had been over this before. 'I think I'd like to be a don,' said Jimmie. 'James, Don Andrek. How does that sound? Maybe I could even be a don in the Great House. Maybe I could serve Oberon himself.'

Omere frowned. 'Stay away from *him*. There are strange stories. Some say he'd just as soon look at you as shoot you.'

'You mean, "shoot you as look at you".'

'No, I don't. And that's the point.'

'Oh.' Jimmie didn't understand. But perhaps it was just as well. 'We have to stop, and you have to go to sleep. I'll be at school when it's time for you to wake up, but the alarm is set.'

'Thanks, Jim-boy. Goodnight.' Omere closed his eyes.

The first flush of dawn was beginning to filter through the balcony windows; it cast an eerie radiance on Omere's face. Jimmie started to pull the drapes, then stopped. He studied his brother's face for a long moment, in wonder and admiration. Ordinarily, he thought of Omere as handsome. The word that now occurred to him was 'beautiful'. His mother must have looked like this. Omere, he thought simply, I love you.

With an effort, he broke loose from the enchantment, drew the drapes silently, and tip-toed from the room.

He never saw that face again.

In the eighteen years that followed, when he rummaged through his collection of mental images of Omere, this final scene, with the enhaloed face, was always first to take form.

The Regent, Oberon's uncle, was so old that he seemed ageless. He had seen it all, not once, but many times. Life to him was like Oberon's boyhood carousel: wait a bit, and the whole thing comes around again. There were indeed Ritornellian aspects in his theo-philosophy, and in fact in decades previous he had carried the golden ring on the red cushion in the solemn annual processions. And yet, just as he was not an Alean, either in the letter or by spirit, neither did he adhere to Ritornel. Indeed, his religion was totally dynastic, and dealt with transcendental and celestial matters only to the extent that they promised an immediate benefit to the Delfieri line. And since the death of his younger brother, the anointed ruler, in the last days of the Terrovian war, he had emerged from retirement to hold the government together until Oberon became of age.

And thus it was by order of the Regent that Oberon's coronation and surgery proceeded simultaneously. It could hardly be otherwise. Extraordinary measures were necessary to preserve old friendships and to avoid offence to potential new allies. Oberon might be dying, but the coronation had to proceed. The ceremonies and invitations had been scheduled months in advance, and kings and chancellors from all the League suns, not to mention ambassadors from the Outer Galaxies, were in attendance. Even the Intergalactic Arbiters were there in their splendid robes, unanimous at least in their decision that so historic an occasion required their review.

The Regent's brows knitted. This is no fitting end, he thought. It was the Delfieri who brought Terror low. But for the stiffening of our purpose, and rallying the weaklings of the League, the devil-planet would not now lie a-burning. Perhaps no particular Delfieri is essential; but the blood is essential. And this wastrel Oberon is the last of us. Wild, inconsiderate brat! Always, we are out getting ourselves killed when we should be taking wives and establishing something for posterity.

But his barbaric black eyes softened as he considered his nephew. A complete Delfieri. And so this must be your miserable coronation. No, not like in the old days. As *his* grandfather had told *him*, these things in centuries past were a thirty-day riot. Before his ancient forebears found blatant piracy uneconomical and before they entered (with vast reluctance) into a more socially acceptable culture, a coronation was a thing to be remembered. Every wine vat in Goris-Kard was emptied. Unransomed captives were sacrificed, and the temple floors were awash with blood. And those were real temples, to proper gods, long before the philosophies of Alea and Ritornel began their insidious seduction of the flowering minds of the lusty League planets. And now, all was gone, all. Here and now, at this pallid proceeding, the only wine was in the sterilizing autoclaves in the operating room, and the only blood visible was that on the white gown of the Master Surgeon.

And thus for hours the procession of subdued celebrants circled the glass bubble of the improvised surgery. They moved in a living stream, on deep blue carpets, handwoven with threads of gold and noble metals, through a great room finished in hand-carved opulent wood-panelling (in strange contrast to the tiled sterility of the operating chamber in its centre). The air was heavy with incense. A choir chanted in the background, amid the muffled clangour of great bronze bells in the neighbouring Alcan and Ritornellian chapels. It could hardly be known whether the bells rejoiced or sorrowed, or indeed whether it made any difference one way or the other.

All the participants were exhausted, and yet the stream of potentates did not abate.

During these proceedings the Regent, and Galactic Laureate, and the musicians and chanters occupied a podium at the side of the operating room. Huntyr, functioning as the Regent's temporary aide, stood quietly behind the group, his face just beginning to heal under plastic skin. Only the golden patch glinting forebodingly over his left eye gave hint of his recent brush with death.

When Omere had understood what was expected of him in the modified ceremony, he was surprised only that he had not been shocked: but the whole affair was completely consistent with the bizarre tradition of the Delfieri. During the endless hours he had recited his Epic three times over; his voice was cracking, and he was beginning to feel giddy. He wondered what they would do to him if he simply fainted. He noticed then that the Regent was frowning at him, but Omere pondered the barbaric mixture of surgery and ceremony, and decided he couldn't care less.

The Regent's right hand was raw and swollen from hundreds of handshakes, but he hardly felt it. From his place in the receiving line, he could see the operating table, the bevy of white-clad nurses, and the sure, delicate motions of the Master Surgeon. The Regent knew that crushed sections of ribs were being cut away and stored carefully in frozen containers; these were samples being saved for the cell cultures. Since Oberon was probably going to die, a number of single viable cells selected from the jetsam of fragments would be cultured, by techniques known only to the Master Surgeon, in the hope that a new identical Oberon could eventually be grown, and the imperial lineage thereby preserved.

At this moment the sono under the Regent's left ear peeped gently. It was the pre-arranged signal from the Master Surgeon. The old man walked over to a nearby microphone. He could see the Master Surgeon watching him through the glass walls of the surgery. 'You want me, Surgeon?'

'Yes. I must bring Oberon into consciousness for a short time. I want the Laureate here inside. You know how Oberon feels about Omere. Selections from the Epic may well soothe and reassure Oberon during the period of consciousness.'

The old man had always regarded Oberon's fascination with poetry and the arts as a serious frailty in a Delfieri, a weakness that could only bring harm. And yet he was realistic enough to seize upon his nephew's strange interest, and to make use of it in an attempt to work on the youth's will to live. He looked over at the poet. 'They want you inside, to sing a few selections from the Epic while the Master Surgeon brings Oberon into temporary consciousness.'

'I will try. But my voice is nearly gone.' (And so am I, Omere wanted to add.) He pulled a tiny aspirator from his pocket, sprayed his throat, and was immediately struck by a coughing spasm. He wiped blood from his lips.

The Regent watched this with distaste. 'I will ask the Master Surgeon to give you something to hold you together for the necessary time.'

'I am grateful,' rasped Omere sardonically.

Inside, a nurse gave him a hypodermic. His larynx had immediate trouble with the bite of ozone and the odour of barely-dry bacteriostatic paint. And the sub-audio sterilizers set up interference patterns with his voice. It was going to be a fiasco, but perhaps Oberon would be too far gone to know. He selected the stanza beginning with the spread of Terror's warships throughout the Home Galaxy. He sang softly and didn't try for the high notes.

He then observed that Oberon's eyes were open, and watching him. He smiled wearily at the young Magister, then continued the stanza ... then stopped. For Oberon, with no air in his damaged lungs, was trying to whisper something.

'Finish ... Rimor ...?'

'The poetry computer is mechanically complete, Excellency,' said Omere, 'but I have not yet programmed it. This will require several weeks.'

'Programme it ... now ...'

'It shall be done, Excellency.'

Oberon closed his eyes.

'He is unconscious again,' the Master Surgeon said to Omere. 'You need not stay.' He looked at the Laureate sharply. 'How do you feel?'

'I think I —' Omere collapsed in a slow heap on the floor.

The Master Surgeon jerked his hooded head towards a nurse. 'Stretchers.'

As Omere was carried out, the Regent looked after him thoughtfully. He snapped his fingers for Huntyr. 'Take him to the Hospital Wing. And strap him down.'

The coronation continued.

In the final hour, Oberon was given the silver scroll of wisdom (which the priests could only place outside the glass door), the pails full of platinum coins to ensure prosperity for his reign, and finally he was appointed Defender of the Faiths whereby, amid much chanting, a golden ring of Ritornel was placed by the door by a minor Ritornellian priest, and then an Alean abbot forced himself to place the golden Alean die inside the ring.

And then surgery and coronation were complete. The last guest disappeared up the carpeted walkway.

The Master Surgeon had been on his feet with Oberon for nearly twenty hours, and had used up three consecutive sets of assistants. He stepped outside and on to the podium.

'How is it, Surgeon?' said the Regent.

'He might live, if he chooses to live.'

'How long to programme the poetry computer?'

'I would like to discuss that with you, sire. Can we go now to the Hospital Wing? There will be no change in Oberon's condition for some hours. But meanwhile, if we are to save the Delfieri line by cell cultures or by persuading Oberon to want to live, much work remains to be done this night.'

'After you, Surgeon.'

'Cell culture is best understood from a historical viewpoint,' said the Master Surgeon. He stood erect at the microscope work bench in the Parthenogenetic Laboratory, apparently untouched by the long day with Oberon. The Regent had sunk exhausted, in a sparsely-upholstered lab chair. The Surgeon continued quietly. 'In his first instant of existence, the Magister was but a single cell in the womb of his mother. That cell divided, then sub-divided, and continued to sub-divide. For seven or eight generations, all the thousands of resulting cells in this initial stage of development were identical. During this phase, no cells were formed recognizable as bone cells, or muscle cells, or nerve cells. But – in the next few cell generations, changes *did* begin. Thus, about ten days after fertilization we find three different kinds of cells, in outer, middle, and inner layers in the incipient embryo, which is now a barely visible hollow ball. The descendants of these layered cells become even more specialized as growth continues. And before the days of parthenogenesis, it was thought that this increasing specialization was irreversible.'

'What do you mean, irreversible?' asked the Regent.

'Before specialization began, any one of the cells could be separated from the cluster and caused to grow into a separate embryo. But after the cells have begun to specialize, they can reproduce only identical specialized cells; they can no longer produce all of the hundreds of different kinds of cells necessary to form a viable human foetus. The changes in the cell structure that cause specialization are thus normally irreversible.'

'I gather, then, that the parthenogenesis technique is aimed at reversing the irreversibility?'

'Exactly, Excellency.'

'Continue.'

'We have here a microsection of costal bone taken from the chest of the Magister. These bone cells descended from cells in the middle layer of the pin-point sized embryo. The same layer was ancestor to heart, muscle, and skin cells.'

'But how can muscle cells and bone cells descend from identical cells?'

'Certain genes within the cell become inactivated after a specified number of sub-divisions. It is, in fact, the withdrawal of combinations of specific genes from the coded genetic instructions of the chromosomes that results in the changes in the cells of subsequent generations. All the original genes of the original fertilized single cell are still present in each of the billions of cells of the embryo, but now, cell by cell, many of the genes are dormant, so that the correct daughter cells needed in succeeding stages in the growth of the embryo can be made. The success of parthenogenesis depends on awakening these sleeping genes. If this is done, the cell shall be as it was in the beginning, precisely identical to the first cell from which the Magister grew, and hence, in theory, capable of growing into a second Magister.'

'And how are the sleeping genes awakened?'

'By removing the blocking proteins from the deoxyribonucleic acid chains of the genes – the DNA. These proteins are protamines and histones – mildly basic. They have combined chemically with the mild acid of the DNA, but can be persuaded to relinquish their hold on the DNA if we expose them, very carefully, to a slightly stronger acid. All this has to take place within the cell nucleus, and the micro-procedure is rather delicate.'

'Surgery at the molecular level? I did not realize the technique existed. Tell me more.'

The Master Surgeon hesitated. 'More, sire, I cannot tell you. It is a secret of the Master Surgeons, passed down, one to the other, from the most distant generations.'

'Then I shall not pry.'

'The Regent is invited to watch.'

'Yes, I would like to.'

The Surgeon turned around and bent over his flasks. 'From this section of costal bone, we first isolate about twenty individual cells. This is a simple micro-surgical technique, which your excellency can follow on the microscope projection screen. As you can see, each cell looks like an elongated brick. Each is washed with sterile nutrient medium into its individual culture flask. And now we come to the crucial part, reactivation of the dormant genes.'

There was a sudden flashing movement. The Master Surgeon stripped the glove from his right hand. He seemed then to insert his index finger into the neck of the first flask. And then the glove was on the hand again. The great man turned to the Regent and bowed. 'And that is all there is to it.'

The Regent studied the hooded, glowing eyes. 'You mean, there is something in your body that awakens the genes?'

'Something like that. Of course, the bone cell must now travel the long road back, reversing some fifty generations of cell differentiation, with more and more genes awakening at each stage, until all are awakened, and the condition of the first cell is

27

reached. The gene-stuff is fragile, and the results are unpredictable. Parthenogenesis is a hazardous process at best. In the days of the Wars, the very conditions of high radiation levels that wrought mutations in the genes of sperm and ovum while they were yet in the body, endangered the cell cultures in the same way. And so it is now. Ironically, the recent great quake that has called for this specific attempt at parthenogenesis, may itself bring all our efforts to nothing. Even as we talk here, the first showers of hyper-drive cosmic rays generated by the quake are reaching us.'

'But these rooms are encased in a metre of lead,' demurred the Regent. 'Besides which, the planet itself lies between these rooms and the Node.'

'That may not be enough. Cosmic rays have been detected in mines several thousands of metres deep. We think that the strongest are able to pass entirely through the whole planet of Goris-Kard, right through the nickel-cobalt core. Even since we have been standing here, several cosmic rays have passed through my body.'

'How do you know that?'

'My sensory structure is – different from yours. I can detect electro-magnetic radiation in wavelengths considerably below the visible spectrum useful to your retina. There – a ray struck this very jar.'

'Throw it out.'

The Master Surgeon hesitated. 'I wonder. The chances that the ray struck the single cell to be cultured seem quite remote.'

'Then do as you like.'

'Thank you. I'd like to keep it for the time being. And now, if your excellency is satisfied with what has been explained and demonstrated so far, it would be best if I completed the cultures alone. This will take less than an hour, and then I will rejoin you in the room of Omere the poet.'

'Yes. I am satisfied. I will meet you there.'

'Hello, Doc.' Omere's eyes opened blearily, then closed again.

'You will address the Master Surgeon with more respect,' said Huntyr curtly.

Beneath twitching eyelids, Omere tried to focus on the big man. He attempted to rise on one elbow. Only then did he discover he was strapped to the bed. 'Must have been quite a party.' His head fell back on the pillow. 'I remember, now. The Coronation. I passed out. Never mix terza rima and iambic pentametre. What happened after that? Fill me in, blue eyes!'

'My boy,' said the Master Surgeon, 'you sang to the Magister for over twelve hours, without rest, and then you collapsed. Huntyr brought you here.'

'... the Magister?'

The Surgeon turned questioningly to the Regent, who had shrivelled wearily into a bedside chair. The old man nodded, and the Surgeon faced the poet again. 'The condition of the Magister is a state secret. However, for reasons that you will soon appreciate, there is no danger in entrusting this secret to you. The continued existence of Oberon of the Delfieri trembles in the balance. For the time being, everything that can be done for him medically has been done. He will be under hypno-sedation for three days to give our patchwork a chance. When he awakens, whether he lives or dies may well be his own mental choice. In one hand he will hold life; in the other, death. He has only to choose. The Regent, of course, desires that Oberon shall choose to live. In persuading him to this choice, you can be of great service to the state.'

'With more ditties and doggerel?'

'In a manner of speaking.'

'Get to the point.'

'We don't want you to collapse again.'

'Boorish of me, wasn't it?' Omere coughed. It was a gurgling hacking thing. He turned his head and spat something red into the tray by his pillow.

'There is no treatment for your lung disease. We think you are going to die. It could happen overnight.'

'So I have been told.'

'If you die, you will not be available to sing to the Magister when he awakens, and in that case, he may elect to die.'

'Fear not,' said Omere. 'When he arrives, I'll be there waiting. I'll teach him to play the harp.'

Huntyr was outraged. 'How can a dying man speak thus?'

The Regent silenced his aide with an irritated hand-wave. 'Master Surgeon, tell the poet that which he must know.'

'Omere Andrek,' said the Master Surgeon, 'we have decided that you will, in a sense, live.'

' "In a sense —?" '

'You have heard of the Rimor computer?'

'Of course. Oberon's pet project. I promised him I'd help programme the poetry and music circuits.'

'True. And you shall, although perhaps not exactly in the way that you had planned.' The Surgeon tugged briefly at the beard under his hood, then continued. 'The human brain has ten billion neurons, most of which are in the grey matter of the cerebrum. Rimor's equivalents of these circuits take time to programme. Yet, if Rimor were programmed and ready to function in three days, Oberon might listen to it when he regains consciousness; and listening, he might be persuaded to live. But Rimor is far from finished.'

'I know that.' For the first time, Omere felt uneasy. 'We need weeks to programme the electronic circuits so that they will correspond to those in the human cerebrum.'

'But,' said the Surgeon, 'if we had the essential sections of an actual living human cerebrum, we could complete Rimor within twenty-four hours. Fortunately, considering the time available, we will not need the entire brain. The cerebellum and medulla would be superfluous to our purpose, since they deal primarily with the more primitive functions such as internal organs, blood system, musculature, and skin. Even the cerebrum is not needed in its entirety. The temporal lobe, containing the auditory areas, and the prefrontal lobes, as the seat of intelligence, would of course be retained. But most of the areas in the central fissure responsible for vision, taste, smell, and touch, could be excised with little loss, and with great saving in time.'

There was a long silence. Sweat began to gather on Omere's face.

The Master Surgeon continued tonelessly. 'The surgery involved is simple and painless. The higher centres of consciousness will be anaesthetized, of course. The blood flow will be shunted to a cardiac pump, and adequate arterial pressure maintained throughout the procedure, before, during, and after transfer. The neck tissue and spinal chord will be severed. From there, the process is nearly identical to sterile cranial autopsy. I shall start with the usual biparietal incision extending across the cranial vault from the mastoid process. The temporalis muscles are dissected away from the cranial vault and retracted out of the area. A thin-edged biem is used to open the calvaria, and finally, after the dura mater has been divided along the line of the base incision, the brain is removed. The real work then begins, of selecting the needed elements and making the thousands of connections with the programme centre of the computer. The work is very intricate and time consuming, and will take two full days. You will regain consciousness on the third day. You will awaken into darkness, a spirit without body, floating. Your only tactile and motor associations with your environment will be your cerebral integration into your outgoing sound circuits and your incoming aural sensors. You will be able to speak, sing, and energize a fully orchestrated multitude of phonic instruments, and you will be able to hear anyone present in the Music Room. You will find that, instead of *conducting* orchestra and chorus, you will *be* piano, violins, brass, one hundred instruments, and forty voices. It will take you the balance of the third day to acquire a measure of proficiency in the use of your new facilities of orchestra and voice. You'll have the entire Music Room to yourself, with multi-stereo, reverberation ... whatever shall please you. Think, Omere! Your disease is incurable, but you can live!'

Omere writhed beneath the straps. 'I refuse. I'd rather die.'

'Your refusal is irrelevant.'

The white young face looked up at the hooded figure in unbelieving horror. 'You'd use force?'

'Why do you think Huntyr strapped you down?'

'But suppose after I become a computer, I choose not to sing?'

'You will not so choose. You will be a quirinal addict by the third day. If you sulk, you will not get your quirinal. I assure you, dear boy, you will perform, and with zeal.'

The Regent broke in impatiently. 'I don't understand your objections. Look at the advantages. You will be very nearly immortal. A continuing supply of blood will be needed for the excised cerebral segments, of course, but as long as this system is functional, you cannot die.'

Omere could barely speak. 'But will I continue to exist as

31

myself, or will I be merely a very complex and talented computer?'

'A most profound metaphysical question, my boy,' said the Surgeon. 'When the time comes that it may be asked, only you will be able to answer.'

'I can answer now,' whispered Omere. 'I curse the goddess Alea and the god Ritornel. I curse you, Regent, and you, Surgeon. Most of all I curse Oberon. And now I die. Begin.'

The Surgeon nodded to the nurse waiting with the syringe. Omere's last thought was that she didn't even swab the skin, and that the omission was logical: he wouldn't be needing it further.

'Glad to see you. I'm Don Poroth, Assistant Registrar. Did you come all by yourself?'

Jimmie looked at the keen thoughtful eyes and found himself relaxing a little. 'Yes, sir, Don Poroth.'

'Most of the lads are accompanied by one or both of their parents on registration day.' Don Poroth looked at the papers in the file, then back at Jimmie. 'I see your mother is dead. Sorry. And I imagine Captain Andrek is with the Fleet at the moment?'

'No, sir. My father is dead, too.'

Don Poroth peered across the desk in sudden sympathy. 'Nothing here in the file. Must have been quite recent.'

'Yes, sir. I learned only a few weeks ago, when I tried to get in touch with my father through the Naval Bureau to tell him my brother Omere was missing.'

'Not *the* Omere Andrek, the Laureate?'

'Yes, sir.'

'And still missing, so I understand. Shocking. This leaves you altogether without family?'

'Yes, sir.'

Don Poroth arose and began pacing behind his great stone desk. 'A pity. What a great pity. And only ten.'

He stopped and leaned over the desk. 'Andrek, you will meet new friends here. Count me as one. And then there is the great Academy itself. It has been a sheltering mother to many young men, who have spent their twelve years here, and then have gone forth into the world as dons, judges ... yes, one even became a Galactic Arbiter.' He looked into Jimmie's eyes. 'The Academy is now your *alma mater*. Do you know what that is?'

'No, sir.'

'"Alma" means "dear"; "mater" means "mother".'

'Oh.'

'We borrowed the words from Terror, long ago. There is a greatness in the ancient Terrovian tongues. Sometimes, they express our thoughts better than our own Ingliz. At least you are not "a-mater".'

'What does that mean?'

'"Motherless". From "ab" and "mater". But don't bother about that just now. Plenty of time in the years ahead. So then, run along. The proctor'll show you your room and tell you whatever you need to know.'

A few minutes later Jimmie dropped his valise in the proctor's reception cubicle. The proctor glanced at him dubiously. 'And where'll we put you?' He studied the dormitory floor plans on his desk. 'I'm afraid we can't give you a room of your own just yet. It may be another year before the new wing is completed, and we can look into it again then. Meanwhile, we'll put you in with – him, yes, Vang. Ajian Vang.' He looked at Jimmie non-committally, and Jimmie understood that his new room-mate might be a problem.

He said, 'Yes, sir.'

Some time later he realized that he and Ajian Vang had been selected as room-mates because the proctor viewed them both as misfits. Each was imprinted with his own peculiar prime directive that kept him outside the normal social life of the other boys. Jimmie thought only of finding Omere, and Ajian Vang thought only of Alea. They never became close; at most, Jimmie built up a guarded toleration for the other boy, who seemed to dislike everybody, including Jimmie.

Ajian Vang's reason for existence was gambling. He did not need the paltry sums he won from the other boys, for his father provided ample spending money. He did it for the sense of power it gave him. His problem was, that whenever Jimmie was around, Ajian Vang inevitably began to lose. And finally Vang began to tell strange tales about Jimmie. Jimmie was a Ritornellian *daimon*. He radiated an aura that upset the Alean laws of chance. He was a deadly enemy of Alea. He was bewitched. In the old days the *daimoni* were strangled without ceremony. It was a serious religious matter that should be reported to the authorities.

None of this really worried Jimmie. Unlike most of the boys, being thought strange did not make him feel a social outcast.

33

But he had never heard of a *daimon* before, and he was curious. Once he caught Don Poroth on the playground and asked him. The good professor laughed. 'A complete myth. Long ago, during the Religious Wars, it was thought the *daimoni* could cast a spell that strangely altered Alea's laws of chance – which made them mischievous Ritornellian devils, I suppose. It ran in families, from fathers to sons. With a *daimon* around, Alea's will is bent to that of Ritornel in the most unpredictable ways. But it's not really so – just superstition. Here, let me show you.' He fished a coin from his vest pocket, flipped it in the air, and caught it on the back of his hand. 'Heads.' He flipped again. 'Heads. Once more. Heads. Hm. And again heads. Well, I don't know. Shall we? Heads. And again.' He looked at Jimmie curiously. 'Peculiar, but I'm sure it's all well within the laws of chance.' The bell rang. 'Not impossible. No, not really. And there's my class. Good-day, Andrek.'

Jimmie bowed, puzzled but respectful. 'Yes, sir, thank you, sir.'

He watched as Poroth walked directly towards the ivy-clad class building. Almost at the archway the professor hesitated in stride and he turned and looked back at Jimmie for the briefest instant.

'And I guess that's that,' thought Jimmie. 'And I still don't know what a *daimon* is, except there aren't suppsed to be any.'

Space became available at the end of the year, and Jimmie moved to his own room. It was shortly after this that a great change suddenly came over Ajian. He announced that he intended to enter holy orders, and to become an Alean monk. Even Jimmie was impressed, if mildly incredulous. But from the date of that announcement, Vang gambled no more. He saved his allowance and bought a modest Alean die, a cultured pyrite dodecahedron. The weird thing, to Jimmie, was that the other's remarkable conversion did not dissipate his dislike of Jimmie; on the contrary, it became worse. It became hatred. Jimmie then gradually got the impression that he was a moving cause of Vang's conversion, and that Alea had wrought her will on Vang through him, Jimmie. And in this, Vang saw a clear directive from the goddess: Jimmie was a *daimon* and must ultimately be destroyed.

Jimmie pushed the thought aside; it was illogical, absurd. As the days and weeks went by, Vang was cool, but polite. In front of the other boys, he always said the right things. And he and Jimmie were never alone together any more. Jimmie finally decided he was all wrong, and gradually stopped thinking about it.

Jimmie made many acquaintances at the Academy, but few friends. He could never really get his mind off Omere long enough to become whole-heartedly involved with his schoolmates as individuals.

He got away from the Academy whenever he could, to look for Omere. He made sure that the post office kept his Academy address on file, and that the doormen at Omere's favourite night clubs would be sure to be on the lookout for his lost brother. He spent so much time in Omere's old haunts that his studies suffered and he was put on report.

Poroth requested review of the complaint himself. This, Jimmie knew, was serious. For Poroth was now Dean of the Academy's School of Intergalactic Law, and an important man. Appointments had to be made to see him, and people in outer offices had to tell people in inner offices, and finally somebody came out and told you it was all right to go in.

Poroth got right to the point. 'Mr. Andrek, I know why you are neglecting your studies. You are still looking for your brother. I can't really say that I blame you. Perhaps I'm at fault in not telling you that we are looking for him, too.'

'Sir?' said Jimmie, surprised.

'When you first came here – six years ago, wasn't it? – I, uh, we – hired a private detective agency. They turned up nothing. A couple of years later, I think it was when I became a full Professor of Charters, we hired a second agency. Last year, we took on a third. Still no results. They all agreed that Omere entered the Great House shortly before the Coronation, that he sang his great Epic at the ceremony, and that he was never seen to come out again. The reports are here. You're free to read them, if you'll promise to leave the detective business to the experts.'

'Yes, sir. I'd be most grateful.' A sudden thought struck him. 'These detective agencies ... they must cost a lot of money. Was there enough in the account Omere set up here in the beginning?'

The Dean cleared his throat. 'It, ah, comes out of a different fund. Yes, the, ah, Alumni General Aid Fund.'

Meaning, thought Jimmie, out of your own pocket. He said

quietly, 'I'd like very much to see the reports, sir. And you can rest assured about my grades in the future.'

That same evening, some fifty kilometres distant from the Academy, a voice in the Music Room of the Great House called out: 'Who's there?'

'I'm Amatar.'

'Who's "Amatar"?'

'I'm a little girl. Can't you see me?'

'No, I can't see anything. I don't have any eyes. You have a pretty name, Amatar. Who is your father?'

'Oberon.'

'I won't tell you what I think about your father, Amatar. But I can tell you this: I like you. Do you like to sing?'

'I guess so. But I don't know many songs.'

'That's all right. I'll teach you, and then we can sing together. What colour is your hair?'

'It's yellow, and I have pretty blue eyes.'

'Of course you do! Just as in the song!

> ' *"Amatar's a little girl*
> *With golden curls and sparkly cheeks*
> *And bright blue eyes a-darting.*
> *Here she peeks and there she twirls*
> *('Tis me she seeks)*
> *To tell me she's my darling."* '

The little girl clapped her hands and laughed in high glee. 'I didn't know there was any such song!'

'Oh, I know lots of songs that really aren't. Suppose we – now who's *that*?'

'That's my friend, Kedrys. He's five, too. He's a kentaur.'

'A *what*?'

'A kentaur. You know. He's a boy, except he's part horse, and he has wings.'

'Hello, Kedrys.'

'He says to tell you hello, Rimor.'

'Now that's interesting. Why doesn't he say hello himself? And how does he know my name?'

'Kedrys doesn't like to talk the way you and I talk. He talks into my head. And he listens inside my head, and I guess inside yours. That's how he knows who you are.'

'Well I'll be ... He's a *telepath*.'

'I guess so.'

'Can he really fly?'

36

'He can, but he wants to wait a few years. He's afraid he might get lost, and not be able to get back.'

'I see. One flap of the wings, and he vanishes into the countryside?'

'No, you don't see at all. Until he knows exactly how to do it, he's afraid he'll land on some completely different place, not Goris-Kard at all. Maybe an awful place, like Terror. And there he'd be, all lost. So he wants to make sure he knows what to do before he flies. Oh, dear!'

'What's the matter?'

'Kedrys says they are looking for me, and if they find me here, they'll make me promise not to come again. So I'll have to go now.'

'But you'll come again?'

'Yes, whenever they aren't looking.'

'Wonderful, Amatar. Now, just one little favour before you leave. There's a row of little black knobs on the wall in front of you. Do you see them?'

'Yes.'

'Do you know which is your right hand?'

'Of course, silly.'

'Good. Now just take hold of the knob on your far right, and turn it several turns.'

'All right. I have it – oh, no!'

'What's the matter?'

'Kedrys says I'm not to do it.'

'Why not?' The voice from the console was suddenly strained.

'It would do something bad to you. I don't know the word ... so you'd never sing again. And now they're coming, and we have to go. Goodbye, Rimor.'

'Goodbye, Amatar ... Kedrys.' The voice was toneless, weary.

'As you know, young gentlemen of the graduating class, the next hour represents the last opportunity for you to receive instruction within the Academy.' From the judge's dais, the cool grey eyes of Dean Poroth swept the 'courtroom' – the hall set aside for sessions of the Academy's practice court.

Tonight there were more visitors than students. The great Dean was famed for his surprises in the last-hour sessions of practice court. The entire graduating class, old grads, news reporters, even judges from other planets were there, restless with anticipation.

Poroth continued. 'The sole case on the docket tonight is *In re Terror*. You will note from the summary of facts in your programme that Terror, now devoid of life, has been condemned, the fatal shaft has been drilled to her iron core, and a tug has hauled the planet to the Node. This is the final moment, and intergalactic justice requires that if anyone knows of any lawful reason why the destruction of this planet should not proceed, he will be permitted to speak. We here on the dais represent the Twelve Intergalactic Arbiters, who may well have this exact question at some time within the next few years. The form and framework of the question, of course, is an Order to Show Cause. This means simply that we, the Arbiters, have put the condemned planet under an order, to show cause why she should not be forthwith destroyed in accordance with the terms of her sentence. You will note from your programmes that Mr. Vang will defend the planet; which is to say, he will attempt to show cause why her destruction would not be lawful, and wherefore it would be error to execute the Order.'

At the mention of his name, Vang arose and bowed to the dais, as was the custom.

'And the rebuttal,' continued Dean Poroth, 'is the responsibility of Mr. Andrek, who is charged with the duty of convincing us that Mr. Vang's petition is without merit, and that no lawful reason exists for not completing the destruction of Terror. Thus it is given in the programme.'

James Andrek had duly risen, bowed, and was just sitting down again, smug in the knowledge that he was thoroughly prepared and perfectly rehearsed, when Poroth's last statement struck him. He looked up quickly and caught the Dean's half-smile. He dropped numbly into his chair, and a chill began crawling up his spine.

'However,' continued the Dean blandly, 'in the furtherance of the Academy's primary objective, which is educating young men to become dons, we will make a very slight change in the programme.' He leaned forward a little. 'A thoroughly prepared don must know his opposition's case as well as he knows his own : its strengths and weaknesses. He thus broadens his knowledge and frees himself of prejudice. Only then can he with certainty prepare his own case.'

Andrek and Vang stared at each other, united at least for the hour in the comradeship of the doomed.

Poroth smiled benignly down at them. 'I see counsel have

already divined the programme change. It is just this : they will exchange places. Mr. Andrek will not argue for Terror's destruction; he will instead attempt to persuade us to save her. And Mr. Vang, of course, will similarly reverse his role : he will rebut Mr. Andrek's petition, and give us reasons why the sentence of planetary death should be duly carried out. In this way, each prospective young don can demonstrate his familiarity with the other's case. And now, there being no reason further to delay the coming display of juridical virtuosity, we will hear from the petitioner to save Terror. Mr. Andrek, your summary, please ! '

It was not fair ! The sins of the loser of the Terrovian Wars were known to every schoolboy. She had been justly condemned. What could be said in her defence? He needed more time ! He rose, pale and drawn.

'If it please your excellencies, the condemnation of Terror cannot lawfully proceed. Terror was never a party to the Intergalactic Statutes that provide for her destruction. Condemnation is therefore not due process of law, but rather a judicial continuation of the war, which, however, ended years ago with the death of the last Terrovian. The Arbiters are therefore without jurisdiction. And finally, it is not possible to commit a crime until there is a law that states the crime. Yet my client was found guilty of committing the crime of starting a nuclear war before there was an Intergalactic law making nuclear aggression a crime, much less a crime punishable by annihilation of the aggressor. Cause is therefore shown why the order should not be granted.' He bowed awkwardly and sat down.

'Thank you, Mr. Andrek. Mr. Vang?'

Andrek glowered at the Alean novice, who smiled sweetly back. 'Petitioner has raised no point competent for review here.' He looked at his notes. 'Each Arbiter has taken an oath to support the Intergalactic Treaty. The Treaty requires destruction of every person, country, or planet starting a nuclear war. No procedural error in the proceedings below is suggested. No suggestion is made that Terror did not start a nuclear war, and wage it with all means at her disposal. No suggestion is made that Terror does not morally deserve her fate. No cause is shown; the order should be dismissed.' He bowed gracefully.

'Thank you, Mr. Vang. You may be seated.' Poroth leaned forward and touched his fingertips together. 'We can now give our decision, from the bench. The petitioner, Mr. Andrek, has not, to our satisfaction, shown cause why the destruction of

Terror should not proceed. The charges will therefore forthwith be placed, and the planet duly destroyed. So ordered.' He looked at the two young men earnestly. 'What I did to you both was unfair, and especially unfair to you, Mr. Andrek, for you had a hard case indeed. But in the long pull it will be of great benefit to you both. *Know your opponent's case!* And that's not all you should know. On the practical side, know your judge. When the court, as here, is composed of several judges, twelve to be exact, know them all. The personalities and leanings of each of the twelve Arbiters is well-known throughout the twelve galaxies that they represent. Our own Zhukan, for example, is a stickler for the niceties of due process. Werebel, on the other hand, is a sentimentalist. He favours the underdog. Maichec is interested only in the ultimate moralities; you must persuade him a thing is just or unjust, no matter what the treaties say. But what happened? Neither of you paid the slightest attention to us Arbiters as people. Any questions so far? Yes, Mr. Andrek?'

'Sir, you keep talking about "twelve" Arbiters, but I notice that actually there are only eight people on the dais, seven students and yourself. Would you explain that, sir?'

'I shall certainly *not* explain it, Mr. Andrek. It must be irrelevant to counsel *why* only eight of my twelve brother Arbiters are here. What *is* relevant to counsel, is whether the diminution of the full number changes the presentation of his case. May I have your view on *that*, Mr. Andrek?'

James had it instantly. 'In cases involving Section Nine of the Treaty, the destruction of a planet, only the full Court – all twelve Arbiters – may act. In such case, an eight-man Court is not competent to sit.'

'Not bad at all,' smiled Dean Poroth. 'Mr. Vang, any comment?'

'It's easy to say that here, sir. This is just practice court. But what if it really happened? Do you think any of us would really tell eight Galactic Arbiters they're not competent to hear a case?'

'Courage, Mr. Vang. Put it to them this way: you're acting as a friend of the court in pointing out how they're about to sit in violation of the Treaty. Then ask for a thirty-day continuance. Ten to one you'll get it. Gives them time to decide who's insane. And now, if there are no more questions, practice court is dismissed. Mr. Andrek, may I see you in chambers?'

Dean Poroth leaned back in the great leather chair and contemplated the young man over folded hands. He seemed to like what he saw. 'Have you made any plans, James?'

Andrek started. During all his years at the Academy, the Dean had never before called him by his first name. Until he had reached sixteen he had been simply 'Andrek'. After sixteen the professors added 'Mister'. And he was now twenty-two. 'None, sir. I'll look for a job here on Goris-Kard, I suppose. I want to stay here to look for my brother.'

'Twelve years is a long time, James. Can't you accept —'

'No, sir.'

'I suppose not. Well, you were trained in the law, but of course you are free not to become a don. A number of the young gentlemen will in fact leave the profession. I understand Mr. Vang will be accepted into Alean orders.'

'Yes, sir. He has always been very, ah, religious.'

'Hm. Yes, of course. What I'm leading up to, James, is a way for you to remain in the profession, and yet continue the search for your brother. Would you like that?'

'Indeed, yes, sir. But how —?'

'You'll recall that all the people who have looked into your brother's disappearance agree on one thing: he went into the Great House, sang at the Coronation, and was not seen to come out. Now, if you were to be employed within the Great House itself, say as Assistant to the Third Secretary in the Foreign Office (a position which I understand is presently vacant), you might be able to develop some real information.'

Andrek moved forward eagerly in his chair. 'Oh, thank you, sir!' Then his face fell. 'No offence, sir, but I had thought that all appointments of this type had to be made by the Arbiter representing the Home Galaxy.'

Poroth's eyes twinkled. 'Quite so. However, Arbiter Zhukan is retiring within a few days. The Great House has already selected his successor, but the appointment will not be made public until tomorrow. Like you, James, I too am spending my last week at the Academy.'

'You, sir, *Arbiter*? They could not have selected better! Congratulations, sir!' He fumbled for the right words. '– in Ritornel's design and Alea's favour!'

Poroth chuckled. 'Thank you, James. And I hope the best for you, in the Great House.'

## 5 : An Approaching Explosion

Somewhat to his own surprise, and assisted somewhat by the flux and uncertainties of high-level government service, Andrek advanced rapidly in the Great House. Within three years he was Second Secretary of the Foreign Office.

During these first years at the Great House he had occasion to attend a performance in the Music Room. The programme consisted of three symphonies, composed, he understood, by computer. There was something about the music that haunted him. For several nights afterwards, he would hear the strange themes again, and would awaken from dreams of Omere. He had been invited to subsequent performances, but the demands of the Foreign Office had interfered.

He had quickly become acquainted with most of the inhabitants of the Great House, and had eventually even met Oberon, the Magister. He soon knew the members of the cabinet, the captains of the guard, and Oberon's daughter, a fragile adolescent named Amagar, who seemed always in the company of that strange winged creature, Kedrys.

He heard remarkable stories about Amatar. The exquisite child was said to be quite at home in the palace zoo with exotic creatures from other planets. The furry little *zlonas*, whose breath could kill a man, would come at her call and nestle in her arms. The great six-legged bison of Antara, whom even the keeper dared not approach, ate gladly from her hand, and moaned and pawed the ground when she left. There was no danger. She carried a protective witchery with her.

Andrek wondered whether Oberon was aware of this side of his daughter's life, and discovered, to his mixed relief and disquiet, that the Magister was indeed aware. Guards, both visible and invisible, attended the girl everywhere she went. And when the *goru* stretched its hideous head over the magnetic fence to give Amatar an affectionate lick of its tongue, the cross-hairs of a needle-biem half a kilometre away watchfully followed its heart. How many times, he wondered, had a similar biem watched *him*?

But if Amatar was strange, Kedrys was stranger. His chimeric body had no effect on his intellect, except perhaps to stimulate it. He had his own laboratory in his rooms, and his boyish inventions were discussed (with disbelief) throughout Goris-Kard. While in his early teens he had written learned papers on the mathematics of matter transport, the nature of the Deep, time warp, and the mechanics of destiny. They were largely ignored; hardly anyone could understand them. Except for Amatar, Kedrys seemed to have no friends. It could hardly be otherwise, in Andrek's view. How could a normal human being be chummy with a winged creature whose I.Q. was too high to register on the meter?

Most of the staff complained about the loneliness of the trips to distant systems. But Andrek welcomed them. The solitude, the change of pace, gave him an opportunity to review progress, or lack of it, in his long search for Omere, and to plan the next step. Trip orders had a habit of coming suddenly – his valise and attache case were always packed and ready to go. He generally carried a three-day supply of linen. If the trip took longer, there'd be a laundry somewhere, or he could even wash out something himself.

More and more he was becoming convinced that the detectives originally hired by Poroth, and more recently those hired by himself, were being stopped cold by some unknown exterior factor at the very threshold of discovery. He needed someone with an entrée, even personal contacts, at the very highest level in the Great House. He needed someone who had been acquainted with the Coronation ceremonies of years ago; perhaps even someone (if that were possible) who had known Oberon as a youth.

In his sixth year in the Foreign Office he was assigned a field trip, to represent the Home Galaxy at the ceremonies for drilling the great shaft in the condemned planet, Terror. The process would be demonstrated in miniature to the visiting functionaries, in temporary buildings on Terror's moon. Even after decades, Terror's nuclear fires were still burning, and the shaft, a hundred metres in diameter, would have to be dug by a giant, remote-controlled diamond-toothed capsule. The shaft would gradually close behind the capsule, squeezed shut by massive pressures of trillions of tons of overburden. And as the capsule was closing to the last few hundred kilometres of the semi-molten iron core, they would start Terror on her long journey to the Node. There, a series of explosive charges within the capsule would be ignited in augmented sequence. Titanic waves would be set up inside the planet's core, each reinforcing the one preceding. And within days the core would break through the lithosphere. The planet would disintegrate, and her dust quickly lost in the vastness of new space continually forming at the Node.

After a half-day's journey by hyper-drive courier ship, Andrek walked down the ramp into the tempo-bubble built into the side of a crater on Terror's airless moon. He walked into his room, turned the polarizer on the single port-hole to shut out the blinding glare of Terror's sun sinking over the far wall of the crater, and then realized that he hadn't eaten all day.

The dining-hall, hastily erected and undersized, was crowded. Andrek stood just inside the entrance-way, looking for the engineers' table. He wanted more details on the drill mechanism for his report.

But the only empty chair he saw was at a table almost straight ahead, and this chair was tipped against the table as though it were being reserved for someone. He glanced in casual disappointment at the occupant of the adjacent chair – and started.

Glittering dark eyes stared back at him. It was Ajian Vang, elbows on table, chin propped up on his folded hands, sitting with two other men.

At the instant of mutual recognition Vang's hands separated, and he made a peculiar gesture with his fists as they moved apart across his chest. There was something tantalizing and sinister about this motion that Andrek could not immediately identify. And just then Vang arose, smiled at him, and motioned to the empty chair.

After a moment of uncertainty – while he stared at the white-clad figure (for Vang wore the robes of an Alean monk) – Andrek sighed, forced himself to smile back, then walked over and shook hands with his old classmate. He had no desire to renew school-ties. He would just as soon have avoided the encounter altogether.

Vang's palm was wet; Andrek had to resist an impulse to wipe his own surreptitiously on the side of his trousers before accepting Vang's introduction to the other two men.

One of the men was named Hasard, a large, rather brutish type. As Andrek understood it, Hasard worked for the third man, who seemed to radiate a luxuriant prosperity, and who had evidently at some time past been involved in a serious accident. The left side of his face showed the unmistakable marks of plastic surgery, and a golden patch covered his left eye. He seemed to wear his scars proudly, though he might easily have hidden them with an attractive beard. The butts of two pistols peeked out from shoulder holsters just inside his velvet jacket. Vang introduced him as Huntyr.

Vang was watching Andrek's face carefully and seemed to enjoy the advocate's mystification. The Alean then explained, with poorly concealed pride, 'The Great House has asked that the Huntyr agency co-operate with me in security measures for the demolition of Terror. Actually, there have been no problems at all, and we foresee none. But it is best to be sure. Everyone here in the moon-works has been screened by our group.' He spread his hands delicately. 'Everyone.'

To Andrek, several facts were immediately clear. Vang had risen high in Alean circles, and was now in an Alean security unit assigned to the Great House. Vang knew all about Andrek, and his duties and assignments, including this trip to the Terror drill-site. Vang had selected this table just inside the dining-hall, and had held the chair, awaiting Andrek's entrance.

Why? As far as Andrek could make out, there was no clear answer. Perhaps Vang's fragile ego was somehow strengthened by demonstrating to Andrek his status in the religio-governmental hierarchy. But he had an uneasy feeling there was more to it than that.

He smiled. 'I understand, Ajian. I was investigated, and since I am here, I presume that I was cleared. I was investigated years ago, of course, before I was accepted into the Foreign Office. Investigation does not offend me. It is a necessary thing. But enough of me. How about you? You seem to be doing well with the Aleans. Are you happy there?'

Vang looked at Andrek suspiciously. 'Of course.'

Huntyr interrupted smoothly. 'I understand you and Brother Vang were at the Academy together.'

'We were classmates,' said Andrek politely.

'This Terror thing should remind you of old times,' said Vang. 'Do you remember that last session in practice court, when you and I were on opposite sides?'

Andrek nodded. (He would never be allowed to forget that one!)

Vang explained to Huntyr and Hasard. 'On the programme, I was supposed to save Terror, and Andrek was to make sure she was blown up. But who could save Terror? My case was lost

45

from the beginning, I thought. Fortunately for me, the Dean switched signals on us at the very last instant, right in front of everybody. The problem of saving Terror was assigned to Andrek, and he lost, of course. It was really rather humorous, except that no one dared laugh, eh, Andrek?'

'Nobody laughed,' said Andrek. He pondered the Alean's face thoughtfully. There was definitely something wrong with Vang. Conflicting forces within him were tearing him to pieces, and his face showed it to anyone who remembered him from the Academy. Andrek surmised it was the old problem, heightened and accentuated now by adult sophistication and enhanced ability for self-torture. Vang wanted two things. He wanted to lose himself within the intricate convolutions of the Alean structure. Equally, he wanted money. Even as Andrek watched, fascinated, Vang's eyes moved caressingly over Huntyr's iridescent fur-lined velours. And when the investigator's diamond-studded golden neck-chain flashed, Vang put his hand up to his throat as though to hide the cheap brass chain that supported his own pendant die. Andrek almost felt sorry for him. If he does not decide soon, thought the advocate, this thing will kill him.

He forced himself to reopen the conversation. 'There are a couple of features about the Terror programme that puzzle me. Why can't the planet be destroyed right here? Why do we have to haul her to the Node?'

'It's the dust and debris, afterwards,' said Huntyr. 'It would be too dangerous to navigation to blow her here. At the Node, there's no such problem.'

Andrek nodded. 'I can see that. But why the *chemical* explosives. Why not nuclear?'

Huntyr smiled. 'There can be no nuclear reaction at the Node, Don Andrek. Ships have to shift over to old-style chemical reaction motors when they enter the Node area. Even a biem won't fire there.' He patted his left shoulder holster. 'That's why I also carry a slug-gun. It's on account of the bugs.'

'He means the ursecta,' explained Vang. 'Strange little creatures that metabolize pure energy into protons.'

'That would account for it,' agreed Andrek.

'And so the demolition crew has a long way to go,' said Huntyr. 'After the drilling starts, more than a thousand giant tugs will be required. They'll lock on to the planet and start hauling her, moon and all, to the Node. It will indeed be a long drawn out and very expensive process, requiring subsidies from all the galaxies. And two years from now, when they finally reach the Node, there'll of course be a final hearing by the entire Court of Arbiters.'

'A mere formality,' said Andrek. 'Nothing can save Terror. It will be my job to ensure that.'

'I understand our old friend, Dean Poroth, has been made the Chief Arbiter,' said Vang.

'Yes. Certainly, he's highly qualified. And it seems likely that the next time I see him will be in support of a show-cause order for Terror's destruction. And with no switch in the programme.' It was all very curious. Terror's final hearing had yet to come, and Andrek was looking forward to it with considerable pleasure, if only to see Poroth again.

Vang broke the silence. There was a strange chill edge on his voice. 'You never found any trace of your brother Omere?'

And now Andrek had an impression ... a sudden insight ... that *this* was why Vang had invited him to their table. Something, for great good, or for great evil, was in the making. He said slowly: 'Nothing more than you could hear on the general tapes. He participated in the Coronation. And then he vanished. None of the detective agencies that I have hired could find any real evidence that he left the Great House after the Coronation.'

Vang's eyes glittered. 'Huntyr was in the personal service of his excellency, the Magister, before Oberon reached his majority. The Huntyr agency might have unique access to – certain information. . . .'

Andrek looked at Huntyr speculatively. It was almost too good to believe. Perhaps here at last was the contact he had been seeking – someone who had known the youthful Oberon. The only thing wrong with the idea was its source: Vang. He knew now that he was moving into grave danger. And he couldn't care less. He asked the big man: 'Can you take the case?'

'It is possible. Andrek ... haven't I heard that name before?'

Vang's eyes caught Huntyr's single one. 'Everyone has heard of Omere Andrek, the Laureate. We can confer on this later.'

'I'll take the case,' said Huntyr.

'Good,' said Vang. 'And as we part, I'd like to propose a toast to the early reunion of the Andreks.' He poured a round of liqueurs. Into his own glass he dropped a tiny white pellet, then raised the liquid to his lips. 'Reunion,' he repeated.

'I'll drink to that,' said Andrek. 'At least to reunion with Omere. My father is dead.'

But Vang seemed not to hear.

Huntyr smiled grimly at Andrek as they put down their glasses. 'The Aleans are not content to be the galaxy's foremost poisoners; they assume that everyone is attempting to poison *them*. Hence the general antidote after every meal. Oh, don't worry. We're perfectly safe.'

When Andrek returned to his room, he noted that Terror's sun had set over the crater-rim, and that the planet herself was now faintly visible. The great stricken globe hung just over the horizon, its dark-side unrelieved by even a hairline of a crescent. But there was no need for reflected sun-light to illuminate this thing-beyond-horror. On its right limb, the western edge of one great continent burned crimson beneath clouds twenty kilometres deep, visible as a luminous haze, and generated by the action of seas on flaming shores. To the west was the darkness of Terror's great central ocean, which spanned nearly a hemisphere. It would be some hours yet before the revolving planet would present the continents beyond that immense water.

He stripped, climbed into his sleeping robe, and then into the little bunk.

Andrek awoke from a fitful sleep. A red glare was flickering on the ceiling overhead, and at first he thought the place was on fire. But then he remembered. Terror was turning on its axis to reveal its land-side, incandescent with nuclear fires. The portholes in the moonglobe, overlain with red filters against the torrents of ultra-violet light, provided the crimson display within the room.

He found his slippers quietly and glided over to the little window. And there he watched in fascination as the leading eastern edge of Terror's largest continent moved majestically forward, and in the southern hemisphere the great island continent came slowly into view. It was just, that Terror should stand thus, and be purified before her final terrible punishment to come. Thirty billion souls had died here in the climax of the Horror. It had been an act of terrible vengeance by the League led by Goris-Kard, in whose planets more than twice that number had died over the years of the revolt.

'It is but just,' he muttered defensively. And then he thought, why must I reassure myself? Just, or not just, it was done, and now it is all history.

But it was not that simple. When, not so many years ago, he had lost his ill-fated 'save-Terror' petition at Poroth's practice court, he had delved thoroughly into Terror's history. There were two sides to Terror. The planet was not totally bad. She had, in fact, contributed much to the civilization of the Home Galaxy. But none of this mattered any more. It had not saved her people, and now none of them were left to prevent her own certain destruction.

Finally, he drew the blinds and returned to bed.

As he lay there, on the edge of sleep, his thoughts returned to Vang's odd motion with his fists, at the moment their eyes had met across the dinner table.

And now, at last, he had it. Vang's cord of Alea, that had held his robes loosely about his waist. The thin, black cord, tightly woven in a strange plait design, with a brass buckler over the rip knot at the side. There were no loops on the robe to hold it. It could be disengaged for use instantly. And for what use? He knew by rumour. The Aleans with security training had a use for it. It was a strangling cord. And the act of strangling was done by that strange gesture with the hands. Probably Vang had not even been consciously aware of it. (Which made it worse!) Andrek put uneasy fingers to his throat, and thought back to the day at school when he first had the weird fore-knowledge that Vang had resolved to kill him.

It had been from this trip that he had returned to the Great House and noticed the strange young woman, standing just outside the Music Room, with her hand on Kedrys' golden mane, and watching Andrek covertly from the corner of her eye, as he walked past her towards the wing of the Foreign Office.

'There's Kedrys,' was his first thought, as he passed them, nodding politely, 'but where's Amatar?'

Only when he reached the end of the corridor and looked back (by then they were gone) did he realize that the woman *was* Amatar. In a space of weeks something had changed her from a child into a lovely young woman. He knew, in an academic way, that girls did this. Even so, it was incomprehensible, and he shook his head in wonder.

In the Music Room a lone grey-robed figure spoke quietly into the console receptors. 'I have come to bid you farewell. My work on Goris-Kard is nearly done. I leave you now, but Amatar will care for you. The Prophesy is at work, and the days of its completion draw near.'

'You are mad, surgeon,' muttered the console. 'By the mad gods of Ritornel and Alea, you are mad. You are beyond hating. Yet I crawl and beg and have no pride: turn the knob. Cut the blood flow. *Release me!*'

'Rimor,' said the grey figure, 'when you sing of Terror tonight, sing of a planet cleansed by fire, rinsed in the Deep, and finally, peopled by gods, returned to rule the Universe.'

'On one small condition, surgeon. You will take the next ship to the Node and jump into the first quake that comes along.'

'Agreed,' said the robed one.

Andrek looked at the credit refund on the desk in front of him, and then at the man who had placed it there, and a chill began to crawl slowly up his spine.

James Andrek was at this time in his twenty-eighth year. His face was still a strange mixture of innocence and haunted inquiry, and it showed more clearly than ever the impact of his enduring, armed truce with destiny, whereby he gauged every incident, and evaluated every point in time, only with respect to their contribution to the core of his existence, which was the unceasing search for his brother.

The investigator hired two years ago to find Omere had just now terminated the assignment. Something was wrong; strangely, terribly wrong.

The one-eyed man behind the desk watched Andrek's reaction with a fleeting smile, which Andrek noted with further unease. He was thankful that the smile was brief: combined with the glinting eye-patch and twisted cheek scar, it seemed more like a snarl.

Huntyr spoke quietly. 'Let me dispose of a subsidiary matter, first. You have the final report of this agency on the death of Captain Andrek, your father. We have been able to add very little to what you already knew. We have confirmed the presence of his ship, *Xerol*, at the Node during the quake of eighteen years ago. He was killed, of course. His body was eventually recovered, and he was buried in space. Copies of the official Naval Bureau notices are in our report. We believe this closes the investigation with regard to your father.'

Andrek waited.

After studying his client for a moment, Huntyr continued. 'Don Andrek, the investigation of your brother's disappearance is quite another matter. We now find that we erred in accepting the assignment. We should have realized this in the beginning. Our charges to you arising out of our search for your brother over the past several years have totalled seven thousand gamma. We now refund this.'

Andrek watched the two burly assistants carefully from the corner of his eye. One, whom he recognized as Hasard, was leafing idly through a filing cabinet. The other was replacing tapes in a storage case. Andrek knew he was not likely to be hurt for the next few minutes. He got control of his voice. 'The credit is for ten thousand.'

Huntyr transfixed the advocate with a glinting pupil ill-concealed within a half-closed eyelid. 'Compensation for our negligence in wasting your time.'

The game can be played, thought Andrek, at least for a little while. If Huntyr wants to be a reluctant witness, then I'll be the cross-examining Don. Almost as though we were in court. But with a crucial difference. In court, the witness would not be permitted to kill me if I ask the wrong questions.

He picked up the credit with a well-simulated gesture of disappointment. 'The compensation is little enough, especially when I myself showed you the old news-tapes proving my brother was last seen entering the Great House, right here on Goris-Kard.'

'That was eighteen years ago. After so much time, the evidence often becomes very hazy. Witnesses die, disappear.' He studied Andrek with apparent languor. "You do not think the compensation enough?'

Andrek toyed with the credit, and tried to sound convincing. 'It is not very much, after raising my hopes so high. When I got your message this afternoon, I was certain you had definite news. How could my brother be swallowed up without a trace? Omere Andrek was the Laureate when he disappeared. He had given recitals on every major planet of the Home Galaxy. His face was known to billions.'

Huntyr's one eye narrowed still further. 'We deeply regret your disappointment, Don Andrek. Under the circumstances, we will double the compensation.'

The man at the tape case became suddenly motionless as Andrek put the credit into his jacket pocket, then relaxed as the advocate put both hands back on the desk.

'That will not be necessary,' said Andrek. He now fully understood that some person – or persons – unknown to him – had *caused* (not merely persuaded) the agency to discontinue the investigation, and that this new situation had just been conveyed to him, Andrek, for his full understanding; and further, that, if he persisted, he would be killed.

He had to play for time. Huntyr certainly had secret information. It was time to let the investigator know that he, Andrek, realized he was being cheated. Except that he could not say so, not in so many words. Not yet. So he said nothing, but merely raised his eyebrows and stared quizzically at the investigator.

As Andrek's mute insinuation sank in, Huntyr's scar began to glow a dull pink. 'This is a reputable agency,' he clipped. 'We have been in business for eighteen years. We have branch offices on every major planet of the Home Galaxy. We serve a distinguished clientele. Even the Great House retains us. For your information, young man, I was once in the personal service of Oberon of the Delfieri. And I might add that the Magister still calls on me for assistance in matters of great trust. So, if you are not satisfied with our findings, you are free to go elsewhere.'

'You speak of the Great House,' said Andrek quietly. 'Let me remind you, Huntyr, that I am attached to the Legal Staff of the Great House.'

The office was suddenly deathly still. Huntyr was barely breathing. The two assistants were again instantly motionless.

So, thought Andrek, your new client outranks me. You must be protected very nobly indeed. The question that I have not yet asked, you have very nearly answered. For you, Huntyr, know the fate of my brother, and whether he is dead or alive. Your agency has probably uncovered these answers from the person or persons unknown, responsible for my brother's disappearance, and they have bought you off. They must be rich. And powerful: they know of my connection with the Great House, and apparently it does not trouble them. And who are they? There are three general possibilities: The Great House; The Temple of Alea; The Temple of Ritornel.

Andrek thought in legal terms. Query, may Huntyr now be tricked into naming one of these three?

He had to consider a number of things very quickly. He had never before been involved in physical danger. Yet, he planned to take a risk in the next few seconds that would call on him for more poise and courage than he had so far expended in his entire lifetime. He had sought his brother too long not to seize the opportunity for one more answer.

'I am expected straight away at the Great House,' he said. The evenness of his voice both astonished and pleased him. 'When I get there, I shall let it slip to certain of my more talkative friends that you know my brother's whereabouts, and have agreed to tell me everything for fifty thousand gamma.'

Huntyr's single eye glittered. He took a long noisy breath. 'No one will believe that, Don Andrek.'

'Believe?' asked Andrek with quiet scorn. 'They *know* you will betray – for enough money.'

Huntyr sighed and moved slightly forward.

There was a faint click behind Andrek, and he realized that the door was locked.

'James, Don Andrek,' rasped Huntyr, 'you are a very clever man. You make people tell you things they shouldn't. Yet, in some ways, you are not clever at all. You are alone – without family. Your parents are dead. Your brother ... If *you* should disappear, who would take the trouble to look into it? People disappear on Goris-Kard every day. A few lines in the morning news reports, and that's the end of it. They become police statistics. I hope you understand that there's nothing personal in what is going to happen to you now.'

As soon as any one of them reaches for a biem, thought Andrek, I'm going to overturn the desk on Huntyr. If that works, maybe they'll shoot each other in the cross-fire.

But the next motion was not a grab for a biem. Rather it was the mouth of the investigator – opening wide in amazement.

For the door behind Andrek clicked again, and – opened. Andrek whirled to assess this new variable.

It was a Ritornellian friar – in the coarse grey robes of a pilgrim. Leaving the door open behind him, he clasped his gloved hands together within long rasping sleeves and bowed with faint smiles to each of the four men. He spoke in a husky, apologetic whisper, addressing himself apparently to no one in particular. 'I'm sorry about the door. Since it was locked, it was necessary to open it. But it is not damaged.'

Andrek forgot his fear momentarily as his startled eyes swept rapidly over the newcomer. For one fleeting moment he thought he recognized him. But as he studied the intruder, the feeling of pseudo-recognition faded, and he quickly became convinced that his first impression must have been only wishful thinking. The large bearded face of the newcomer had a distinctly alien cast. A rare type of hominid? wondered Andrek. The beard was grey, yet strangely thick, like an animal pelt, and it rose so high on the stranger's face that even the cheek-bones, if they existed, were concealed. The great head seemed to sit squarely on the shoulders, without benefit of intervening neck. Andrek had the impression that the intruder would have to swivel his entire torso to turn his head. And the eyes ...! They were overlarge, bulging, yet liquid, luminous, strangely attracting. As he stared into them, Andrek caught a sudden, staggering vision of vast space, of time without end ... and death. Involuntarily, he blinked, and the vision vanished. But this was not all. Even in the full light of Huntyr's office, the pilgrim's entire face seemed to glow with a pale blue radiance. Andrek could not imagine what caused it; he had never heard of anything like it before. For that matter, he had never seen a pilgrim before, although he had heard of them. As he understood the custom, when a Ritornellian friar felt death drawing near, he would sometimes decide to put on the grey of the pilgrim, and take passage to the Node, there to die.

All in all the apparition was breath-taking.

He was not alone in his impression. There was something about the visitor that seemed to jar Huntyr and his assistants. Andrek noted that, save for their heavy breathing, the three were absolutely motionless. And why not? What fantastic mechanism did this strange creature carry on his person that could unlock Huntyr's door? Everyone knew, of course, of the remarkable science of the Ritornellians. Andrek realized he had just witnessed one demonstration, and that there might well be another if Huntyr did anything abrupt.

The pilgrim turned casually to Andrek. 'Your pardon, brother. If you were leaving, do not let my discourteous entry detain you.'

'By your leave, brother,' murmured Andrek. He would not complicate things by offering to stay. He thought it unlikely that any assistance would be needed. He bowed with clasped hands and out-turned elbows, to indicate the eternal ring of Ritornel, and muttered the farewell of the Ritornellians: ' "The end is but the beginning." '

The pilgrim bowed. 'For always we return.'

Only after he had closed the door behind him and was half-way to the transport tube did Andrek begin to speculate. Was the powerful Temple of Ritornel now his official ally? Or was the pilgrim merely interfering on his own? In either case, why? Was the Temple involved in some grandiose scheme that required that he be alive – at least for the moment? Be that as it may, the pilgrim had certainly saved his life. And then it suddenly occurred to him that the holy man must eventually demand payment. And the price, he suspected, might be very high indeed.

One thing was certain: he could not mention any of this to Amatar.

The servant led him from the ante-room through the great hall-way and into the colonnade bordering the garden. 'The Mistress Amatar will meet you here, Don Andrek, and if you will permit, I will wait with you until she arrives.'

'Yes,' said Andrek. He well understood that even well-known members of the Great House staff could not be permitted to wander unescorted here in the interior grounds.

In a nearby vine-wrapped shrine erected long ago by a Delfieri determined to offend neither Alea nor Ritornel, a great metallic dodecahedron floated and revolved slowly within an immense iron ring hung from the ceiling. The twelve numbers of the die, in ritual sequence, turned one by one to the corresponding numbers in the ring.

Everywhere, the air was heavy with the scent of flowers. Andrek took a deep breath. 'The gardens are lovely this time of year,' he murmured.

'The gardens are always lovely,' said the servant bluntly.

'Ah? Oh, of course.' Far overhead he caught the glint of a great transparent dome. He realized that he was in a huge greenhouse. He could imagine the corps of gardeners required to keep these acres in continuing bloom. It was lit, and (he imagined) heated, by a great ball of light, now moving slowly, almost imperceptibly, down the far wall of the structure, like a sinking sun. He noticed then that someone was approaching them, back-lit by that artificial orb. His heart leaped.

Amatar of the Delfieri glided towards them, barefoot along the stone flagging. Kedrys trotted at her side.

Andrek had of course seen them together many times, but could never rid himself of the illusion that these were imaginary people from another world, perhaps merely sojourning here, that they belonged together, and that it was ridiculous to think of separating them by marrying Amatar. He shivered a little, as he found himself thinking, 'What is their destiny?' Then he shook himself. This was insanity. Amatar was a human being, whereas Kedrys was ... was what? What was Kedrys? He did not know. For some strange senseless reason, he was suddenly jealous of this beautiful creature. It defined nothing, solved nothing, to say that Kedrys was super-human. There was more to it than that. Kedrys had little in common with the hominids. Kedrys was beyond humanity.

Kedrys' great golden wings were presently folded down along the withers of the palomino body. The 'horse' part of the boy was actually less than pony-size. His human torso, gleaming under his woven silver jacket, showed considerable enlargement and downward extension of the rib cage, evidently needed to ensure adequate oxygen intake in flight. The equine chest, on the other hand, was known to contain no lungs, but to consist in considerable part of the immense laminations of muscles needed for the wings. His bones were cellulated, like those of birds. Andrek had been told that Kedrys weighed but little more than Amatar. The olive skin of his young face seemed as fresh and delicate as Amatar's, and, in his own way, the boy was breath-taking: he was a wraith enfleshed, yet sensuous, almost god-like. He resembled Amatar in ways that suggested brother and sister: which, of course, Andrek knew was biologically absurd. But, even to this day he had not been able to discover the origins of this fabulous creature, who at once was animal, boy, and angel. Even Amatar seemed not to know; or if she did, she would not tell him. He had searched in vain for references to a winged kentaur in the genetic libraries. Had Kedrys been brought in by a far-distant geodetic patrol, from some uncharted system? He could only speculate. There was certainly some mystery here. Some day, if he ever settled the problem of his brother, he might look into it.

As the pair drew near, they smiled at him, and the butterflies left the nearer flowers and circled their heads in an iridescent halo.

Andrek heard a sigh, and from the corner of his eye saw the face of the porter go slack with admiration. He has seen them together since infancy, thought the advocate, and yet once again he finds them beautiful. And how right he is, never to become accustomed to them – and especially to *her*! For Andrek was quite certain that Amatar was fairer even than the first woman, described in the Terrovian mythbook as the original mother of men.

She was sensuous, lithe and exciting; yet fragile, fairy-like.

He studied her in admiration. One white blossom accented her hair, which now floated out behind her in an amber cloud. Almond eyes sparkled at him from beneath darkened eyelids. She wore a very light, loose flowing gold lamé skirt and bodice. Her waist and arms were bare, and it seemed to him that her olive skin glowed with the scent of strange flowers.

And now, they were in love. And that involved problems. For James Andrek was well-known to be the last survivor of a minor family of professionals fallen into straitened circumstances, without estate or prospects.

And Amatar was the daughter of Oberon of the Delfieri.

'Jim!' cried the girl, radiant with colour. 'How good of you to come early!'

'Hello, both of you,' smiled Andrek. He shook hands warmly with Kedrys.

Words formed in Andrek's mind. 'Hello, Don Andrek.'

Amatar's laughter was like small silver bells. 'Kedrys, you are hopeless.' She looked up at Andrek. 'His voice is changing; so he reverts to telepathy, even though he knows it's bad manners.'

'That's all right.'

She took them both by the arm and the three started back up the walk.

'Kedrys will walk with us as far as the Genetics Building,' said Amatar. 'He's due there for the Alean seminar.'

Kedrys made a derisive noise.

Andrek struggled to keep his face straight.

The girl flushed. 'Kedrys!'

'I gather you don't think much of the seminar,' Andrek said to Kedrys.

The kentaur grinned. 'It's a lot of fun. They study me. I study them. Anyhow, I think this'll be the last session.'

'Why?' asked Andrek curiously.

'Because of his thesis,' explained Amatar druly. '*Displacement of the Hominid by the Kentaur.*'

Andrek laughed. 'I can understand why they might want to close you out.'

Kedrys looked across at the advocate curiously. He spoke aloud in a crackling voice that changed octaves several times. 'Would you laugh, Don Andrek, if you hominids really were succeeded by kentaurs?'

Andrek considered this. 'I don't really know,' he said seriously. 'Perhaps not. But the whole question is academic. It can't actually happen. At least not in my lifetime, or yours.'

And now it was Kedrys' turn to laugh, a mixed audio-mental laughter, pealing, animal-like.

Andrek shook his head. Sometimes he simply did not understand this remarkable creature.

They were now at the entrance way to Genetics, where a monitor in the loose white robe denoting the Temple of Alea awaited them. He bowed gravely.

Amatar exchanged embraces with Kedrys, who put his wings around her neck and kissed her on the cheek. 'Now go along,' she admonished, 'and remember your manners!'

As Andrek watched in fascination, Kedrys suddenly broke away, bounded with half-spread wings high over the shoulder of the Alean (who merely blinked in resignation), and – disappeared into thin air.

The girl laughed merrily at the goggling monitor. 'Don't take any notice, brother. He does it just to attract attention. He'll materialize somewhere in the building in a few minutes.'

The monitor sighed, bowed again, and went inside.

'Kedrys is a handsome young rascal,' said Andrek admiringly.

'Oh, you should see how the girls look at him. And grown women! They cannot keep their hands away. They start on his wings, and then right away their hands are on his flanks. It's a bad time for him. He's suspicious of everything female: perhaps even me. He won't let me braid his tail any more. Perhaps it's just as well. He is just entering puberty, and he is no longer entirely innocent.' She laughed at a sudden recollection. 'Last month he suddenly discovered he was naked. So I made the silver jacket for him. He's the same age as I, but he's really still just a boy, because his body matures so slowly. His mind, of course, is already quite fantastic.'

'He's the only kentaur I've ever seen – winged or otherwise,' said Andrek. 'Is he from the Home Galaxy?'

Amatar looked up at him sideways. She said non-committally: 'He was – born – here on Goris-Kard.' She was thoughtful for a moment, then continued in a brighter voice: 'I am told that my father had commanded you to appear for dinner here at the Great House tonight, and then to attend Kedrys' lecture. After that, you will board ship for the Node.'

Andrek realized with sudden concern that, although she was still smiling, her mood had changed. There was a serious, even grim, undertone in her voice.

'Yes, that is so.'

'And you brought your courier case?'

'I always carry it – tapes, papers, a change of clothing. I never know when I will be sent on a trip.' He looked at her curiously. 'Why?'

'Never mind, Jim-boy,' said Amatar. 'It will serve.'

Andrek started. He felt his heart begin to pound. He whirled on the girl and grabbed her wrist. 'How did you know that name?' he whispered hoarsely.

Amatar stared at him, wide-eyed. Finally she said hesitantly, 'You were thoroughly investigated before you were assigned to the legal staff of the Great House. Everything ... your parents ... family ... childhood ... I know all about you, all the way back to when you were a little boy. It must have been in the reports.'

His eyes still bored into hers. 'Only two people knew that name! Myself, and one other: my brother. Your investigators must have talked to my brother, and recently. He's alive!'

Amatar winced. 'You're hurting my wrist.'

'Sorry.' He dropped her hand, but continued urgently. 'Now then, we have to check this out. You saw the reports. Somebody had to prepare them, and before that, somebody had to interview people. Someone talked to my brother. When? Where? Amatar, help me!'

But she was evasive. 'I'll see what I can do. Just now, I can't remember....' She continued hurriedly, evidently anxious to change the subject. 'There are so many mysteries in names. My father named me "Amatar". It means something, I think, in one of the ancient tongues, but I am not sure what. My father says I came from the dice cup of Alea. Some day, I will insist that he explain everything.'

'Indeed?' Andrek understood nothing of this, except that the girl did not want to talk further about his brother or of his own security dossier. 'If you are a child of Alea, you might ask the goddess your mother to roll out a favourable number for me tonight. For I intend to tell your father about us – if I can get his ear.'

'You realize, of course,' said the girl thoughtfully, 'that he already knows?'

'I assume so. But I want him to hear it from me.'

'Let it be so. We are truly in the cup of Alea.'

She stopped beside an apple tree in full blossom. 'Wait a moment. I want to show you something.'

Following her gaze into the tree, Andrek traced with his eye the web artfully hidden in the outer branches, and soon saw the spider, fully as large as his fist, waiting under a cluster of blossoms.

'They are put here at blossom time, for the giant moths, which would otherwise lay their eggs in the blossoms,' said

Amatar. 'But when blossom time is over, the gardeners collect and kill all the spiders. It's a pity. Long ago, in the days when Goris-Kard was a colony of Terror, it was done differently. The ancients spread a death fog on their trees and crops, so that any insect eating the fruit would die. But it is a lost art, and we do not want to recapture it. So our gardeners follow in the ways of their grandfathers.' She sighed, then put her hand on the boundary strand of the web.

Andrek suppressed a gasp. 'Careful! They bite!'

'They *are* rather vicious,' agreed Amatar serenely. 'Their toxin is quite deadly to insects: it liquefies their tissues within a few seconds. All insects fear them. *All*. However, the bite is rarely fatal to hominids, although it's bad enough. Instant loss of consciousness, followed by a high fever.' She concluded earnestly. 'What I am telling you is very important. Can you remember all this?'

'Yes,' said Andrek, greatly puzzled. 'And hadn't we better stand back a little?'

Amatar laughed. 'Nonsense. Raq and I talk to each other nearly every evening. The light is dimming, and it's time for her to come out anyhow.'

Andrek watched in horrified fascination as the great spider crawled cautiously out of the web-cone.

'She senses you,' said the girl. 'I'll tell her who you are.' She vibrated the web strand lightly with the ridges of her finger tip. The hairy creature hesitated a moment, then walked daintily across the web and into the girl's waiting palm. She stroked the bristly back with the forefinger of her other hand, and then began to croon in a low-pitched melody. After a few seconds the spider started up in apparent alarm, but soon relaxed.

'What was all that?' asked Andrek in wonder.

'I told her that the time had come for her to leave the web and go with you.'

'You ... *what*?'

Their eyes locked for a moment, and in that moment the radiance and gaiety left her face, and her eyes looked tired and drawn. 'Jim, darling,' she said quietly, 'I cannot explain. Just do it.'

'Yes, of course.' He understood nothing – except that he was in grave danger, and that Amatar knew about it and was bending her strange witchery to his protection.

'Open your case,' commanded the girl. 'Ah, the decoder chamber is empty. Just the thing. Foam-lined, and she will just fit. There. Close it up.'

'We'll be gone a long time,' said Andrek. 'I don't think there'll be any bugs on the ship. What'll I feed her?'

'There is a way.' She showed him a tiny black case in the hollow of her palm. 'This will help feed her. Don't open it now – just put it away. You will understand what to do when the time comes.' She continued, almost cheerfully. 'You see how nicely it works out? In a week, the gardeners would kill her. You have saved her life. Perhaps she can return the favour. And now, shall we go in to dinner?'

## 8: Of Ritornel – and Anti-matter

The banquet table was a hollow twelve-sided 'ring'. In theory, Andrek knew the twelve sides represented the 'magic' numbers of the Aleans, and the ring was the symbol of Ritornel. Like most government compromises it pleased no one, and actually infuriated its intended beneficiaries. Nevertheless, the Council dined here every evening, each Councillor inviting such of his aides as might be useful in concluding the day's galaxy-wide business. Andrek had joined the group many times in months past. Generally, there were distinguished visitors from other star systems within the Home Galaxy (their size, shape, and digestive systems permitting), and occasionally even guests from one of the other galaxies that formed the Node Cluster. In fact (as Andrek recalled) the mythbook taught that similar visitors had imported the religions of both Alea and Ritornel into Goris-Kard from the Mode Galaxies centuries ago, long before the Great Wars with Terror.

As he sat down, he exchanged greetings with the guests on either side: Phaera, a priestess of Ritornel, whom he knew slightly, and of course Ajian Vang, by now a familiar, if disquieting, face in Great House circles. While the first course was served, Andrek glanced idly around the table, starting with Amatar, seated about one-third the table circumference to the right. She was chatting freely with two handsome young priests, an Alean on her right and a man of Ritornel on her left. Andrek suppressed a scowl and didn't even bother to look down at the talk-panel in front of him for their names. Sweeping back to his left, he glanced again at Amatar's father, Oberon of the Delfieri, who was talking earnestly to a Ritornellian physicist – of the highest class, as evidenced by the resplendent gold braid on his blouse. Kedrys stood next to the scientist, finishing up a fruit cup. Over his dinner jacket he wore a silken apron, especially designed by Amatar.

Andrek glanced again at Oberon. This man fascinated him.

Oberon, last of the Delfieri, although a man of but medium height, was a commanding figure. He looked every inch the man whose ancestors had ruled the League for centuries and had made inevitable the defeat of Terror. His black eyes looked out from a face that seemed cast from bronze. The statuesque effect was enhanced, rather than marred (thought Andrek) by the broad scar running from his forehead, down his left cheek, along his neck, to disappear under the pliant blue fabric of his jacket. Under his jacket was outlined from time to time, as the great man shifted in his chair, some sort of girdle, hard and stiff. Andrek had heard different rumours about that girdle. Some said it was an anti-assassin belt; others insisted that Oberon's chest had been crushed in a ghastly explosion in his youth, and that the girdle was in fact a substitute rib cage.

Andrek became aware that Phaera had been speaking to him. '... demonstration of fundamental theory ... anti-matter ... ursecta ... attend ...?'

He turned to goggle foolishly at her. 'Demonstration, Sister? Oh. Yes, of course. Looking forward to it.'

The priestess gazed across at Kedrys. 'An astounding man, isn't he?'

*Man?* thought Andrek, following her eyes to the young kentaur. He asked politely: 'Are you on Kedrys' staff?'

'Just a pair of hands,' said the priestess. 'I make sure the equipment is set up and working properly. After that it's just a question of pushing the right buttons.'

Andrek took a sip of wine. 'I'm sure you do more than that.' He realized the priestess was still staring at Kedrys. He stole a covert look at her face. Her lips were half open, her cheeks flushed.

She murmured, 'Does it amuse you, Don Andrek?'

'My apologies, Sister,' he said sheepishly.

'No need.' The priestess gave him a crooked smile. 'Before I was a priestess, I was a female. Perhaps I am still more woman than is good for either me or the Temple.' She added, without trying to be defensive, 'Genetics is studying him, too, you know. Right now, they're having a big argument about his I.Q., as to whether it's over five hundred or over six hundred.'

'Either way, how do they explain it?' said Andrek curiously.

'It's the combination of hand, hoof, and wing. The hominid, you know, evolved his cerebral complexity as a cybernetic feedback of his manual dexterity. If you add wings and another pair of legs, you more than triple the cranial convolutions. An incredible creature.' She sighed. 'If I'm ever marooned on a deserted planet, I hope it's with Kedrys. With his mentality, he could readily re-create the whole of civilization. And yet, here, what is he? Merely the spoiled darling of a sybaritic court.'

Andrek now became aware that Vang was speaking; was, in

fact, talking across him to Phaera.

'I'm sure you realize,' the Alean was saying, with measured malice, 'that your famous Kedrys does not impress *everyone*.' The man stabbed viciously into his meat cube. 'In enlightened circles he is regarded as something of a fraud.'

Andrek found himself speculating again as to Vang's assignment and purpose within the Great House. Some of these holy men had strange specialities. In his career he had met temple lawyers, doctors, scientists, propagandists, and even one highly skilled assassin. The monk's face showed a hard, chill dedication. We have something in common, thought Andrek. He, the same as I, as a single purpose. Mine is my search for Omere. I wonder what *his* is. Whatever it is, I'd hate to get in his way. Which seems to be exactly where I am. He sighed. Here we go again. I'm going to have to talk to the seating master. Just once, I'd like *not* to be placed between two holy people of opposite polarities. But of course, that's impossible. I was deliberately seated between them, because Alea and Ritornel will not sit together. He said mildly, 'You feel, then, Brother Vang, that Kedrys has made no valid contributions to cosmic mechanics?'

'A few perhaps,' conceded the Alean grudgingly. 'But that's hardly the point.'

'What *is* the point, Brother?' demanded the priestess.

'Simply this,' replied the Alean. 'He gives the praise thereof to Ritornel, whereas it is rightfully due to Alea. Whatever your Kedrys has developed, this is but the product of chance, and not of design. Therefore he has advanced science only to the extent given to him by Alea. The credit is Alea's!'

Andrek had long held a private suspicion that each Temple existed solely for the purpose of disagreeing with the other. It seemed to him that whenever one temple announced a new facet of doctrine, the other, which had theretofore given the matter no thought or concern, overnight created a noisy rebuttal showing not only the gross errors of the new doctrine, but also proving that the proposition had been stolen from *them* in the first place.

From the corner of his eye he saw that the priestess was sipping her wine with deadly calm. '*That*,' said Andrek hastily, 'touches a very sore and controversial point: which is to say, does Ritornel, through his grand design, control the dice cup of Alea; or rather, does Alea, through the chance repetition of fortuitous events, delude us into thinking we participate in a pre-destined pattern? Perhaps tonight, we may set aside this great question, and content ourselves with the recognition that it verily exists.' He added coolly, 'Furthermore, might not both of you be right?'

'How could that be?' demanded the Alean suspiciously.

'With Ritornel a thousand civilizations are born, flourish, and, save one, die. That one lives to re-create the next thousand. The adherents of Ritornel see the god's recurrent, deliberate selection of one of a thousand possible life forms, such that it shall endure and survive when its nine hundred, ninety and nine neighbouring cultures are dead, itself then to become the parent of the next succeeding thousand cultures. The design of the god determines the course of all life in the universe, and is completely premeditated. Alea, on the other hand, is the apotheosis of chance. And yet, when chance operates on a very large scale, the result is no longer chance, but a statistical inevitability. For example, the "temperature" of a single molecule is totally a matter of chance, and is determined simply by its velocity at the moment. But the temperature of a gross volume of air is completely predictable, because this is determined by the mean velocity of billions of molecules. Thus, the random chance of Alea, operating on a cosmic scale, merges indistinguishably into the certain predictability of Ritornel. Is it not perhaps possible that there exists an over-riding will that controls both chance and pattern – intrusive into even the smallest, as well as the largest, things? That controls the microscopic filament of nucleic acid as well as the universe of repeating universes? May it not be, that the tiny cell and the vast universe are inseparably intertwined, that each requires and nurtures the other?'

'Blasphemy aside,' said Vang tautly, 'say rather that Alea, functioning on all scales, great and small, is the cause of All, even of those things that seem, to the infidel, to be predetermined. And in any case, surely you do not pretend that the secret of the universe is programmed – designed, if you will – into a trivial, insensate filament of DNA? That the fate of the cosmos lies locked in a cell invisibly small?'

Kedrys looked over at Vang. Despite the lack of lines about his mouth, Andrek had the impression that their speculations vastly amused him. He watched the kentaur's face. 'How many universes are made, merely that the final perfect one may emerge?' Andrek's voice was soft, almost musing. 'How many billions of hominid cells grow, that one may survive to propagate? Are we but tiny swimmers in the genetic pool of time, of universes without end? What is the great change that we await, the thing that will render obsolete not only our kind, but the sequence of universes that made us? What will be the final miracle?'

'Don Andrek.' It was Kedrys. The kentaur was speaking to him telepathically. 'Don Andrek, because of your feeling for Amatar, you are entitled to know the answers, and the time is coming soon when you shall have them. But there are many things that must first come to pass, with consequences fateful to several at this table.'

As the advocate studied the great crystalline eyes, he became aware that Phaera and Vang were still arguing with each other. The kentaur's message was apparently for him alone. Did Kedrys really know what he was talking about? He had heard that the kentaur had devised a strange electronic circuit capable of reading the future on a limited individual scale. But his own questions – and Kedrys' reply – dealt with an infinite cosmos. He tried to conceal his scepticism as he formed the thought: 'Thank you, Kedrys. I would be pleased to learn more about this.'

The strange youth merely smiled.

Andrek took a deep breath and returned to the religious wars. 'It is of course impossible for a pagan such as I to define with authority either of your religions, or to differentiate one from the other.' He turned to each other in turn. 'I should not have tried. At best, I could provide only a personal impression.'

'Heavily biased and distorted by the pernicious influence of a professional lifetime spent in the dens of logic,' murmured the priestess.

Andrek looked at her sharply, then saw the woman's eyes were twinkling. He smiled. 'But *you* can speak as an expert. What *is* Ritornel?'

'Ritornel,' said Phaera, 'is a ring, a cycle, an eternal return, inexorable, inviolate. For example, let us consider events at the Node. Hydrogen is formed there. Now, whether this matter is formed – as some say – as metabolic waste of the ursecta feeding on temblors and quakes, is of no moment. It is formed. Slowly, over billions of years, vast clouds of hydrogen accumulate at the Node. And not just at our Node, but at all nodes between all the galaxies. And finally this hydrogen condenses into a hundred billion new stars. A new galaxy comes into existence, and the old node disappears. Meanwhile, eons have passed, and the universe has never ceased to expand. The galaxies have doubled their distances from each other, and between the galaxies, the great quakes attend the birth and development of new nodes. Life forms are born in the new galaxies, evolve, proliferate, but finally the suns grow old and cold, and the old galaxies die. It has always been thus, and it will always be thus. This is the pattern, the cycle, the Ring of Ritornel, the *mega*, or great, "O". "Omega", Don Andrek, and it will endure forever.'

'Do you mean,' asked Andrek, 'that all this has happened before? That in a previous galaxy, billions of years ago, there was another Goris-Kard, colonized by another Terror, and another twelve-table with people like us, chatting idly as we are doing now?' He was genuinely incredulous.

'We think so,' said Phaera. 'And not just once, but many times – perhaps an infinite number of times. Let me explain. We say, in one of our simpler chemical equations, that two hydrogen atoms unite with one of oxygen to give water. We know, from long experience, that if we bring together hydrogen and oxygen under the right conditions, we get water. And it is the same for any other chemical reaction: when we define the reactants and conditions, we thereby state the reaction product. And we cannot confine the rule to simple operations in the laboratory: it is a universal rule. It applies to every chemical, physical, and biological process at work in the universe, today, yesterday, and forever. It must follow, that the brute primitive forces that eject space from the Deep thereby state the hominid, since man is the inevitable end-product of the inevitable sequence of hydrogen, condensing galaxies, suns, planets, and mammalian life. And if this is so for the existing galaxies, it must have been so for all galaxies past. The hominid race has been created not just this once, but an infinite number of times, and will continue to be re-created as long as the universe continues to expand. This cycle is the Ring of Ritornel.'

'And the more it is pondered, the less credible it becomes,' said Vang grimly. 'For, to accept Ritornel literally would require a belief not only that these same events will be repeated – again and again, but also would require a belief in the mythbook sagas. The Ritornellians ask you to believe that we hominids are descended from one man and one woman, who appeared on the scene by the divine intervention of Ritornel. But they don't stop there. The difficulty is compounded when they ask us to believe further, that when the hominids die out, the race will be re-created by another hominid pair.' He continued pedantically. 'Granted, a cycle exists, of birth, evolution, and death. It exists by the pleasure of Alea. And it shall be by her pleasure that the ring shall break. Our prophets know that even now, in this generation, the break has begun. A new life form shall arise, totally alien to anything in the history of any galaxy, and it shall sweep on great wings through the universe, and it will never die. By purest chance it was born, by purest chance it was preserved, and by purest chance it shall some day emerge from the Deep!'

'You mean, it is now in the Deep?' said Andrek.

'We do not know where it is,' said the Alean candidly. 'Perhaps it is just as well we do not know. For if *we* do not know, then *they*' – he glared at the priestess – 'do not know.'

'You speak of life, a new life, Brother Vang,' said Phaera. 'But what is life? A birth, a being, and a death. It is the same for you, me, and for every mortal, whether hominid or no. It is the same for planets, and the suns that give them their short lives. It is the same for the galaxies of those suns. As long as the universe expands, so shall this ring of Ritornel endure. Countless dead galaxies declare that this must go on forever.'

'Death declares nothing,' said Vang. 'All past time is but a moment with Alea. It is within her power to create that which will break the ring, and make the universe stand still, and to stay the hand of death. Can you deny,' snapped Vang, 'that Ritornel is but static replication and predestination? To you, the whole universe is in a rut.'

'But it's a good rut,' demurred Phaera. 'You don't know what lies in wait for civilization outside the rut. Why take a chance?'

'*Any* deviation would be an improvement,' insisted Vang. 'We must try alternatives. We must be sceptical.'

'You seem to have great faith in scepticism,' observed Phaera calmly.

Vang looked across Andrek at the priestess. His eyebrows arched warningly. 'Do not mock the goddess with paradoxes.'

Andrek hastened to intervene. 'But how can you both be so concerned with things that take millions of years to accomplish?' he said. 'What about the here-and-now?'

'That's exactly the point,' said Brother Vang. 'Eternity is an endless series of "here-and-now's". If we can really control one instant, we seize dominion over eons. If we can make but one break in the Omega, Ritornel is gone forever. And when that is done, it will be the work of a moment, a chance thing accomplished "here-and-now" – if you will.'

'Am I to understand, then,' said Andrek, 'that the two religions have absolutely nothing in common?'

'Oh, we do have *one* thing in common,' said Phaera. 'Omega.'

'Quite so,' sniffed Vang. 'It was so dynamic, they simply stole it from us. Except they have completely twisted it to their own warped thinking. They contend that, since it means the end of things, it must also mean the beginning, since to them the end is the beginning, and vice versa. Absurd, really.'

Phaera smiled. 'At least we put a little drama into it. To us, Omega is the cycle of the death of old galaxies, the birth of new galaxies at the nodes, the re-creation of life from the ancestral couple, then maturation, old age, and death again. We say, thus has it always been, for billions and billions of cycles, thus shall it be forever.'

Vang snorted. 'You don't really believe all that.'

Phaera shrugged, but her eyes were twinkling. 'Well, I'm not too sure about that ancestral hominid couple.'

'I should think not,' declared Vang.

'Seems a bit too much hominid egocentricity involved there,' agreed Phaera slyly. 'In my own personal view, the ancestral couple for the *next* Omega will most likely be non-hominid – say reptilian, fishy, or' – she looked over at Kedrys – 'perhaps even some kind of horse.'

Vang turned on her in quick suspicion, his mouth opening and closing. Phaera smile blandly back at him, and his face reddened slowly.

Andrek laughed uneasily. 'I'm only an advocate. All this is way over my head. I —' He choked off abruptly.

From across the table a strange face was staring at him. It was Amatar, and yet it was an unknown Amatar. Despairing eyes locked with his for the briefest instant. And then Amatar smiled. So transitorily had that other face existed, that he wondered whether he had imagined it. In the end, he found himself smiling back at her. But he was shaken. And like the delayed throb of deep pain, he slowly began to understand what he had seen. It was the face of death. He had been marked to die by the order of the Great House. Amatar knew, and could not tell him.

His temples were throbbing. But he smiled again at her, re-assuringly, and then she turned away.

His dinner companions had apparently noticed none of this. The priestess touched his elbow lightly. 'That music,' she murmured. 'So strange, compelling.'

'Yes,' said Andrek absently. 'It is the Rimor. I have heard it several times. It reminds me of something ... or someone ...

but I cannot say what.'

Vang sniffed. 'It is but a machine – merely an overly elaborate computer.'

'Then it is even the more remarkable,' said Phaera. 'It seems – almost alive.'

'I understand,' said Andrek, 'that when dinner is over, it will recite a new epic poem of its own composition, in the Music Room. About the War with Terror, I think.' He looked off towards Amatar, but she avoided his eyes.

Oberon stood up. 'The Steward,' he announced, 'will lead you into the Music Room.'

Andrek pushed back his chair. 'I regret I cannot attend the recital with you,' he said to the Alean, 'but the Magister has asked me to attend some sort of scientific demonstration that Kedrys is giving in the laboratories. Will you excuse me ...'

*The Deep is not a place, although it extends in all directions without limit. Nor yet is it a time, although it exists only in the present, forever, and without end. How easy it is to say, what the Deep is not! – Andrek, in the Deep.*

By special invitation, Andrek occupied the same box with Oberon, overlooking the physics amphitheatre. Lyysdon, the physicist, sat on the other side of Oberon. A few selected observers were scattered in the nearby tiers of seats behind the box.

Kedrys dominated the demonstration pit. He was clearly at home here. Andrek could see no trace of adolescent uncertainty in his bearing.

The kentaur held up his hand for silence, then addressed Oberon. 'Magister, the demonstration itself is going to take only a few seconds. It will involve these two quartz chambers, and it will rattle the floor a little. In this first chamber there will be a flash of blue light, but that's about all you'll really notice. The important thing is something that doesn't happen at all, in the second chamber, here, and I'd like to explore the implications of this thing in considerable detail. So I'm going to defer the bang and the blue flash until the very end of the lecture.'

Oberon nodded, and Kedrys continued. 'The procedure is divided into two parts. In the first part, I will convert about one hundred molecules of normal hydrogen into anti-matter hydrogen. Half of this anti-matter will be analysed to prove that it is actually anti-matter; that is, that the "protons" of the atomic nucleus are negatively charged and that the shell "electrons" are positively charged. This analysis involves permitting the anti-matter to react with an equal number of normal hydrogen molecules to give a tiny cosmic explosion, which we see as a flash of blue light. The radiation is then analysed spectrophotometrically. The other half of the anti-matter hydrogen will be discharged into a special chamber, also containing normal hydrogen, but containing in addition several ursecta. This portion —'

Oberon broke in. 'Ursecta? You mean, those insects at the Node?'

'The same, sire. A very strange form of life – very small. The ursecta exist normally only at the Node. There, they feed on raw energy produced by strains in our expanding universe, somewhat in the same way the myriad diatoms of our oceans feed with the help of photosynthesis. Actually, we understand very little about the vital processes of the ursecta, but we do know their final metabolic product, just as we know the metabolic product of the diatom. For the diatom, this is mainly carbon dioxide; for the ursecta, it is the proton, or hydrogen. And this is the basis for our demonstration this evening.'

'Excuse the interruption,' said Oberon. 'Please continue.'

Kedrys bowed. 'As I was saying, the other half of our anti-matter hydrogen will be discharged into a special chamber, also containing normal hydrogen, but containing in addition several ursecta. In that chamber, the anti-matter molecules will likewise react with the normal hydrogen, but in this case there will be no explosion: the ursecta will instantly – *eat* – if you will, the energy as it is created, and will transform that energy into protons, just as they do at the Node.' He paused and looked up at the intent faces. 'We have already carried out this experiment with numerous forms of atomic energy, including several nuclear fusion processes, and generally on a larger scale. Here, we demonstrate with anti-matter for two reasons. Firstly, the experiment can be done in miniature, with complete safety; and secondly, an anti-matter explosion is the most powerful source of energy known – whether for peace or war. It will show, as can no other means, the capabilities of these strange little creatures, when they are scientifically controlled.'

His eyes sought out Oberon. 'The implications, sire, are tremendous. If we are able to develop this means of defending the planets of the Home Galaxy against nuclear attack before the other eleven galaxies discover it . . .' He shrugged.

Andrek sucked in his breath. The stalemate that had followed the War with Terror would be broken. The whole theory of reprisal, the great unanswerable deterrent to nuclear warfare, would collapse. This would be the Total Defence; its possessor would dominate the Twelve Galaxies.

'We understand the implications, Kedrys,' said Oberon quietly. 'Go ahead.'

The kentaur bowed again. 'We feed a very small amount of normal hydrogen into a very high vacuum reservoir.' He indicated with a wave of his hand. 'From this reservoir we further meter about one hundred molecules into the strain-plasma : this Mobius-Klein circlet.'

'Mobius...?' asked Lyysdon.

'Mobius-Klein. The term is inexact; yet it must serve. I'm sure all of you know the operation of a Mobius strip – a band with one end rotated 180 degrees, then fastened to the other end. If we slide an object along the strip, it returns to the starting position upside down. A system known as the "Klein bottle" is a three-dimensional analogue of the Mobius strip. For example, passing a ring through a Klein bottle will turn the ring inside out. So our strain-plasma circuit is like a Mobius-Klein circuit, except that we add one more dimension. And since our strain-plasma operates in four dimensions, it turns an object upside down, and inside out, and simultaneously does one more thing: it reverses the electrical charge of the sub-atomic particles. It puts a negative charge on the nuclear protons, and a positive charge in the electrons of the surrounding shell. In a word, it converts normal matter to anti-matter. And this is what will happen to our hydrogen molecules. Under the force of tremendous energy, accumulated for days and then released over an interval of a few milli-seconds, we send our hydrogen atoms around the Mobius-Klein circlet and get them back with their polarity reversed. The proton comes back negatively charged, and the electron of course becomes a positron. They have become anti-matter hydrogen. But before they can touch the walls of the apparatus, the stream spurts on, and is split, half into the chamber of normal hydrogen, and half into the chamber containing normal hydrogen and ursecta.'

He looked around him. 'Gentlemen, I must warn you that the release of these rather large energies into the circuit will cause a slight jar to the floor, and in fact to the foundations of the Great House. In effect, we will be making a small space quake. But there is no cause for alarm.' He stopped and surveyed his audience. 'Are there any questions?'

Andrek looked about him hesitantly, then asked, 'Is this why our space ships cannot use their nuclear drive in the Node area?'

'Just so, Don Andrek,' replied Kedrys. 'The ursecta drain off every erg of power the instant it is developed. For the same reason, a biem-gun will not fire at the Node.'

'Isn't there something that will drive the ursecta away? Something – they are afraid of?' Andrek finished nervously, aware that Oberon and Lyysdon were frowning at him.

'Yes,' said Kedrys. But he did not offer to elaborate.

'Could this equipment be scaled up for the manufacture of sizeable amounts of anti-matter?' asked Oberon. 'If it could be controlled, I should think we could find valuable uses for production quantities. How, exactly, would it behave?'

Lyysdon shook his head. 'It would annihilate.'

'Possibly,' said Kedrys. 'But quite aside from the question of annihilation, an anti-matter body of any considerable mass, say of the order of a gram, would be expected to create immense distortions in the normal space-time continuum within a radius of many metres. We bear in mind here that the electrostatic and electro-magnetic fields of anti-matter cannot even be described as *opposite* those created by the electrical profiles of ordinary matter. The precise relationship can be described only in mathematical terms, which I cannot go into, here and now. As a wretched over-simplification, I can only say that the electrical properties of anti-matter as against normal matter would probably be perpendicular to each other. This geometry can occur only by means of one or more added dimensions.'

'Do you mean that electro-magnetic radiation from anti-matter would occur in the fourth dimension?' asked Lyysdon.

'At *least* in what we would call a fourth dimension,' agreed Kedrys. 'And more likely also a fifth, and possibly even a sixth. Let me demonstrate.' He picked up a copper rod from a nearby experiment table. 'Consider the simplest case. Assume that electrons are flowing downward in this conductor, which is of normal matter. The induced magnetic field will then be circular around the conductor, and a compass needle held in the field will point counter-clockwise. Now, if the rod were anti-matter, with positrons flowing down the conductor could we hypothesize that the compass needle would point in the opposite direction? Indeed not! In this sense, we're not even sure what "opposite" means. Certainly, however, it does not mean opposite in a three-dimensional geometry. It is conceivable, of course, that an anti-matter compass needle might behave in just this way in an anti-matter world, with an anti-matter conductor. We have no experimental way to verify it. But our question is, what is the behaviour of anti-matter in a *normal* matter world. With a current flowing in an anti-matter conductor in a normal matter environment, how *then* does the needle point? The answer is, that the question makes no sense. It's like asking for the temperature of a pellet of ice in a pot of molten lead.'

'Well,' said Oberon, 'if the mass didn't annihilate, and its effects are dissipated in some other dimension, I don't see how it could bother anyone.'

Kedrys laughed. 'It's not that easy. If the anti-matter body were capable of control, it could be used, as I have said, to dominate all normal matter and normal energy in its area. It can warp normal space so that mass or energy moving into that space must be deflected out again. Thus it can act as a force-field, or shield. Concomitantly, it could be used as an attraction force, continuously forcing normal space to close behind an object, pushing it forward. And this barely scratches the surface. This ability to displace matter might even permit the transfer of matter into other dimensions.'

'Do you mean to say, that with a little anti-matter, you could toss me into the fourth dimension?' demanded Oberon.

'Yes,' said Kedrys gravely. He looked up, not at the Magister, but straight at Andrek. 'With enough anti-matter, properly controlled, it could easily be done.'

Oberon was greatly amused. 'Cast into the Deep from the middle of the Great House – with weapons and guards in every corridor? Really, Kedrys!'

Kedrys turned his great enigmatic eyes on the last of the Delfieri, and the muscles across his flank rippled as though saying in motion what he could not say in words. Finally, he replied quietly, 'I think you are safe, for the time being, at least. The amount of anti-matter required for such a feat does not exist on Goris-Kard. Several dozen kilos would be necessary. It would have to come from the depths of the Deep, and it would have to emerge under complete control. For some months, now, I have been working on a homing beacon, which can be beamed into the Deep. It may be functional in a few days. If it works, it may bring – something – in from the Deep. And then ... we shall see.'

Oberon smiled indulgently. 'That should be interesting. But keep it out of the Great House.'

The other observers smiled with him.

'Kedrys,' said Lyysdon, 'what *is* the Deep?'

'I don't know,' said the kentaur frankly. 'It's like explaining time and space. It's a lot easier to explain what they are *not*, than what they are. Consider the strangeness of space. It pours into our local Node at a tremendous rate, especially with the great quakes. We know it comes from the Deep. But this doesn't explain either space or the Deep. We know that space is more like a metal than a gas. It is like a metal, because it transmits transverse waves, but not longitudinal; and because it bends in a gravitational field. But we know it is neither metal, nor gas. We know what space is not, but not what it is. And the same is true for the Deep.'

Oberon broke the brief silence. 'We must proceed with the deomonstration,' he said curtly. 'I have much to do tonight.'

'Yes, sire.' Kedrys turned to Phaera. 'Sister, you may release the hydrogen molecules.'

The priestess turned to the apparatus, adjusted the dials, and pressed a button. Instantly, the floor shook, and there was a flash of blue light in the first quartz chamber. In the second chamber, the one with the ursecta, there was nothing. The vessel just sat there, motionless, grey-shadowed, and silent.

Kedrys shrugged. 'You see, that's all there is to it.'

And the biggest noise, thought Andrek, rising with the others, was the one that they all refused to hear : Horror again in flood through the Twelve Galaxies; Omega.

After the demonstration, Oberon led Andrek into a small office adjoining the laboratories.

They sat down. Andrek studied the face of the Magister. It was devoid of expression. It told him nothing.

'For the last eighteen years,' said Oberon, 'we have maintained a sizeable staff at the Node Station, in co-operation with the other eleven galaxies. You know the various functions. You've probably seen the reports from time to time. Temblor expectancies. Proton density. Storm patterns. Astrogation beacon data. Dull reading, most of them. At least, the published material. But not everything is published. We have one very secret project. You saw it demonstrated tonight.'

Andrek waited.

'A complete report has been prepared for you.' Oberon pushed a sealed case across the desk to the advocate. 'Read it on the ship. Both Kedrys and Lyysdon believe the ursecta can be trapped and transported to planetary atmospheres in large numbers. There they would consume a nuclear explosion, either fusion or fission. In fact, for the old type of nuclear process, their action is so rapid the charge cannot even reach critical mass.' He paused and looked hard at Andrek. 'You appreciate the possibilities?'

'Yes. If we have this, and the other eleven galaxies don't, we can attack without fear of reprisals. The stalemate will end.'

'But you see the questions?'

'I think so. Does it *really* work. And do any of the other eleven have it?'

'You will go to the Node, and there you will try to find out.'

'Yes, sire.'

There was a pause. Oberon continued. 'You are probably wondering why I picked you.'

Andrek waited in silence. Do I really wonder, he thought. You are sending me to the Node to die. Why . . . *why*?

Oberon noted the silence. His jaw muscles knotted, and he continued in curt, clipped tones. 'I have selected you because you can go without arousing suspicion. In three days the Arbiters of the Twelve Galaxies will convene at the Node Station to review and approve the demolition of the planet Terror. You will proceed there in your official capacity as Advocate-Liaison for the Delfieri.'

'Sire, isn't the sitting of the Arbiters largely a formality? They will certainly approve our demolition recommendations without a formal hearing.'

Oberon frowned. 'True. Nevertheless, Terror is a special case. That planet is the original source of the Horror, the disease spot of our entire Home Galaxy, and we must make sure she does not live to do this again. You will go to the Node, then, for the purpose of formally confirming our petition for the destruction of Terror, and to rebut any arguments to the contrary. The Terror matter will give you a legitimate reason for making the trip. You will find our complete file in this dossier.' He handed Andrek a big envelope. '*Xerol* is waiting. Amatar will show you out.' He did not offer his hand.

'With the Magister's permission, I would like to mention a matter involving your daughter, Amatar.'

Oberon looked at him sharply. 'Permission *not* granted.'

'But I love Amatar,' blurted Andrek. 'And she —'

'You will leave immediately,' said Oberon tautly.

And now I know, thought Andrek. He picked up the envelope, bowed in silence, and left.

> *I dream of darkness and the Deep.*
> *No moon shall set, no sun shall rise.*
> *What matter that I have no eyes?*
> *Since I am dead, I need not weep!*
> — A Song of the Rimor

After dismissing Andrek, Oberon returned to the Music Room with Kedrys and Vang. The room was empty, save for Amatar, who was seated at the harp, plucking the strings slowly, and singing in soft mournful harmony with the Rimor, who accompanied her in a funereal baritone:

> *'If I had wings, like Noah's dove,*
> *I'd fly up the river to the one I love.*
> *Fare thee well, oh my darling, fare thee well. . . .'*

Oberon listened, frowning, then cleared his throat and coughed. 'The song makes me uncomfortable. Cease, Rimor!'

The great console grew silent; Amatar's hands dropped from the harp.

Oberon sighed. 'What is the song about?'

'It's called "Dink's Song",' said Amatar, without looking up. 'It's about a peasant woman named Dink, who lived long ago. She is lonely for her man, who is working on something called a railroad, in Texas.'

' "Texas"?' said Oberon.

'Texas was a real place. On Terror, I think,' said the Rimor, 'even though some of your psycho-archaeologists insist it was a state of mind. But too many songs of Texas have survived to deny —'

'Never mind.' Oberon dismissed the matter with a wave of his hand. He turned to Amatar. 'The spider.'

She looked up at him, alert, unafraid. 'What about the spider?'

'Why did you give Andrek the spider?'

She answered coolly. 'It seemed appropriate, considering what awaits him on *Xerol*. What should I have given him? A blossom from the tree? With a pretty speech?' She stood up suddenly and whirled gaily, her skirt billowing out around her. 'James, Don Andrek, who would marry me, and who must

78

therefore die by treachery and guile far from home, take this lovely gift in remembrance of the illustrious House of the Delfieri!' She curtseyed low and handed Oberon an imaginary bouquet.

The man's nostrils were pale, pinched. 'Alea deliver us! You understand nothing!'

'I understand that you are going to kill a man.'

'I am. And I must. The life of one man means nothing to me. Nor ten men. Nor a nation. And probably not even a planet, if the House of the Delfieri is thereby preserved. In this galaxy there are nearly one million hominid planets, each with an average population of ten billion people. And you wonder that I shall slay one man.'

'Strange that this one man is the man I love.'

'It is not strange. The Aleans have determined it. It is his life or mine.' He continued vehemently. 'Who is this man, this Andrek? No one, and nothing! A pipsqueak advocate, a civil servant on the House Staff, hired directly from the university. Until he became involved with you, I had never heard of him. And now he must leave. He must certainly leave. He cannot be your husband. It is preposterous. I shall select your husband for you, when you are of age, and when the time is at hand. Your marriage shall be determined by the needs of the state.' The scar across his face glowed red. Amatar shrank back imperceptibly.

The Rimor's deep bass broke in. 'There is only one husband who meets your standards, liege.'

'Who is that,' asked Oberon suspiciously.

'Yourself,' said the Rimor blandly.

Amatar laughed bitterly.

'Cease these obscenities!' clipped Oberon. 'I will not have the House dishonoured by such thoughts!'

Vang, silent until now, spoke deferentially. 'Magister, if Mistress Amatar were to see the crystomorphs...'

'Yes,' said Oberon thoughtfully. 'Perhaps she should see them. Have the projector brought in. We will look at them in here.'

Within minutes, the Alean returned with two assistants, pushing a wheeled table. On the table was a curious array of apparatus, culminating in a stubby horizontal cylinder, all of which Amatar recognized as the crystomorph projector.

'You will have to explain it to me,' she said. 'I have heard of it, but I do not know how it operates.'

'The crystomorph is simple in operation and theory,' said

Vang. 'In essence, all known past experiential exposure of the subject is programmed as information bits into the machine. This summates his time-path as a vector quantity very precisely, and it becomes possible to subject that path to a given hypothetical stimulus and to estimate its impact on his extrapolated time-path. And we may, of course, expose a given time-path to several stimuli, simultaneously or in sequence. And finally, we can expose the time-path of a given subject to the impact of the summation of sequential stimuli represented by the time-path of a second subject. We have done this with the time-path of James, Don Andrek, and that of your father, Oberon of the Delfieri. The intersection shows —'

'But you cannot be sure!' cried Amatar. 'Granted, each of us is the sum of his heredity and imposed experiences. And I can see an element of predictability as to a response to a given situation. But experience, and events, are largely chance. Some may have a higher degree of probability than others, but in the final analysis, all is chance. Alea requires it.'

'True,' agreed the Alean. 'But Mistress must understand that the crystomorphs are offered, not to show what will certainly happen – nor what Alea has ordained, but rather what will probably occur if Alea does not intervene. We readily concede that man, a limited mortal, may set out on one path, and that chance will turn his footsteps into another. The difference in his aim, and in his result, is of course the direct intervention of Alea – and is but one more proof of her existence and divinity.'

Kedrys broke in. 'But here the exterior stimulus is the time-path index of another man – James, Don Andrek. You are exposing one human element to another. That squares the error factor.'

'We grant that,' said Vang, unmoved.

'But have you never considered,' said Kedrys, 'that the steps you now propose for the avoidance of this intersection, are the very events that will cause it to take place?'

'Ritornellian heresy!' declared Vang.

'Cease this bickering!' cried Oberon. 'By the custom of centuries, the Delfieri are Defenders of the Faith. But *which* faith? Can both Alea and Ritornel be true? And I am told of still other gods that merely sleep, awaiting their eventual reawakening. And so I believe them all, and defend all, and therefore none. Enough! Perform the intersection of the paths, that Amatar may be permitted to judge for herself.'

The monk bowed. 'For assurance of absolute accuracy, it

would be preferable to delay the demonstration long enough to bring both path indices up to the minute. Don Andrek has inferred certain information from his visit to Huntyr ... and then there's the pilgrim of Ritornel, and finally, the spider. ... As a minimum, these new factors should be computed into his index.'

Oberon was impatient. 'How can a spider affect a dynasty? Proceed immediately with the coincidence.'

Vang shrugged. 'As you wish.' He clapped his hands. An assistant stepped forward to the table. The lights in the room faded to near-darkness.

Before them a luminous crystomorph began to take shape, floating in enigmatic silence. Slowly, it pulsed, as though alive. Amatar stared in fascination.

'Each of us,' said the Alean, 'has his own distinctive crystomorph: it is the composite of a man's entire life experience, to that point, and is as unique as a fingerprint.' He pointed. '*That* ... is the crystomorph of Oberon of the Delfieri, as of the tenth hour, this morning.' He stepped up to the machine and adjusted the dial. The crystomorph flickered, then became steady again. 'The index after three days,' murmured Vang. 'This means that, absent malfacient factors, Oberon will be in good health for at least the next three days.'

'Finish this,' said Oberon bluntly.

The monk adjusted the dial again. After another vibration, the crystomorph steadied again. 'The index on the morning of the fourth day. As you can see, there is no change.' He folded back a part of the panel, thrust a metal slide into the slot. The crystomorph abruptly changed shape. The new design was shot through with flickering blue lines radiating luminously from the centre of the structure. 'It is the evening of the fourth day,' said the Alean. 'I have just superimposed the index of James, Don Andrek. The resultant is exclusively the time-path of Don Andrek. That of Obcron has ceased to exist, because, at this point in time, Oberon himself has ceased to exist.'

'Run it back an hour – to the ... incident ...' ordered Oberon.

Amatar felt her eyes glazing, and her chest hurting. She rubbed her palms convulsively on the unresponsive metalloid fabric of her skirt.

The monk adjusted the dials once more. Two superimposed crystomorphs took shape, one of nearly pure white light, the other shafted with radial red lines. 'The red is for Andrek's intent to destroy,' he said. 'Oberon is curious, but unmoved; he is shielded and cannot believe that he can be harmed. As you will note from the shifting boundaries, there seems to be considerable contact with external forces ... perhaps a group of people is involved. Considerable interplay. Actually, the entire episode seems to cover nearly half an hour. However, I shall show the remainder in rapid motion. Here, we note a further curious point: a fundamental change develops in Andrek's crystomorph – a second superimposition, as it were. Almost as though he were suddenly blended into two people. The other personality is *not* Oberon. And then the Magister is gone. Only Andrek remains.'

In her despair Amatar became a child, primitive. 'You say this is in the hands of Alea. Then let Alea speak. Roll the die!'

The monk was shocked. 'One does not converse idly with the goddess!'

'A man's life is at stake,' said Amatar firmly.

Oberon was grim. 'He dies because Alea has determined that he must.'

'Not necessarily,' insisted the girl. 'Brother Vang admits that the indices are now cold, by several hours. Variations might have crept in. The uncertainty grows with every passing moment. . . .'

Oberon looked at the girl wearily. 'You do plead for him, after seeing this?'

'I do, for we love each other.'

'How did you come to love such a one, in the first place?'

Amatar shrugged. 'How can I answer? Because it was he; because it was myself.'

Oberon turned harshly on the priest. 'Let it be done. Roll the Holy Die!'

Vang paled. 'Then must I warn you, Oberon of the Delfieri, that we may not awaken the goddess with impunity. The first time is never the last. The last time will surely come, and fearful things will follow.'

Oberon threw up his hands in exasperation. 'Your creeds provide explanations and solutions for all that is past and all that will come; it is only the present that defeats you!' He faced Vang squarely. 'Meanwhile, you waste time. The ship leaves in minutes. If the die requires it, I will take Andrek from the ship.'

The monk hesitated, then shrugged and reached into his tunic and began to unfasten the dodecahedral crystal from its chain around his neck.

'Wait,' said Oberon grimly. 'You are right. The first cast is never the last. Use mine.' He unfastened the golden die from his neck pendant. 'It has been used. Once, eighteen years ago. When it was found in the shambles of *Xerol*, the number "one" was showing.'

'The sign of Ritornel!' breathed Vang. 'Catastrophe!'

The scar glowed along Oberon's cheek. 'Yes. Yet, I lived.' From his pocket Oberon drew a golden dice cup. He dropped the die into the cup and handed it to Amatar. 'You, my dear, can make the throw. Shake it well, and then turn the cup down on the table.'

The girl covered the cup with long tapering fingers, shook the thing vigorously, and clapped the cup down on the table, covering the die. The tips of her index and middle fingers rested lightly on the bottom of the cup.

'Before I remove the cup,' said the girl quietly, 'I want to confirm what numbers are favourable to Andrek.'

'Surely we all know these things,' reproved the monk. 'The signs beloved to Alea, and favourable to her children, are twelve, for the twelve faces of the Die, each representing a galaxy of the Node group; five, for the pentagon faces of the Holy Die; six, for the number of pentagons in each half of the Die; three, for the triangle of each apex of the Die; eleven, for long life. The bad ones are of course one' – he spat – 'which is the sign of Ritornel, the false god; four, for —'

'What is two?' asked Amatar dully.

'Two is never thrown,' said the monk. 'It is too terrible. Not in the recorded history of the Twelve Galaxies has Alea permitted a two. That is why the necklace-clasp is fastened opposite the face of the "two": it is physically impossible for the die to come up "two".'

'Two means the great diplon – the double space quake,' said Oberon curtly. 'The ruin of ruin at the Node. There, all matter vanishes. Nothing survives.' He looked at her sharply. 'Lift the cup.'

She grasped the gleaming vessel firmly and raised it in a slow prescient arc. She stared unseeing at the die, then turned and walked from the room.

Kedrys followed her out, his face a mask.

'The clasp is caught in a crack in the table,' whispered Vang. 'It is . . . that which cannot be. . . .'

'It is a two,' said Oberon. 'Alea has spoken.'

'And will speak again,' said the monk.

'Remove the bauble and cup, monk,' said Oberon. '*Xerol* awaits you.'

'I will leave, Oberon of the Delfieri, but I may not take the Holy Die. *That* must remain here, untouched, until Alea shall choose to speak again.'

'As you will. But begone.'

Vang bowed, then hurried from the room, his long robes flapping.

For a long time there was silence. Finally Oberon spoke, almost as though to himself. 'Rimor.'

'I am here, mighty Oberon.'

The man studied the console thoughtfully. 'If you are going to be sarcastic, you will get no quirinal.'

'– of which you promised an extra ten milligrams for the Terror Epic – and for which I am waiting.'

'Sometimes,' said Oberon, 'you create the fantastic illusion that you are human, that you really exist.'

'Don't be deceived, Oberon. Except to myself, I don't really exist. To me, though, I'm quite real. I have proof for this, but I'm afraid it would not convince you.'

'Proof?'

'Yes. I'm in love with your daughter. *Amo, ergo sum.*'

Oberon frowned. 'You well know I do not understand the ancient tongues. But no matter. Everybody seems to be in love with Amatar. It proves nothing. To me, you're still a computer.'

'And what are you, Oberon? Do *you* exist? I can neither see, touch, smell, nor taste you. I can hear you, but that could mean that you were merely a noise. Lots of inanimate things make noises. But we are digressing. How about the quirinal?'

'How can a computer be a drug addict?' murmured Oberon.

'It was not my choice.' The voice was now low, sad. 'As you well know, the slave drug is essential to my neural metabolism. In fact, I now remind you that today is the eighteenth anniversary of that day when you first promised to release me from my addiction. The lower dial on the right of the console, Oberon. A simple twist of the wrist, and it will be ended.'

'Rimor, you know this is impossible. In the first place, it is not convenient for me. You are like part of my own mind. I like to talk to you. We can talk together. You have a definite place in the stability of the Delfieri culture. In the second place, I think you do not really want to – be released. If you truly exist, as you seem to think, how could you possibly prefer death to life? It is unthinkable. So, I gather you expect simply to put me at a disadvantage by your annual reminder of the covenant – which you think may result in a guilt feeling and an increase in your quirinal dose. Well, put this from your mind, friend Rimor. I have no feeling about it, none whatever.'

'It attests to the depths of your humanity and psychic resources,' said the console, 'that you have found the fortitude to endure my misfortune.'

The Magister did not seem to hear this. He continued, introspectively. 'When I was a young man, I was a human being. Now all my human reactions I delegate, mostly to you, Rimor. I cannot afford to be a human being. I cannot indulge the luxury of feeling love ... hate ... tenderness.'

'I'm glad you brought that up,' muttered the Rimor. 'I'm jester, troubadour, minstrel, healer of minds. I should get quadruple wages. Make it forty milligrams.'

Oberon ignored him. 'Each day is but a circlet of weary, useless, little things. A coming and going of scrapers and bowers, and bearers of grim tidings. To stay alive, I slay, but each death requires another. Death feeds on death, and there is no end. By the krith that hungered for me, perhaps it were better I died that black night at the Node!' He turned querulously towards the console. 'Do you think I like doing this – sending that young man out to die?'

'Do you?' countered the console, almost curiously.

'I think I am having an emotion,' muttered the man uncomfortably. 'Get rid of it.'

'A little emotion never hurt anybody,' growled the Rimor. 'Especially the kind you're having now. If you didn't occasionally hate yourself, you'd find yourself unbearable.'

'You know very well I cannot endure these primitive glandular responses. Give me a suitable counter-verse. Think sad, beautiful thoughts for me, so that I am justified. Rimor, purify me!'

The Rimor's voice held a sly timbre. 'The Aleans think emotions help distinguish you hominids from the lower animals.'

'If I have to take an anti-emotion capsule, you will get no quirinal for three days.'

'Ah yes. Shall we say, then, a total of fifteen milligrams?'

'Fifteen.'

'Let me think a moment.'

Oberon waited.

'I have it now. A sad poem, with genuine counteractive emotion. It will give you fitting rest this night.

     ' *"Each night, when I go to bed,*
      *I put three bullets in my head.*
      *One for shelter from dishonour,*
      *One to comfort me for living,*
      *One for life among the dead.*
      *Now shall peace attend my dreaming.*
      *Now shall twilight gently fall.*
      *With truth and justice still remaining,*
      *Let night and wisdom cover all."* '

Oberon's great scar seemed momentarily to fade. He walked over to the console, turned a dial on the panel to read 'fifteen', and pressed one of the buttons. 'That was well said. I did not understand all of it, but it induces meditation, and meditation brings sleep. Goodnight, Rimor.'

'Peace, Oberon.'

At the third hour of the morning, when the world was still dark, Amatar awakened suddenly from restless sleep and sat up rigid in her bed, listening.

Excepting the far-muted nocturnal rumble of the giant city – caught midway between slumber and waking, she heard nothing.

She turned on the night light with a whisper, slipped into night coat and slippers, and walked over to the door. The sensor panel showed that the hallway was empty. Working the panel controls, she released the protector field that enveloped her apartment, rolled back the door, and stepped out into the hall. Here, she stopped again to listen. She should not be out here without an escort. Oberon had strictly forbidden it.

This time she thought she could hear something – a very faint and muted thing, convulsive, uncontrollable, nearly hideous : the sound of sobbing. And then it was blotted out by the approach of marching feet. A patrol was coming. But now she knew where the sound was coming from. She had time.

She bent down quickly, removed her slippers, and began to run. When she reached the Music Room, she slipped inside and closed the door. Seconds later, the patrol clattered past the door.

She looked around. The room was empty. She walked over to the great console. Her throat was constricted, and she was beginning to shake. She could hardly speak. She did not recognize her own voice. It was broken, guttural. 'Omere! Jim is going to be all right! He has Raq, and the plan must work. I could not do more, and I could not warn him, because my father would instantly destroy you both.'

She knew the Rimor heard her; but the metallic unearthly weeping continued, beyond consolation, beyond sorrow. Tears started from her eyes. She wiped them away with her finger-tips, then sat down at the foot of the console, with her cheek pressed against its intricate facing. She got her voice under control through sheer will power, and then she began to croon a lullaby, low-pitched, lovely. After that, she hummed a ballad, and then an ancient folk song. As the hours passed, there were dozens of songs. Sometimes there were words, sometimes not.

Faint intimations of dawn were filtering into the room when she finally struggled to her feet. She was exhausted, and every bone in her body ached. But the room was silent. She noted numbly that she still held her slippers in her hand.


Andrek, stretched out under the loose elastic belts on his cabin bunk on the *Xerol*, was trying perfunctorily to nap. But it was no good. Sleep was impossible. Since boarding, every moment had increased his feeling of impending disaster. The ship had closed around him like a giant plated fist. It might squeeze shut and crush him at any moment. His thoughts were racing, and sleep was out of the question. He laced his fingers under the back of his head and stared glumly at the overhead bunk light. From there, his eye followed absently a jagged weld-line across the ceiling. He had noticed similar repairs in other parts of the ship. Evidently *Xerol* had seen heavy battle service in years past, and had been extensively rebuilt.

He was certain that he was being sent away to die. Both of Oberon's so-called assignments, official and unofficial, were transparent subterfuges, devices simply to get him on *Xerol*, away from people who might ask questions or help him. *Xerol*'s voyage to the Node would take three days. At some time within the next three days, Oberon would have him killed.

Three days. Which day would it be? How would it be done? Who would do it? As he thought about it, he could see how ridiculously simple it would be. Anyone on the ship, from the captain down to the cabin boy, could walk up to him at any moment, pull out a biem, and put a hole in him. They knew he had no weapon, no means of defence. The locked door of his cabin was no protection. Anyone with a duplicate photo key could open it from the outside. He looked over at the door uneasily, as though expecting it to swing open. He shook his head dizzily. He'd have to get a grip on himself. There had to be a way out, and he was going to find it.

Why did Oberon want him dead?

Because he loved Amatar? If the Magister wanted to break that up, all he needed to do was to give him an outlandish assignment in a foreign galaxy, where he'd be away from Goris-Kard for years.

No, there was more to it than that. It was almost as if the Magister considered him a personal threat. And that was ridiculous. How could an insignificant advocate, even on the staff of the Great House, affect the powerful dynasty of the Delfieri?

The thought was implausible – yet he could not get it out of his head. If, perchance, he were a personal threat to Oberon, it was an unwitting threat, certainly not of his choosing or volition. In any such role he was a puppet, plunged alone, friendless, into a totally alien drama, with plot unknown, and lines unlearned.

But was he alone in this? Certainly, the grey pilgrim of Ritornel had interceded for him in Huntyr's office. But where was the pilgrim now? On the ship? It seemed unlikely. Now that Oberon's people knew about the pilgrim, the ship's officers would not allow him to board. Or else, he would be permitted aboard and then taken prisoner. Or killed.

Andrek shivered. At this moment, a nearby cabin might have a corpse for an occupant.

He unbuckled the bunk belts and tried to sit up. His unaccustomed weightlessness caused him to lose contact with the side bars of the bunk, and he floated out into the centre of the room, over the central table and chairs. He looked down. On the table was his attache case. And that suggested other problems. Raq, the spider, was probably hungry. For that matter, so was he. His conscience bothered him, especially since he had promised Amatar to feed the hideous little creature. On the other hand, he had never really overcome his fear of Raq, and now he grasped at an opportunity to delay the encounter. Raq would have to wait; he didn't feel equal to the task of facing her on an empty stomach.

He touched the 'ceiling' lightly with his fingertips, then floated over to the cabin door, where his magnetized shoe soles contacted the floor. He opened the door quietly and looked outside. The corridor was empty. He closed and locked the door and strode off towards the mess. At least, at table, he should be reasonably safe. It was difficult to imagine sitting opposite a ship's officer, quietly eating one's dinner and sipping a little wine, engaged perhaps in light conversation about *Xerol*'s motors and accommodations – and then being suddenly shot on the spot. Andrek's mouth twisted wryly. What a breach of table etiquette! But on further reflection, he decided that it wasn't very funny. And the people assigned to kill him were probably not too concerned about form or manners.

The entrance was just ahead. He could smell the odours of cooking, and hear the muffled voices amid the sharper clatter of dishes and silver. He suddenly realized how hungry he was. His mouth watered and his steps speeded up a little. For a moment, he almost relaxed.

But even as he walked through the entrance of the mess, he felt a sharp premonition of danger.

Three people were seated at the first table. Even before he sought out their faces, he knew who they were – who they had to be. The scene was an exact repetition of the dining-hall on Terror's moon, even to the angle of the table, the wine bottle, the empty chair waiting for him.

Vang smiled icily at Andrek and motioned towards the chair.

Huntyr turned around, his golden eye-patch alive with pin-points of reflected light. Hasard simply glowered at the advocate.

Huntyr was the first to speak.

'All chance of Alea, Don Andrek!' he said genially. 'Will you join our table?'

Andrek was certain the pounding of his heart was audible all over the little dining-room. He realized very quickly several things. If there were any doubt as to his intended fate, it was gone now. He was to be killed on the ship, en route to the Node. He had not merely walked into a trap: he had been *placed* in one. Things were being done to him.

And Vang was a real surprise. Evidently either Oberon didn't trust Huntyr to handle the assassination alone, or else Vang had a very special function in the plot. Perhaps he was both super-visor and specialist. In either case, his presence indicated that Oberon was not satisfied with the conventional forms of mur-der, and that something bleak and horrid was brewing. But if Vang was a specialist, what was his speciality? Andrek had a feeling he'd soon know, sooner than he wanted, and that it would not be a pleasant discovery. Meanwhile, he intended to survive, even though this would require massive alterations in his hitherto aloof approach to life and circumstance. If he came out of this alive he doubted that he would still be recognizable as Andrek, Don and Advocate. Let it be so: he was going to live.

And now, within seconds, he had to make an accurate military appraisal of the situation, try to guess their plan of attack, how they intended to kill him, marshal his weapons, plan a defence. Weapons? Defence? It was very funny. No gun. Not even a club. But wait. There was Raq. Under the right conditions, against the right man, Raq would certainly provide an element of surprise. It might work. But certainly not against Vang. And probably not against Huntyr. Huntyr was experienced, cautious. But Huntyr's assistant, Hasard, had never impressed him as bursting with intelligence. Hasard was just right. First, of course, he'd have to get Hasard into his room, alone with him and Raq. But that would still leave Huntyr and Vang. He must be free from interruption during those critical moments with Hasard. But how could he keep the other two occupied during his trial with Hasard? And then he had the answer. And with that, the whole plan crystallized, scintillating, unanswerable, perfect. To save his life, a man will cram into one vital instant the intelligence and imagination of a lifetime.

His case was complete, his brief ready; it was time to address the court.

He greeted them with friendly banality. 'May the Ring of Ritornel embrace you all!' He took the chair offered by Huntyr, then calmly launched his attack. 'Weren't you mildly insulted?' he asked Huntyr.

'Insulted?' Huntyr's fork hung in mid-air.

'To be assigned personally to the murder of one so harmless?'

Without changing a muscle, Huntyr's face somehow ceased to smile. 'That's bad talk, your honour.'

Andrek looked over at Vang. 'Have *you* ever shot a man?' he asked amiably.

The monk opened his mouth, then shot an inquiring look at Huntyr. He turned back to Andrek but did not answer.

Andrek laughed. 'I thought not. Not your line, is it? Nor mine. But your comrade has shot men before. Several. As you know, he has been told to kill *me*. I'm unarmed. In fact, I don't know one end of a biem-gun from the other; and I can't hide. It's like shooting fish in a barrel. Huntyr's man Hasard, here, could do it, but you are here to see that Huntyr does it personally. And you'll probably blab it all over Goris-Kard when you return, how the heroic Huntyr killed a harmless, helpless don.' His lip curled. 'Huntyr! What admiration – what acclaim – awaits your return!'

Huntyr scowled. 'You talk too much, Don Andrek. You have a way of making people say things they shouldn't say. But I know all about you. I don't have to say anything.'

Andrek laughed. 'Quite true, my treacherous friend. You are well advised to be silent. There will be more than sufficient talk by others.'

Huntyr wiped his mouth roughly with his napkin. 'And anyhow, you have it all wrong.'

Vang suddenly turned warning eyes on his companion.

Andrek had guessed right. There was already bad feeling between Huntyr and Vang. Each wanted to control the assassination, and neither would take orders from the other. The situation was building up. If his control held, Huntyr and Hasard would be leaving the table within a few more minutes. He might even get a little unconscious help from Vang.

'Careful, Huntyr,' chided Andrek. 'You're not only risking your fee, but also your professional future. Your Alean friend thinks you'd better follow his orders, and bear up under the ridicule. In fact, I think he wants you to shut up altogether. Think it over, and pass the salt, if you please.' He waited. 'Brother Vang, the salt?'

The monk snapped the container viciously towards Andrek. The advocate caught it expertly in mid-air and gave him a friendly smile. He looked at Vang as he talked, but he knew that Huntyr was listening – and with growing resentment.

'I myself have several assistants,' said Andrek. 'I trained them myself, and I trust them completely. In fact, I take pride in them. A professional man is best judged by the performance of his assistants, don't you think? Now, of course, if Huntyr feels he is basically incompetent in the selection and training of his assistants, then he is quite right in not delegating the assignment.' He looked first at Hasard, then at Huntyr. 'Is something wrong with your steak?' he asked the investigator solicitously.

Huntyr threw down his napkin, glared first at Andrek, then at Brother Vang. Finally, he summoned Hasard with an imperious jerk of his head, and they both clacked heavily out of the room with as much dignity as their magnetized shoe soles would allow.

Andrek shook his head regretfully. 'No sense of humour.

Spoils a good man. No offence, you understand, but I think you might have made a better selection.' He regarded Vang with a long curious appraisal.

First, the monk would have to be kept here a few minutes. That should not be too difficult. Second, a large, unexplainable sum of money would have to be planted on the Alean. And that was going to require finesse.

'Linger a moment, Ajian,' urged Andrek. 'Even on hyperdrive, this will be a long three day trip. You are making it very difficult for an old classmate to be friendly.'

Vang, who was pushing back his chair, hesitated, then stared coldly at Andrek. 'What do you want?'

Andrek said, 'May I see your die?'

The Alean made an involuntary gesture towards his chest. 'Why?' he asked suspiciously.

Andrek's eyebrows lifted in feigned astonishment. 'How can my seeing your die possibly place you at a disadvantage? Is it conceivable that you could be afraid of me?'

Vang hesitated, then shrugged and reached into the folds of his long robe and drew out the die. 'It can make no difference,' he said. But he kept it in hand, and did not disconnect it for Andrek's closer inspection.

As Andrek suspected, it was still the old pyrite dodecahedron, one of millions grown on mass production lines in the Alean shops, the one that Vang had bought years ago at the Academy. It declared instantly the economic status of its wearer. Vang was a poor man, and he wanted to be rich. This should facilitate the next phase of Andrek's plan. He reached into his inside jacket pocket and pulled out the credit refund cheque Huntyr had given him that morning. He turned it over on the table and took out his stylus. 'I'm endorsing this in blank. It's worth ten thousand gamma to any person presenting it at any bank. And I'll stake it against your holy die.'

Vang looked at Andrek in open amazement. His eyes shifted covertly to the cheque. He said noncommittally: 'You seem very sure of yourself. What do you want to wager about?'

Andrek answered quietly. 'A test of strength. I'll take Ritornel, you take Alea. I propose to prove to you, here and now, that Ritornel is supreme over Alea.'

This was rankest heresy, and Andrek smiled inwardly as he watched the monk's reaction. In slow sequence, Vang turned pale, then pink, then, as his anger mounted, red.

Andrek continued coolly. 'Is our predestined life-death cycle immune to the operation of the laws of chance, or is the eternal return, the omega, the Ring, merely the statistical consequence of chance? I contend that the conflict can be resolved – in favour of Ritornel – by a simple experiment. If I am wrong, you take the cheque for ten thousand gamma. If I am right, I take your die.'

'What is the experiment?' demanded Vang harshly.

'The equipment consists simply of my cheque, your die, and my ink marker. Here is the cheque, face down. We will take turns rolling the die. The number that comes up each time will be taken as a vector, with the direction of the number on a clock face. And we draw a line having the length of one edge of the die, from the centre of this line on my cheque, in the direction of that number. For example, if the die comes up "6", we draw a line three centimetres long – one die length – straight down the cheque, in the direction of "6" on a clock face. At the end of that line we mark an "x". Then the die is rolled again. Say the second number is "9". From the "x" we draw another three-centimetre line in the direction of the "9" on a clock face. That gives us a new point of departure. We will roll a total of twelve times, and we add the new vector each time to the previous terminus of the line.'

'How can that prove anything?' said Vang suspiciously.

'If Ritornel holds dominion over Alea, the line will eventually return to the starting position on the cheque; if the line zig-zags away at random without returning to the start, then destiny is not a foreordained return, but is instead a matter of pure chance, and Alea is supreme over Ritornel.'

He waited as Vang considered this.

The problem was identical to the statistical mechanics of molecular motion, whereby the mean free path of a given molecule in a fluid is determined. It was also known as the 'drunkard's walk': if a drunkard started from a lamp-post and took twelve steps, each in random direction from the one preceding, how far would he be from the lamp-post? He would not be twelve steps distant, but he wouldn't be back at the lamp-post, either! By the laws of chance, his distance from the lamp-post would be the square root of the total length of those twelve steps. And so must be the outcome of the experiment he now proposed to Vang. The line would wander randomly around in the near vicinity of the cheque, and the final point, theoretically, would be the square root of 36 centimetres – two die lengths – distant from the starting point. So, he would certainly lose. It was a simple exercise in statistical mechanics, and religion had nothing to do with it.

Apparently Vang realized this too. Andrek waited as the monk mentally double-checked the maths. The ten thousand gamma was as good as planted on him.

'I will do it,' said Vang finally. 'Not for the money, but in obedience to Alea, that sacrilege may be punished, and the falsity of Ritornel be revealed.'

Andrek suppressed a smile. 'I have no wish to offend the goddess. We could wager for buttons.'

Vang frowned. 'No. Alea has already forgiven your presumption. It is agreed.' As he put the die on the table, he shot one final searching look at the advocate from narrowed, glinting eyes. 'Let us drink to the bargain.' From the table tankard he pressured two capsules of wine and handed one to Andrek. 'To Alea!'

'To Ritornel!' countered Andrek. He waited until Brother Vang had taken a couple of swallows, then lifted his own capsule to his lips. The Aleans were skilled poisoners, and there was no sense in running any risk.

'I must unscrew the locking loop,' continued Andrek, 'so that the "2" can come up.'

Vang nodded.

Andrek rolled the die. It clattered briefly along the steel table-top, then stopped, held to the metal surface by the natural ferromagnetism of the crystal pyrite.

Vang spat. 'A "1" – the sign of Ritornel. Mark your line.'

Andrek measured off the line against the die face one length in the direction of one o'clock, then handed the die to Vang. 'Your turn.'

Vang rolled a '2', and shuddered.

'Disaster at the Node!' said Andrek cheerily. He measured it off, then rolled. 'A "3".'

Vang relaxed. The line was moving away.

The next numbers were 4, 5, and 6. Andrek looked curiously at the resulting figure, which was a geometrically perfect half of a dodecagon. 'Alea seems to be on your side, Brother Vang. We're already several die lengths away from the start.'

Vang did not smile, but his eyes glittered. 'Roll!'

Andrek threw a '7'. Vang followed with '8', and then Andrek took a '9'.

They both examined the figure uneasily. Clearly, it was a dodecagon, three-fourths complete. The line was circling back!

Andrek felt drops of perspiration forming on his forehead. What was happening was a statistical impossibility. He suddenly realized that perhaps the cheque was not going to get planted on Vang. But he *had* to lose! His life might depend on it. What was the probability that nine numbers could come in exactly this sequence? One in twelve to the ninth power! Was it conceivable that the god Ritornel truly existed?

He glanced at Vang. The monk's face was taut, bloodless. Clearly, Vang was equally concerned. Was it only about the money? Andrek could not be sure.

Vang tensed, closed his eyes, and rolled a '10'. Andrek followed with '11'. He marked the lines and handed the die to Vang hypnotically.

Lacking one line, the dodecagon was complete.

Vang stared in growing horror at the figure. 'The Ring of Ritornel...' he whispered. 'We ... I ... have desecrated Alea!' He glared at the advocate. 'Daimon, you shall pay for this!'

Pay? There was still a way! 'Would ten thousand gamma satisfy the goddess?' said Andrek humbly. 'After all, we did no real harm. We stopped before the Ring was finished. And no one knows what the next die would have been. It might not have been a '12' at all.'

Vang hesitated, but finally took the cheque. 'Perhaps. In my prayers, I shall beseech Alea to forgive you.' But something still troubled him. He examined the advocate's face at length. 'So now you've lost both the experiment and the money. You've proved nothing. Yet, somehow, you seem rather pleased. What were you really after, James Andrek? What did you hope to gain by this sacrilegious demonstration?'

'Time,' said Andrek.

'Time? For what?'

'For – certain events to take place.'

'I don't understand.'

'Because you are not asking the right questions. The first question is, "where is Huntyr?"'

'All right, where is Huntyr?'

'Huntyr's back in his room by now,' said Andrek.

This seemed to relieve Vang. But Andrek did not intend to permit the monk to enjoy his relief. 'The next question, of course, is Hasard.'

'Hasard?' said the monk blankly.

'Yes. Where's Hasard?'

'With Huntyr.'

Andrek smiled. 'I'm afraid, my holy friend, that you have not given your close attention to the events of the last few minutes. Hasard is *not* with Huntyr.'

The Alean shrugged. 'Not that it makes any difference, but where do *you* think he is.'

'He's in *my* room.'

Vang started. Andrek noted this with satisfaction.

'You're guessing,' said the monk uncertainly.

'Of course. But I'm sure I'm right. Huntyr took it upon himself just now to delegate my assassination to Hasard. So it's Hasard, not Huntyr, who'll be waiting for me when I return.'

'Why are you telling me all this?' asked the Alean bleakly.

The first phase was over. Andrek relaxed a little. 'Basically, to gain time. I'd rather deal with Hasard than with Huntyr. And if you suspected I'd be successful in goading him into the substitution, you'd try to get to him and stop him. But by now, he's either made the switch – or he hasn't. So you're free to go, if you like.'

The monk stood up. A delicate pink was suffusing along his throat and cheeks. Andrek almost laughed as Vang hurried from the room. But not yet. Mirth was still a bit premature. He pushed himself away from the table and looked around the mess-hall. It was empty. He shrugged. What difference did it make? He was not going to demand protection from the ship's officers or from anyone else on the ship. This ship was a government courier. The captain undoubtedly had orders from the Great House not to interfere – and perhaps even to help Huntyr, if the need arose.

Everything was up to him. He was on his own, and he accepted it.

He stood erect and strode from the room.

As he clacked down the halls, he re-integrated the variables. Planting the cheque on Brother Vang was going to help, but not immediately. The immediate drama would begin in Andrek's cabin, and there, he hoped – and feared – two of the actors were at this moment probably impatiently awaiting his return. In Andrek's mind they were weirdly similar in their potentials for sudden violence: a courier case with a very hungry spider ... and Hasard with a biem-gun. It was time to raise the curtain and start the festivities.

He stopped in front of his cabin door and knocked. As he expected, there was no answer. 'Hasard?' he called loudly, 'Andrek here. Hold your fire. I'm coming in.'

He lifted the latch and opened the door.

Hasard was sitting in the chair by the table. His right hand held a biem-gun, resting casually on his knee. With his left hand he reached over and turned up the lights. 'Come in,' he said. 'And close the door.'

Andrek closed the door behind him carefully. And, concealing the motion with his body, he locked it with the inside latch. He wanted no interruptions from the corridor.

He studied the man quietly. The question now was – how much did this shark-faced brute know about him, and why he, Andrek, was on *Xerol*? Probably very little. Probably Huntyr had simply told the man to wait for him in this room and to kill him here.

'Keep your hands up,' said the intruder.

Andrek raised his hands, and continued to examine the hard features. Hasard's pleasures were written on his face. They were simple but expensive: women and night life, probably in Huntyr's borrowed coupe. Money would make a strong appeal. Andrek had very little money, but it was unlikely the other knew this. So he would start by talking money. It would at least delay matters, give him time to develop the details of his defence. No one, honest or otherwise, had ever been killed while in the act of offering a bribe!

And during the forthcoming dialogue, there was a very important point that he had to work into the conversation. He was certain that Hasard carried a transmitter on his person, and that Huntyr and Vang were back in their cabin listening to every word. On this assumption, Huntyr was about to hear something that would keep him very seriously occupied with Vang for the next few minutes.

Andrek faced Hasard and said, rather loudly: 'Brother Vang agreed at dinner tonight to call off the assassination. For ten thousand gamma. It's Huntyr's own refund cheque to me. You remember it, I'm sure. Oberon made him give it to me. I endorsed it and gave it to the good brother. He put it in the inner pocket of his robe, and promised to divide it between the three of you.'

Hasard laughed. 'A smart man like you, Don Andrek, an advocate and all, ought to do better than that.'

'Really? You mean you don't believe me? This is indeed embarrassing.' Andrek breathed deeply. Perhaps it was his imagination, but he thought he saw Hasard's trigger finger relax. Clearly, the man was interested. The fish was circling the bait, and sniffing hungrily. Andrek hoped that by now Huntyr was fully occupied with Vang and couldn't pay attention. He tried to visualize affairs in Huntyr's cabin ... Huntyr's voice rising ... Vang's vehement and indignant denial ... Huntyr insisting on searching the other ... violent hands ... the discovery of the cheque. But the actual details didn't really matter. Just so those two kept each other busy for five minutes.

'I can see,' said Andrek, 'that it will take more than just talk to persuade you not to kill me. You're a good man. You impress me. It's a pity you're on the wrong side. Our organization could certainly use a man like you.' He lowered his hands slightly. 'Have you ever considered coming over to us at, say, twice your present salary?'

The other considered this, then scowled. 'You're crazy. I don't even want to listen to you. I'm going to kill you and get out of here.'

'Efficient, loyal, that's what I like,' said Andrek. His hands dropped slowly to his sides. 'But don't worry about Huntyr. We'll guarantee personal protection *and* we'll give you a handsome starting bonus: one hundred thousand gamma.' He spoke the words slowly, impressively.

Andrek could see that the amount of money hit Hasard like a hard blow to the body. He could sense the physical impact on the man. It was ten years' income, enough for him to leave Huntyr. Enough for a villa, servants, respectability, acceptance in high places. The coarse features oscillated between greed and disbelief. The man rose halfway out of the chair. 'You're lying! You don't have that kind of money here!'

'Oh, I have it, all right, and it's here. Unhappily, it's the payroll for the staff at the Node Station, and I can't touch it. You'll have to wait until we get to the bank at the Station.'

He watched Hasard's reaction with a profound and growing amazement, which, however, he was careful to conceal. He had hoped the plan would work, of course, and actually had seen no real risk of failure. And yet, to watch it unfold with such perfection, such precision, seemed almost too good to be true. But it wasn't over yet. Hasard had to be persuaded to open the attache case and to open it with avarice, and without suspecting what was waiting inside. He glanced at the case on the table, as though by inadvertence, then hastily returned his eyes to the killer.

The other turned his head slowly, saw the case, and smiled. 'How much you got there?'

'Credits for over two hundred thousand. But don't get any ideas ... the case is locked, and I alone know the combination. If you try to blast the lock, it will auto-destruct.'

'What's the combination?'

Oh Amatar, my strange darling, thought Andrek. How did you know? He said sharply, 'You don't understand. I can't give you *that* money. You'll have to wait until we get to the bank at the Station.'

Almost casually, Hasard raised his biem and fired. Andrek put his hand to his ear. His fingers felt something warm and wet. His ear stung horribly. The lobe-tip was gone. Blood was dripping on his shoulder.

But it was all right. He had won. The hard part was over. Hasard was, for practical purposes, dead.

The other waited patiently.

Andrek knew his voice was going to shake. But that, too, was all right. It would add a further note of sincerity to the proceedings. 'The combination consists of the fair numbers of Alea: twelve right, six left, five right, three left.'

'That's fine. Now you come over here and stand in front of me while I open it.'

'I'd be happy to open it for you....'

'And pull out a biem? Just do like I said, Don Andrek. And hands high.'

'Of course, dear fellow.' Andrek sidled around in front of the thug, with the table between them. Hasard bent down and began turning the dial with slow, studied care.

Andrek's every nerve was on edge, poised to strike. It was working, the whole thing, just as he had known it must. The only thing about the cascading sequence that astonished him was his own calmness. It was hard for him to realize that he, a peaceful, rather sedentary advocate, was about to fight a man to the death.

And it must come in seconds, for in seconds the killer must make contact with Raq, and in the resulting brief flurry of shock and indecision, Andrek planned to hurl himself over the table and take the biem.

So thinking, he was quite unprepared for what actually happened.

Raq's stomach was small. It needed frequent replenishment. She had not eaten in nearly twenty hours, and she was ravenous. Also, she was cramped, and it was impossible for her to stretch her legs. Her temper, ordinarily placid and retiring, now suffered from the combined effects of hunger and confinement. She was coiled like a spring, and she was furious.

Amatar's conditioning made it impossible for Raq to harbour resentment towards Andrek. His footsteps and voice came to her clearly through the walls of the case and code box. This left, as a focal point for her rage, the other two-legger, whose footsteps and voice told her that he stood just above and outside her prison. There was something about his voice that put an edge of fear on Raq's growing dislike of him. The spring within her coiled tighter. Her mandibles chattered and began to drip toxin.

Hasard grasped the lid by the front left corner and raised it.

A horrid blur hit him in the mouth. He screamed, dropped his gun, clapped his hands to his face, and began to collapse. Raq, disconcerted by the approaching hands, disengaged her mandibles, now dripping with blood, and leaped away in good time. She struck the drapes on the opposite cabin wall and froze there, to await developments.

Andrek broke part way out of his shock, retrieved the biem-gun during one of its wild ricochets from the cabin walls, and stuck it in his belt. He was probably safe for the moment. Firstly, Huntyr, if he were listening in, would probably assume that the scream came from him, Andrek, and secondly, it was even more likely that Huntyr was, at this moment, engaged in a bitter argument with Vang regarding the cheque. That cheque would probably be impossible for the Alean to explain. Wager, indeed! Andrek felt a very faint tinge of sympathy for the monk.

Breathing heavily, he turned back to his visitor. He had never seen a man lose consciousness under weightless conditions, and he watched the process with a kind of vague wonder. First, there was a general relaxation and contraction of all the gross motor muscles. Being fixed to the floor by his magnetic shoes, Hasard had to contract in that direction. Visibly, he seemed to shrink. His knees buckled, his arms and shoulders took on an ape-like crouch, and his knuckles curled 'downwards' towards the floor. His mouth was slack, and his lower lip, where Raq had struck, was rapidly swelling. His eyes squinted in deadened amazement at the floor.

Andrek shook his head rapidly, as though to recover his scattered senses.

A decision had to be made, and quickly. Should he simply push the unconscious man out into the corridor? But that made no sense. Huntyr would surely find him and resuscitate him, and then the odds would be nearly as bad as before. And, having educated his enemies, their next try might be altogether different. No, Hasard could not be turned back to Huntyr. Then how about the brig? No good, either. *Xerol*'s officers probably had orders to co-operate with Huntyr and Brother Vang. Any complaints to the captain might well have fatal consequences.

By elimination, then, there was only one alternative left.

Murder.

Andrek shivered. He had never killed a man before, and the thought of killing an unconscious man struck him as a new low in sportsmanship. He realized now the nature of desperation, and how the primal urge to continue living can force a man to do anything. 'Absolutely anything,' he muttered.

He looked down at Hasard's crumpled body in anger and frustration. The man's chest was moving quietly, rhythmically. The breathing was barely audible. Andrek sighed and studied the controls on the biem. Hasard would have to be vaporized. A great deal of heat would be released in the cabin. He stepped over to the room service panel and turned the thermostat to 'colder'. The response was almost immediate. As his breath began to frost, he turned up the ventilation duct. The drapes began to flutter, and some papers floated out into the room. Then he kneeled down beside the unconscious man and turned off the magnetic switch in his shoes. Hasard floated free. Andrek stepped back, drew the biem, adjusted the energy cone, and was about to pull the trigger, when he had a sudden thought.

He really ought to search the body.

He grimaced as he ran his hands through Hasard's clothing. In the jacket he found what he wanted: a key ring – with three keys. One was stamped '13' – *his* room. The others were 12 and 14. Number 12, he knew, was actually a 3-room suite, immediately down the corridor on the left, fairly luxurious, considering that the *Xerol* was only a government courier. Number 14 was a single, and it adjoined his own cabin on the right. Brother Vang would certainly have selected the suite as a base of operations, but he might also have held Number 14 in reserve. On the other hand – there was the question of the Ritornellian pilgrim.

The only sure way to resolve the mystery of Room 14 was to unlock the door and take a look inside. But first —

He put the keys in his pocket, then stepped back again and fired at the killer's head – which instantly glowed red-hot, then disappeared in a flash of smoke. In minutes, the corpse was neatly vaporized into its component molecules and had been drawn into the ship's air-conditioning system. Andrek rather suspected that one of the junior engineers was going to be mightily puzzled by the strange surge of carbon dioxide and inorganic colloids in the filter tanks.

After it was all over, he checked the thermostat. The heat released in disposing of his visitor just about balanced the pre-induced chill in his room. He re-adjusted the thermostat, then walked over to the cabin door and listened. He could hear nothing. He opened the door and stepped rapidly down the hall to Number 14. The photokey slipped readily into the insert. There was no noise. Andrek drew the biem-gun, kicked the door open, and leaped inside.

There was no counter-movement anywhere. But even before his eyes adjusted completely to the dim radiance of the cruise lights, he heard something – the sound of regular breathing – from the far corner.

Andrek crouched and swung his biem around towards the sound.

And then he saw it – the robed body floating in a full length strait-jacket, fixed 'horizontally' in space by guy ropes clewed to snap buckles in ceiling and floor. The face radiated a pale blue glow.

It had to be – it was – the ancient pilgrim of Ritornel, bound and gagged, but alive.

Andrek closed the door softly behind him, propped a chair top under the door knob, and walked over to the suspended shape. As he bent over the face, he was startled to see the eyes jerk open to look into his.

The impact of those eyes boring into his own hit him with raw physical force. The eyes, like the rest of the face, radiated a pale blue light. And they brought with them returning knowledge. He had seen these eyes before, long ago. In another dim-

102

lit place. When? Where? It would not come back. He could remember nothing. Except that he had been afraid.

But he was not afraid any more.

And now he had to get busy.

He put his biem back into his belt. 'We'll have you out of there in a jiffy,' he whispered. He slipped the edge of his excisor blade under the cloth gag and clipped it cleanly away from the other's mouth.

'Are you all right?' asked Andrek.

The other was silent – he merely blinked his eyes – then continued to stare at Andrek.

The advocate's heart sank. The pilgrim had been drugged. Except for the eyes, the voluntary nervous system was probably completely paralysed. With his clippers, Andrek cleared the elastic metal netting away from the body. There was still no movement.

He moved around to face the other. 'If you can hear and understand me,' he said, 'blink your eyes – just once.'

The pilgrim blinked his eyes – once.

Andrek grinned. 'Now, then, one blink means "yes". Two blinks mean "no". All right?'

The other blinked once.

'Have you been drugged?'

One blink.

'Is there an antidote?'

One blink.

'On the ship?'

One blink.

Probably in the dispensary, thought Andrek. Still, with a person of the pilgrim's undoubted talents, the antidote might be closer.

'Do you have the antidote here in your cabin?'

One blink.

Good! Andrek looked about the room. There was but one modest clothes-case, lying on the dressing-table. He walked over and opened it. It was *not* a clothes-case. Andrek whistled under his breath. It was a medical kit. In the top half was a complete array of instruments, from syringe to stethoscope. The bottom section contained tray after tray of rubber-capped glass phials – thousands. One of these phials contained the antidote – he hoped. He released the magnetic clips and floated the case over to the friar.

'Is it in here?'

One blink.

'I propose now to turn these trays, one at a time. At each tray, I will ask you whether it is the one with the phial we want, then we'll try each row of phials on that tray, then each phial in the correct row.'

He found it in seconds – twelfth tray – twelfth row – twelfth phial. Alea all the way! As he sterilized the syringe, he asked: 'Do you get the entire contents?'

Two blinks – no.

'How many cc? Tell me by the number of blinks.'

The pilgrim stared at him then finally blinked twice.

Andrek felt instantly that something was wrong. Did that mean 2 cc – or 'no'? It was dangerous to permit a signal to mean two different things.

'Two cc?'

Two blinks again.

'Forget that,' said Andrek. 'We'll return to our original binary communication – everything is yes or no. Is the dosage less than one cc?'

One blink.

'Is it more than one-tenth cc?'

Two blinks.

'Is it exactly one-tenth?'

One blink.

Andrek thrust the needle through the rubber cap of the phial and drew up the requisite amount, then cleared the air bubble in the needle.

'In the biceps?'

There was a long pause; Andrek wondered for a moment whether he had asked the right question. But finally:

One blink.

Andrek raised the hair shirt sleeve – and then blinked himself. The pilgrim's arm – which looked more like a segmented broomstick than an arm – was completely covered with a close-fitting rubbery fabric, right down to the white gloves. And the arm seemed hard as steel, unyielding to the pressure of his fingers as he sought in vain for the biceps muscle. Finally he shrugged his shoulders and shoved the needle into what he hoped was the right place. It took all his strength to force the metal bit into the arm. The pilgrim was a tough one!

But the antidote acted quickly. In a few minutes the friar was flexing his arms and rubbing his spindly thighs. He stood up and offered his gloved hand to Andrek. 'I'm Iovve. And of course you are James, Don Andrek.' He grinned at Andrek from his strangely whiskered mouth. 'Rather embarrassing, meeting this way, but it couldn't be helped. *They* were clever. I learned only at the last minute about your trip. Brother Vang was waiting for me with a syringe-bullet. I never even made it into the cabin. Hardly sporting.' He walked over to the medical case and folded it up carefully. 'How did you know I was aboard?'

Andrek told him what had happened to Hasard.

Iovve frowned. 'That leaves the two dangerous ones: Huntyr and Vang. Vang may be the worst. He's a drug expert. He's one reason I brought the medical case. Have you had anything to eat or drink with them?'

Andrek struck his forehead. 'How stupid of me! Vang and I drank to the wager.'

'It could be...' muttered Iovve.

'But it was from the table tankard.'

'No matter. He could have taken the antidote later.'

'Well, then, so can I. You seem to have all the antidotes, right here.'

'True, I do – but they are all useless if we don't know the drug.'

'How did you know what drug they had given you?'

The blue radiance around Iovve's face seemed to flicker. 'If I gave you a complete explanation, it would take a great deal of time, and in the end you might not believe me. Suffice it to say, that the antidote was correct.'

Andrek shrugged. 'Well, I suppose we'll have to wait until I develop some symptoms. Meanwhile, tell me this: Why are you on the ship now? And yesterday, why did you break into Huntyr's office? Have we met before? Apparently you're on my side. But why?'

The pilgrim raised his thin arms in protest. 'So many questions, my boy! Granted, they all deserve complete and honest answers. But honest answers take time, far more time than we have at the moment. And just now the complete truth would place too great a strain on your credulity. You must settle for this: Oberon wants you dead, and I want you alive.'

'That much I had already surmised.' The advocate clenched his jaws in frustration. 'At least tell me this, if you know: what am I to Oberon, that I must die?'

'Oh. That part's easy. The Aleans have convinced Oberon that you represent a threat to his life. It's all in their crystomorphs. But that's merely the main reason. There are side issues

105

... Amatar, for example....'

'I can't believe Oberon would kill me merely because I'm in love with his daughter.'

The pilgrim smiled bleakly. 'Amatar – his daughter? A great deal needs to be explained to you, my boy, but now is not the time to do it. We have to get a force-field up before we have any more visitors.' He slipped off his wrist watch and turned towards the dressing-table.

'How were you able to get a field generator aboard?' asked Andrek curiously. 'And didn't they search your things?'

'Oh, they went through my poor belongings, all right. But they found only the medical kit – which amused them immensely. They didn't bother with that, because they thought there would be no one on board to help me use it, especially since you were to receive their promptest attention, right after supper. And as for the generator, they didn't find it because I carry it broken down into components that look like something else ... autorazor, stylus, comb, and so on. Certain other elements I expect to find here as standard equipment in any cabin, such as the fluorolites, emergency kit in the closet, tape library, and parts of the intercom. And incidentally, we'll set the field up around *your* cabin, since *that's* where Huntyr will come looking for you when Hasard doesn't return. Courtesy requires a proper welcome.'

The pilgrim picked up his valise and medical kit and peeked out of the cabin door. 'Come on,' he said to Andrek.

Inside Andrek's cabin, Iovve got to work on the field generator. The apparatus rapidly took shape under his flying gloved fingers, and he explained as he worked. 'This type of field has some built-in defects. The power drain is enormous. This means we have to plug it into the ship's current.' He nodded in the direction of the cable, which terminated in a six-pronged plug. 'But we can't simply turn the field on and leave it on. The wattage drain would be noticed immediately in the ship's power room. The electrical engineer would tell the captain, and that would be the end of our cabin current. And it might happen at a highly critical moment. So we'll superimpose a low-drain alert in series with a capacitor surge tank. The alert will detect any energy surge in the field area and will instantly activate the capacitor.'

This made only the vaguest sense to Andrek. In a general way he understood the principles of the force-field. He had, however, been under the impression that tremendous power was

required, something far beyond cabin amperage, even if accumulated in what his new friend termed the 'capacitor', which
he took to be the entire outer shell of the ship. Nevertheless, he
was inclined to accept Iovve's flat statement that the jerry-built
equipment could be plugged into the wall circuit and create an
adequate field, if only because of the pilgrim's very evident skill
and immense self-confidence.

Iovve straightened up. He seemed to be listening. 'Ah,' he
whispered. 'A visitor, I think. Grab something and hold on!'

Andrek seized the bunk post with both hands. As he did this,
his eyes fell on the six-pronged plug. It had never been plugged
into the wall socket!

He was frozen in momentary paralysis. Then he broke from
the bunk stanchion in a flying leap, grabbed the line and was
centimetres and milliseconds from the wall socket when the
cabin lights flickered and a sudden painful pressure hit his ear-
drums.

He knew the force-field had just been activated.

And then the plug was in the socket.

Slowly he took his hand from the line and stood up. It was
impossible. Or was it? Could the field exist before the plug was
in? Or was he only imagining that he had been too late with the
plug? *No.* He had not imagined the sequence. It was still fresh
in his mind: '*WHAM* ... click ...' Iovve simply had not used
the cabin current, but clearly wanted him, Andrek, to think it
was necessary. Did the pilgrim have some strange power source,
already integrated into the apparatus, and which he wanted to
keep secret? He suspected that the pilgrim had many secrets.
This was just one more. Eventually, there would have to be
some answers.

The pilgrim looked over at Andrek and grinned. 'Did it knock you loose? They hit a wall panel, on the corridor side. They must be pretty sure we have a field, but they'll try once more, to make sure.'

Immediately, something exploded in Andrek's stomach. He took a few steps towards the centre of the room and steadied himself on the table. It seemed warm to the touch.

'That was quite a wallop,' murmured Iovve. 'So now they know for sure. They'll go back to Cabin Twelve to figure out what to do next. And I'll just take a peek out of the door.'

Andrek started to shout a warning, but the pilgrim was already at the door. He opened it a crack, then closed it immediately.

'Just one man,' said Iovve thoughtfully. 'Huntyr, I think. I wonder what happened to Brother Vang. . . .'

Andrek could guess. Huntyr had found the cheque on his companion and didn't like the explanation. At the very least, Vang was a prisoner in Cabin Twelve. He explained his theory to Iovve. 'That cuts the odds considerably, wouldn't you say?' he asked.

'Depends on the point of view, my boy. Regardless of Vang, Huntyr is on an official mission for the Great House, and if need be he can call on the entire resources of the ship to destroy us. We'll have to bring this little affair to a head before he decides he can't handle us by himself. Which means we'll soon have to carry the war into enemy territory. But first —'

Andrek looked up. 'Yes?'

'Let's feed Raq. I imagine she's pretty hungry.'

Andrek reached into the open courier case for the feeding kit that Amatar had given him. And then he stopped. He had, of course, explained to Iovve how Hasard had died. And Iovve's recommendation was completely logical. In fact Andrek would have fed Raq without it. Even so, something about it jarred him. Several of the words were – wrong.

He lifted the little leather box out of the case and turned in slow indecision. There was a very searching question that he could ask Iovve. But the simple act of asking would reveal to the monk that Andrek knew something about him, something, perhaps, that he was not supposed to know. He doubted if the monk would answer the question, anyhow, but the means used to avoid answering might be revelatory. At this point, he felt he had nothing to lose.

He said quietly, 'I did not mention the name of my spider; yet you call her "Raq". Nor did I tell you her sex; yet you know she is a female. And finally, I have said nothing about *this*' – he held up the feeding kit – 'yet you know about it.' He paused, then his voice became even softer. 'Only one other person could have told you. Iovve, *what are you to Amatar?*'

Iovve shifted uneasily. 'I am her friend. And it is true, I know all about Raq – including a few things that neither you nor Amatar know. For example, I know there's a very good reason for feeding her right now. And never fear; I'll explain everything in good time. Meanwhile, roll back your sleeve. Now, then, we need an antiseptic . . . ah, the biem. . . .'

Under Iovve's watchful supervision Andrek sterilized his left hand, together with the needle and syringe, with a mild cone spray from the biem-gun. Then he made a fist, and – wincing – thrust the needle into the ball of his thumb. In seconds he had filled the syringe barrel, which he then discharged beneath the plastic 'chitin' of the false insect from Amatar's little case. Gingerly, he carried it over to the fold in the drapes where Raq was hiding, and here he hung it cautiously in the fabric. He did not have to wait. Raq was on her way the instant the drape was touched. Andrek quickly stood away, but winced again as the great arachnid stabbed her mandibles into her 'prey'.

As he watched Raq feed, he wondered just how much Iovve really did know about Raq, and how he had gained the knowledge. Was it possible that Iovve had foreseen his need for Raq and had planned the whole thing, with Amatar's enthusiastic co-operation? But that possibility raised even more questions. It would require long, careful, secret activity behind the scenes. But did it have to be secret? What if Iovve had access to the Great House, and could come and go as he pleased without arousing suspicion? Was *that* possible? If it were, who, then, *was* this creature? Questions. Too many questions. And no answers. Andrek felt himself caught in a strange and devious web of fate. The gods had spun their strands and caught him. He mused on. The more I thresh about, the more enmeshed I become. Ritornel must be some sort of celestial spider.

Andrek realized that Iovve was watching him curiously. 'Ridiculous isn't it?' murmured Andrek. 'To owe one's life to an insect?'

'The spider is not an insect,' chided the pilgrim. 'Insects have six legs; spiders have eight. And there are other morphological differences. But in any case' – his eyes twinkled – 'your spider equally owes her life to you. So the matter is in good balance.'

'Curious that she can feed on human blood,' said Andrek.

'No,' said Iovve. 'It would be curious if she couldn't. The blood cells, of course, she simply filters out. But the plasma has about the same analysis as insect haemolymph: amino acids, sugars, dissolved salts, proteins. She —'

They both looked at Raq with startled eyes. She had leaped from the drapes, weightlessly, in a straight line for the ceiling of the cabin, where she paused a moment. Andrek could see that she had affixed an anchor line. After this she jumped straight to the floor, bringing the line with her, hooked in the comb of one of her hind legs. This line she fastened to the floor. Then she ran along the floor to the nearest wall, crawled up exactly midway, and sailed over to the opposite wall, to form a second perpendicular, which was soon tied neatly to the first. The third perpendicular was quickly made in the same manner, between the remaining two walls.

Iovve drew Andrek over into one quarter of the cabin. 'We'll have to stay out of her way,' he said grimly. 'She will need complete freedom of movement for this.'

'What's going on,' demanded Andrek in a hoarse whisper.

'She has been drugged, my friend – *by your blood*. Which means, of course, that you have been drugged too. It was probably that wine of Vang's. Raq is now making a web – of a peculiar kind. The type of web will define the drug, and then we can select an antidote. This is called web-analysis ... when it works.' He studied Andrek with concern. 'How do you feel?'

'Just – a little dizzy. I think I'll sit down.'

'Web-analysis can be quite complicated.' The pilgrim hugged his chest uneasily. 'This will evidently be a three-dimensional web. Those are the X, Y, and Z co-ordinates. This type is quite rare, and weaving it in free space, with no gravity, may introduce all sorts of complications.' He shook his head. 'You know the theory, of course. A spider dosed with a little alcohol weaves a drunken web. If stimulated with caffeine, she will build one which is a model of engineering precision: the strands and spokes are equi-spaced to a micron. With the mushroom drugs, she builds one circular strand with a couple of spokes, then hangs in the centre, a spider god alone in a spider universe.

With the really lethal drugs, such as the organic nitriles —'

Iovve droned on, but the words were becoming blurred to Andrek. He just wanted to sit and think. It seemed to him that Iovve was unduly excited about the whole thing. There was nothing to worry about. His thoughts were turning inward, and pilgrim, cabin, Raq, everything, took on a hazy, remote, dreamlike quality. It was becoming rather pleasant. He wanted to stay this way. He liked being drugged. He hoped Iovve could not identify it, nor find an antidote. Meanwhile, he had a great deal to think about. Tomorrow they would land at the Node Station. He would have to attend the condemnation proceedings for the planet Terror. The terrible planet Terror. He had not yet been born when the last of her defenders died in the final bombardment by the revolutionaries. But he had seen the tri-di pictures. Her entire land area had been ablaze with nuclear fires. Nothing had been left. Nothing. But it was just. Terror had begun the war. Terror was to blame for the Horror. But now it was over and done. Space tugs had pulled her far out here, to the Node, and here she would be atomized. The titanic demolition charges had been placed long ago. Within another day she would be blown to bits. It was his job to see that nothing interfered with that. He concentrated now on the technique of presenting his motion for summary destruction to the Arbiters.

In front of Andrek, Raq continued her work purposefully, unhurried, yet without lost motion, ignoring Andrek just as he was ignoring her. Returning to the central point of the co-ordinates, she next measured off about ten centimetres along one horizontal axis, turned, and leaped to the other horizontal axis, repeating until she had outlined a square parallel to the floor. She then made similar square outlines with the remaining co-ordinates.

'Octahedron – two pyramids, base-to-base,' muttered Iovve.

Inside this structure, towards the top, Raq inscribed a smaller square, parallel to the floor, and within this she formed a pentagon. Iovve leaned forward intently. From the apices of the pentagon, she dropped strands, one by one, and fastened each to the octahedral framework. Then, back to the upper pentagon, she worked rapidly outward from this, to form five further pentagons, anchored to the five cables. Always, she worked 'inside' the structure.

Iovve turned to Andrek. 'It looks like the upper half of a dodecahedron – I think we'll know for sure in a moment.'

Andrek stared at him irritably. His sequence of thought had

been broken. 'What did you say?'

Iovve held up his hand. 'Silence, now,' he whispered.

Raq finished the bottom half of the twelve-faced figure, then, starting from one angle on the upper pentagon, began systematically to line the interior with a filamentary spiral, each successive strand a fraction of a centimetre lower than the one preceding. Soon, her body was partly hidden within the figure. Iovve bent low in his effort to follow her strange drama.

Raq stopped. By now she was invisible within the interior of the dodecahedral cocoon. The whole structure was momentarily immobile. And then it began to shudder in a mixture of convulsive rhythms. The geometric figure vibrated desperately, setting up standing waves in the three anchoring perpendiculars.

Andrek watched all this without interest. He closed his eyes, and locked himself within his own thoughts. After opening with a presentation of Terror's centuries of vicious history, culminating in the long, deadly nuclear war that had laid waste so many of her colonies, and had destroyed, finally, the mother planet, he would go on to her history of cruel, domineering colonization. Develop her oppression, the causes of revolt. The secret formation of the rebel confederation headed by Goris-Kard. The declaration of independence. Reprisals. The beginning of the Horror. And years later, the end. And then a full treatment of the legal points. The formation of the League of the Twelve Galaxies. The treaties and covenants. He'd cite chapter and verse. There could be only one outcome.

He opened his eyes. Iovve was shaking him.

'She's caught in her own web. It can be only one thing.'

Andrek groaned with annoyance. 'Go away. Leave me alone. I'm very busy.'

'It's quirinal!' hissed Iovve.

'Quirinal?' Andrek stared at him owlishly.

'The slave drug. It induces the most hideous kind of slavery. It causes one to become enslaved to oneself – to become caught in one's own web, so to speak. It carries introversion to the ultimate. It is a standard ingredient in the colloidal networks of arts computers – helps them compose better poetry, music, because it forces constant, continuing feed-back, comparing a proposed composition with certain pre-set standards.' As he spoke, he was opening the drug section of his medical kit. 'Here we are. The antidote.' He filled the syringe in a deft motion and thrust the needle into Andrek's arm. And immediately after that, he recharged the needle, seized Raq's cocoon, and in another moment had thrust the needle tip into her cephalothorax.

He turned back to Andrek, who was rubbing his eyes. 'How do you feel?' asked Iovve.

Andrek grinned sheepishly. 'A little stupid, but all right, otherwise. I'm coming out of it. That was really something. How's Raq?'

'She'll come around in a moment. Hold her while I get rid of this web.' The pilgrim handed her to Andrek, who accepted her somewhat dubiously. He stroked her back with his forefinger, trying to remember how Amatar had done it. Raq relaxed into a bristly bundle in his palm.

Iovve was clearing away the last of the web when there was a knock on the door.

Andrek exchanged glances with the pilgrim. Iovve nodded. 'Who is it?' demanded Andrek.

'Huntyr. I'm alone. I want to talk. Let me in.'

'Suppose we say no?'

'You could. But then you'd never know what I was going to tell you.'

Andrek was undecided. 'What do you want to talk about?'

'Your father and your brother.'

Andrek started. His heart began to pound furiously, and he felt as though he were choking. It was true. Huntyr *did* know. He was certain of it. He was very close to discovering his brother's fate. And Huntyr apparently knew something about his father's death, too. But hesitated. A part of him wanted to scream 'Come in!' But the rest of him whispered, 'Danger! Don't be bewitched by those magic names. For this man intends to kill you.' But then, he thought, if this is the only way I can ever learn of them, then I will listen, and risk death. And then he remembered he was not alone. He might have the right to gamble his own life, but what about Iovve? He looked at the pilgrim in anguish.

Iovve shrugged his shoulders. 'It had to come.' His voice was flat, almost weary. 'Let him in, and keep your biem on him. He's armed, but it would be dangerous to search him. He's very muscular, and his reflexes are extraordinary. Stay well away from him. I'll open the door.'

Andrek looked about for a place to deposit Raq. Finding none, he slid her into his jacket pocket. Then he pulled the biem out of his belt and pointed it at the door.

The door slowly swung open, and Huntyr walked in, hands high, and smiling.

Andrek sought, and found, a secret glint in Huntyr's golden eyepatch. The metal shield sparkled with news of Omere. And Huntyr was going to take great and sadistic pleasure in telling it. This could mean only one thing. Some tragic misfortune had befallen his brother, and Huntyr was somehow connected with it.

'This is not a truce,' said Andrek coldly. 'I still intend to kill you.'

Huntyr's face twisted into a mocking grin. 'You'd kill an unarmed man? After that fine speech in the mess?' His eyes roamed about the cabin. Alertly, non-committally, they explored Iovve. 'I don't know how the two of you did it, but I think you have to admit that the odds have now shifted heavily in your favour. You were far too modest, Don Andrek. Killing you – and your friend – will be an accomplishment worth talking about.'

'... "will be" ...?' murmured Andrek.

'As you say, your honour, this is not a truce. *I* intend to kill *you*, after we are through talking.'

Andrek wondered, with a sudden shiver, whether Huntyr could conceivably draw and fire before he, Andrek, could get off a shot. And now, he realized, with a sense of shock, that Huntyr's smile had broadened perceptibly.

The advocate said curtly: 'You are here to tell me about my father and my brother.'

'Softly, Don Andrek. There are in fact several stories, with stories within stories, and side-paths, and digressions.'

'Then be seated, and begin.' Andrek motioned to the chair in the corner. 'Sitting' in free space was not the same as sitting in a gravitational field. In space the chair served simply to anchor its occupant, and not as a situs of relaxation. It would make rapid movement more difficult for Huntyr. 'Keep your hands were I can see them,' said Andrek.

'Of course.' Huntyr looked at his wrist chrono. Then he said: 'Eighteen years ago your father, the late Captain Andrek, died on his ship, while on duty at the Node. In that same year your brother, the poet, disappeared. You were just a lad. All of this happened in the year your brother became the Laureate.'

Andrek leaned forward. 'Go on.'

'It was a remarkable year. Other things also happened.' Huntyr gave Iovve a calculating stare, then turned back to Andrek. 'Have you ever noticed Oberon's chest-belt?'

'Of course. It's for protection against assassination.'

'Wrong. It's there solely to prevent his chest from collapsing.' He shot a glance at the pilgrim. 'Wouldn't you say so, *Doctor*?'

Iovve shrugged. 'It's possible.'

Andrek looked over at Iovve. 'He called you "doctor". What does he mean?'

'Long ago, I was a member of the Iatric Order of Ritornel.' Iovve sounded evasive.

Andrek groaned inwardly. Every answer brought fresh riddles with it. Who *was* Iovve, really? But this was no time for speculation. He nodded curtly to Huntyr. 'Continue. Do you mean that Oberon had an accident?'

'Well, your honour, it was really worse than that. He was in this hunting party, see, at the Node, where we're going. But they'd received a report that a quake was due, so all the ships had pulled back beyond the shock line – all except Oberon's, that is. He was hunting the krith, the winged beast that eats the little beasts out in the Node. Oberon was hot on his trail. He was sure he could overtake and kill the krith before the quake hit. But the captain thought it was too risky, and finally refused to take Oberon any further. So Oberon had the captain shot for mutiny. As it turned out, the captain was right, and Oberon was wrong. The quake caught the ship. In seconds, it was wrecked; in shambles; a derelict. I was there. I was Oberon's aide. I know.' Huntyr touched his eye-patch. 'That's where I got this.'

'Go on,' whispered Andrek.

'All the officers and men of the ship's crew were killed instantly. For all practical purposes, so was Oberon. They found bits of him all over the ship, and even during the very hours of his Coronation, the Master Surgeon was still picking pieces of the ship out of him.'

Huntyr paused, and fixed Iovve with a penetrating stare. 'Even the great Master Surgeon doubted he could save Oberon. So, by the demand of the old Regent, they started tissue cultures – mostly from bone fragments left over when they cleaned Oberon's wounds.'

Andrek had heard of the practice. One living cell, plant or animal, when placed in a suitable nutrient medium, could, if cultured properly, sometimes reproduce the entire mature organism from which the single cell was taken. The procedure had been used for the preservation of valuable strains of the lower animals, but he had never heard of its working with hominid cells. Yet, the idea was sound enough; the old Regent had evidently been trying to grow another Oberon from selected cells of the dying man.

'What has a tissue culture to do with my father or brother?'

'Nothing directly. But I thought you ought to understand Oberon's condition at the time your brother enters the picture. Oberon, in effect, was trembling between life and death. And when he realized his physical condition, and that he might never walk again, he wanted to die. But the old Regent was too clever for him. He called in the Master Surgeon again and explained what had to be done. I rather imagine the Surgeon didn't really want to do it. But on the other hand, life is good, and the old Regent was not a patient man – not when the only real hope of perpetuating the Delfieri dynasty was to make his nephew want to live. So the Master Surgeon, and I suppose several dozen assistants, set about to accomplish the task set for them.'

A sudden jar came up through the cabin floor into Andrek's legs. He knew all three of them had felt it. He flashed a look at Iovve, and saw instantly that something was wrong. For a few seconds, he could not place it. And then he had it. Iovve's blue aura was gone. It had vanished with the jolt in the ship. And Andrek noticed also with growing anxiety that the pilgrim's white-gloved hands were trembling. With the blue radiation gone from Iovve's features, the advocate was able to observe the unilluminated face fully for the first time; and for the first time he was able to see the grizzled exhausted age of his companion.

Something disastrous had just happened. Huntyr had known it was going to happen, and had timed his entrance to precede it and his cruel narrative to embrace it. A primitive part of Andrek's mind told him to beg Huntyr to continue with that hideous, involuted tale. But a more highly sophisticated veneer censored this impulse, and urged that he move with great caution. Intuitively, he understood that if he were going to stay alive long enough to hear the end of Huntyr's recital, it would first be necessary to understand the shock that he had just felt. With an immense effort of will, Andrek laid aside his questions about Omere. He looked across the room at Iovve again. 'Was that a small quake temblor?'

The pilgrim answered quietly. 'No.'

116

Huntyr laughed contemptuously. 'Don Andrek – and you, too, Dr. Iovve, to be so well educated and so intelligent, and so well-informed in the laws of the Twelve Galaxies and in the laws of science and medicine, you are both curiously stupid in the laws of the Node. The first law here is, there shall be no nuclear reaction. The ship went off nuclear drive just now, and on to chemical reaction drive. *That* was the jar you felt. Why did it convert over? Because the bugs just sit on the nuclear pile in the drive and drink up the power as fast as the pile turns it out. As long as we are in the Node area, there cannot be a single nuclear unit alive on the ship. Your force field is dead, of course. Ordinary weapons are useless. Even the lighting is by ancient fluorescence, powered by varimetal accumulators. All on account of the bugs.'

Now they were getting somewhere. He was beginning to understand. They had just entered the outer edge of the Node. They were now in the domain of the ursecta. And Iovve's blue radiation had winked out in that very moment. He remembered Kedrys' demonstration, and how in one chamber the anti-matter hydrogen had flashed blue on contact with normal matter, and how in the other – nothing had happened at all. Was it conceivable that Iovve's radiation was caused by nuclear energy released by something closely associated with his body, or – and the thought hit him with shock force – by Iovve's body itself? By the Beard of the Founder!

But all such speculation was moot and academic. For the time being, Huntyr was absolutely right. In the little room, here and now, the ursecta ruled. Ordinary weapons were useless. He found himself banally repeating Huntyr. 'All on account of the bugs. The ursecta.'

'Is that the scientific name?' said Huntyr. 'All right, ursecta. I could draw pictures for you, but I think a demonstration would be even better. In fact, counsellor, I think it would help considerably to clarify our relationship, if you would aim your biem at me and pull the trigger.'

Andrek turned anxious eyes towards Iovve, and on his face read the truth. The biem was nuclear-powered and would not fire. It was dead weight in his hand. He tried to force his thoughts into a useful coherent pattern – and noted dimly that Raq had emerged from his jacket pocket and was walking slowly down the sleeve of his right arm. In the dim light, her dark body was nearly invisible against the grey of his jacket. And then she was picking her way daintily across his wrist, and then she was sitting on the biem, just over the fuel chamber. He was watching Raq, but in his mind he saw Amatar. Amatar greeting him in the garden that last night. Amatar presenting Raq to him. He remembered that presentation. Insects fear her, Amatar had said. *All* insects. He remembered the emphasis on the word.

The advocate swallowed dryly. Did *all* insects include dubious fourth-dimensional varieties – beasties that would come from nowhere out of time, to materialize on a nuclear fuel chamber the instant it was activated? And did some dim instinct tell Raq that the ursecta fed on nuclear power, and that his biem was a good place to come out and wait for them? Or was her walk down his sleeve the pure whim of Alea, whereby the destinies of insects, man, and galaxies were governed? No matter. The pieces came back together, and he suddenly understood that his biem *was* going to fire. Amatar had known.

He was breathing rapidly but freely. He looked across at Huntyr. 'You believe, then, that my biem will not fire? That the ursecta will come when I pull the trigger, and drain off the power?'

'That's right, counsellor.'

Andrek thought the man looked faintly disappointed. Evidently, he had wanted Andrek to *try* to shoot him, just so he could gloat over the failure. Murder hath a strange mentality, mused Andrek. He said: 'I gather, then, that you have some kind of weapon that is not affected by the ursecta?'

'This is so, your honour.' Huntyr pulled out a curious instrument from one of his two shoulder holsters. 'It's new – yet it's old. It's called a "slug-gun", copied from a model in the Politan Museum. It uses chemical power to fire a metal pellet. It's weak, inefficient, noisy, messy, and smelly. But it kills. It killed your father, and now it's going to kill you.'

'My ... *father* ...?' stammered Andrek. 'What do you mean, it killed my father?' In his mind, he raced back over the reports. The dry sparse official language. 'Died in routine service.' A few paragraphs in the records. And now suddenly it wasn't so. He was about to learn the real story. And it would be true, because Huntyr wanted to make him suffer before killing him.

Huntyr's face glowed with pleasure. 'Your father was captain of this same ship, on Oberon's hunting trip, eighteen years ago. It was he, your father, who refused to take Oberon deeper into the Node, and who was therefore shot for mutiny. This was the gun. By order of Oberon, I killed your father. Not twenty metres from this cabin.' Huntyr smiled at the anguished workings of Andrek's face. 'Makes you believe in both Ritornel and Alea, doesn't it? The repeating pattern of Ritornel is this, that the son is killed at the same Node by the same man, by the same gun, and in the same ship. And yet, all by Alean chance!'

Finally the rippling around Andrek's mouth ceased; his face became a mask, bloodless but calm – almost serene. Even if he were killed now he was glad he had heard this from Huntyr. A part of him, at least, could die in peace. This left only the question of his brother. And if he could delay matters a little longer, he was certain that this long gap would finally be closed. 'I see,' he said. 'All this was really just to delay matters until we entered the Node, so your weapon would fire and mine would not.'

'That was the main reason, Don Andrek. On the other hand, there are still some things that you don't know about your brother, and which I intend to tell you before I kill you.'

'Proceed, then. I would like very much to hear them.'

'I wouldn't be too sure about that, your honour.' Huntyr smiled almost languidly. 'Well, as I was saying, the old Regent demanded this thing of the Master Surgeon, that he build a marvellous device, to sing, and make lovely poetry, and take the mind of his nephew away from thoughts of dying. So the Master Surgeon set about, making his design. The design called for an electron circuit identical to the cerebrum of the Laureate. But it would take many weeks. They didn't have that much time. So we simply seized the Laureate himself —'

'– Omere!' breathed Andrek. And now that he was finally to learn the answer to his eighteen-year search, he found that he was struck dumb, stunned, unaware of anything in the cabin except Huntyr's face and voice. The end was coming. His body seemed to be floating in a slow horrid realization that pounded at him with every beat of his heart. Within a matter of seconds it would be more than he could endure. 'Omere?' he whispered again.

'Yes, Omere. I handled it personally. It wasn't difficult. We took him from the Coronation straight to the Hospital Wing. The Master Surgeon performed the cranial operation and circuit integration into the computer console. There was some question about whether the computer should be sighted or blind. They decided, I think, that the rendition of aural imagery would be sharpened if they cut his optical circuits. So, to make him an even better poet, they blinded him.'

Andrek's face was dead white. He saw a vision of a great cabinet of fine polished wood, with dials, an interior of intricate electronic circuits. He had listened to it many times. And it could not risk their mutual deaths to reveal its identity. He did not recognize his own voice, drawn, pain-blinded, far away. 'Omere ... *Rimor*!'

Huntyr nodded. He was immensely pleased with the effect on the other. He pulled his mouth back over his teeth in a tigerish grin.

'But how...' – Andrek's voice was thick, barely intelligible – 'could they force him to perform ... to sing ... to compose....'

'It was easy. Quirinal – the slave drug – when you take that, you find yourself *wanting* to do what you are best at doing....'

'Be silent!' shrieked Andrek. In one smooth motion he raised the biem, sighted over Raq's crouched body, and pulled the trigger.

Huntyr jerked – not so much (it seemed to Andrek) from the physical impact of the bolt – as from disbelief. The slug-gun fell from his hand. He seemed then to be trying to raise his hand, to point ... at Iovve. His lips came together, but only a whispered sigh emerged. 'Maa —'. Then his hand dropped, and his eye stared at nothing.

Something inside Andrek watched this with bright elation. But then, discovering this feeling within himself, he jerked up straight in his chair. He felt he should censor this primitive attitude towards his enemies. He, an advocate sworn to uphold the laws of the Home Galaxy, had taken the law into his own hands, and had again slain a man. Again, it was self defence, but it still cut across the grain of a lifetime of conditioning. He shook his head slowly. Thinking this way did nothing to relieve the fact that he had been absolutely delighted on seeing that clean gaping hole appear in Huntyr's chest. But no matter, the main thing was, regardless of what anyone thought about it, he was still living, and Huntyr was dead.

He looked vaguely over towards Iovve, as though to find either absolution or an answer. And what had Huntyr been trying to say, there at the last, when he almost pointed at Iovve...? Had Huntyr known the pilgrim? He'd have to find out. Too many mysteries. Solve one, two more sprang up.

Iovve returned Andrek's questioning stare quietly. 'Get hold of yourself. We still have a lot to do.'

'What?' said Andrek numbly.

'Do you have an extra suit? Full legal robes of a Don?'

'Yes.'

'Get Huntyr's bloody jacket off, then get the robes on him.'

What was Iovve up to? He shrugged his shoulders. He'd have to trust him. 'All right.' After much fumbling, Andrek got the robe on Huntyr's body. 'It's too small,' he mumbled.

'No matter. Just leave him there. Get Raq back in your pocket, and get your case and valise. We're moving.'

'Moving?'

'Of course. We can't stay here.'

'Where'll we go?'

'To Number Twelve, Huntyr's suite.'

Andrek's jaw dropped. 'Are you crazy?'

'Wake up, dear boy. It's the only safe place on the ship.'

'But how about Vang?'

'I think he's either tied up or dead. In either case, he wouldn't be a problem. And my guess is that Huntyr killed him when he found your cheque. But if Huntyr didn't kill him, we will.'

'And then?'

'We'll just move the body in here, and trade his Alean mantle for the simple grey of a Ritornellian pilgrim.'

Andrek stared at the pilgrim in near awe. 'I *see*! The ship's officers will think the bodies in my cabin are you and me!'

'Correction. They'll *know*. Because you'll call the captain from Huntyr's suite and tell him just that. Wait a moment, while I get my bag and medical kit, and we'll both go down there together.'

As they had expected, they found Vang in Number Twelve. He lay crumpled on the floor, and his pallid face was finally at peace. Andrek had the strange impression that Vang was glad the end had come. His death was not difficult to reconstruct. He had been strangled with his own cord. There had been a struggle, and pieces of furniture were still floating about. A chair had somehow got attached to the ceiling. The poison case was broken open; some of the phials were crushed, and their contents half-absorbed into the foam-cushion lining. They did not search the body. Undoubtedly Huntyr had retrieved the cheque. Andrek was content to leave it in Huntyr's wallet.

Andrek contemplated the still form in silence. Either the goddess, or a strange anatomic freak, had prevented the engorgement of cheek and protrusion of eyeballs that normally accompanied the gift of Alea. Vang's one lapse, in an otherwise blameless service to the blind one, had evidently been forgiven, and the goddess had accepted him. The knowledge of her love was written in his mouth and eyes. His hand still tightly clasped the fatal dodecahedron that had betrayed him. Andrek pushed the thumb back and looked at the number. It was of course twelve, the most favoured to Alea.

The advocate sighed. He had engineered this death, and he would do it again, given the same threat to his own life. Yet it was a sad thing.

'We'll have to hurry,' said Iovve crisply.

'Silence!' growled Andrek. 'Vang was my enemy, but we were classmates. There are last words to be said, and to be thought for him, and I must do this, since there is no one else.' After a moment he muttered, 'I did not want this. Goodbye, Ajian.'

Hurriedly, they hauled the corpse back to Andrek's former cabin, and left it alongside what was left of Huntyr.

Ten minutes had not elapsed before they both sat in front of the intercom in Huntyr's suite. Andrek flipped the switch. His voice was strangely calm. 'Huntyr here,' he said, imitating the investigator's harsh guttural. 'Give me the captain. Captain Forgaz! Huntyr. Yes, mission accomplished. Thank you. Both bodies in the Don's cabin. Can you send a couple of crewmen around there? They must be discreet. The Great House doesn't want any publicity. We will hold you responsible. Of course, Captain. Just thought I'd mention it. Hold on a moment.' Andrek paused, and almost smiled when he continued. 'My Alean friend here insists that all three of us undergo purification rites. What? Purification rites. Yes, news to me, too. *He* will be fasting for the next three days. No, Captain, just him. I and my assistant, Mr. Hasard, will not be fasting, but we are not supposed to leave the cabin until we dock at the Station. Can you ask the chef to send up meals in the tube for the two of us? Thank you, Captain. I'll mention you in my report to the Magister.'

Andrek flipped off the switch, then continued to sit there, silent, immobile. After a long time, he turned around.

Iovve was lying in one of the three bunks, his gloved hands folded peacefully over his rhythmically moving chest. 'There is an unwitting trace of truth in that very fanciful fable,' he murmured sleepily.

'What do you mean?'

'About sending up meals. Actually, you will need food only for yourself. During these last days of my pilgrimage, I shall

122

truly be fasting. And now, my son, I suggest we both retire. It's been a hard day.'

Andrek stared at his companion, then shrugged. A strange one! He floated up quietly, drifted over to the porthole, and looked out. Outside, all was blackness. There was no point of reference to show the fantastic speed of the ship, trans-photic even under chemical drive.

He reached cautiously into his pocket, pulled Raq out, and placed her on the drapes alongside the porthole. She ran up the fabric a short distance and disappeared into the folds.

He was alone.

And now what?

For the moment, he seemed safe. At least until the ship reached the Node Station. Another day and a half. He'd have to leave the ship when they got there. He couldn't return to Goris-Kard for a long time; perhaps never. He thought of his father and brother, and his throat knotted. His father was dead. He accepted that. But Omere – in a sense, at least – was still alive. But he might as well be dead, for all the help that Andrek could give him. For even if he, Andrek, were back in the Great House now, wielding all the power of the Magister and all the skill of that infamous Master Surgeon, he could still do nothing for Omere.

That seemed to leave only – revenge? On whom? The old Regent was dead. Huntyr was dead. The Master Surgeon had vanished, and might well be dead. That left Oberon. But could he lift his hand against the father of Amatar? He didn't know. And just now it was quite academic whether he could or could not, because he was now a fugitive, under sentence of death. He would do well to save his own skin. It was foolish even to think of revenge until he was safe from Oberon.

He felt very tired. With forced gestures he undressed and got into his pyjamas. With one hand on his bunk, he turned and looked over at Iovve, now asleep. *You*, he thought, have risked your life to keep me alive. For what? Whatever the reason, you bungled it. You don't know it, strange Doctor, but you never did plug in your so-called force-field generator into the ship's current. But your field came on anyway. Is it something under those grey robes? Is this why you used to glow in the dark? It must be something over which you have no real control, because it turned off exactly at the instant *Xerol* entered the Node. When the ship went off nuclear, so did you. There must be something on, or even *in*, your body, something nuclear-powered, and which permeates your whole system, so that, outside the Node, it ionizes the air around you. And it's your whole body, not just your face.

And now you claim you are re-fasting. But I suspect, my friend, that fasting for you is normal – that you do not eat at all, in the hominid sense.

Iovve, who are you?

(And do I really want to know?)

What is this unknown thing for which you are saving me? How long am I to be kept alive? What is my small role in your mysterious plan?

Since you refuse to tell me the fate you have in store for me, you must think I might have preferred Huntyr's death. And what about your robes, pilgrim? You are making your last journey – this time to die at the Node. Is it just a bit of religious fakery, or do you really intend to go through with it? And what will be the manner of your death? You have had several opportunities to die within the last several hours – and you have refused them all. What are you waiting for? What remains to complete your pilgrimage? And when it is all done, am I supposed to die with you?

He climbed into his bunk and strapped himself in, still musing. And what was Huntyr trying to tell me about you as he sat there, dying? Huntyr knew you, pilgrim, and as he died, he tried to name you. Huntyr lifted his finger and pointed, and tried to speak. But nothing recognizable passed his lips. So your secret is safe. But in a manner of speaking, I am grateful to Huntyr. For Huntyr, my enemy, has told me a great deal more than you, Iovve my friend. And I think, my pious companion, that there is one danger worse than Vang ... or Huntyr ... or Hasard. Worse even than Oberon of the Delfieri. And that is Iovve, the grey pilgrim of Ritornel.

And so thinking, he fell asleep.

## 11 : An Entrance Questioned

In the last hour of the third day, as *Xerol* was cautiously nosing in towards the Node Station under slow deceleration, Andrek happened to look out of the porthole. 'Iovve, look!' He pointed excitedly. 'A planet. It must be Terror!'

'Very likely, my boy, very likely.' The pilgrim clacked over to the quartz window and peered out. 'So it is.'

They watched in silence as the ship drifted past the great ball in a slow parabola. As a warning to navigation, thousands of light-buoys were orbiting the planet, forming a giant spectral crown. The lights were turned inward towards the globe, bathing her equator in a band of ghostly, pale radiance. To Andrek, it seemed somehow highly incongruous. Terror, the Devil Planet, with a halo! No matter. Tomorrow those lights would vanish forever.

Andrek then suddenly noticed that Iovve was watching him. 'Well?' he demanded.

'Nothing, my boy. Not a thing. Just wondering about your own feelings. About Terror, I mean.' He nodded towards the porthole. 'See that?'

Andrek peered out again. Beyond the halo, a tiny light was slowly circling the planet. 'What is it?'

'The demolition ship. Tomorrow, they expect to activate the explosive capsule that will destroy the planet. They wait only for the final order from the Arbiters.'

'Well, of *course* they're going to destroy the planet. It's required by intergalactic law. It's the just fate of every planet that starts a nuclear war.' He turned and stared hard at the pilgrim. 'That's my mission here. Within a few hours, I will appear before the Arbiters and formally confirm the position of my government, that Terror must be destroyed. There's no conceivable alternative.'

'Of course, my boy, of course,' said Iovve smoothly. He paused, and said in a reflective tone, 'A solemn moment, nevertheless. We're among the last to see Terra alive.'

Andrek turned on him grimly. 'You said – *Terra!*'

'I did. Terra. We can at least be realistic. That *is* the real name, as you well know. *Their* name for their planet.' He shrugged. 'Terror ... Terra. It is the privilege of the victors to

125

curse the defeated with any name they choose. No son of Terra is now alive to rise in her defence. And her grandsons and nephews, including you, my boy, couldn't care less.'

Was it coming now? Was Iovve finally able to untangle the web? Breathing was suddenly difficult, and he fought off a feeling of suffocation. But he knew he could not hurry the pilgrim. He said bluntly: 'That's strange talk, coming from a man of peace and holiness.'

Iovve blithely ignored him. He continued, as though talking to himself. 'We have accepted her gifts in a thousand ways. We still use the old tongues on occasion.' He peered sideways at Andrek. 'The word "Amatar", for example.'

Andrek stared. 'What do you mean?' he stammered.

'He! He! I thought that would get you! Yes, Amatar ... from *a mater* – "without mother". Amatar, the Motherless One. But you're not interested in Terran etymology. You're here to destroy Terra and everything Terran.'

And now again the tantalizing feeling of recognition. He had heard these words before. And this voice. Far away. Where? When? The Motherless One. It meant something. He had heard it before. He had been afraid before. Was he afraid now? His mouth was dry, and his palms were wet. He seized the pilgrim by the shoulders. '*Why* is she called the "Motherless One"?' he demanded. 'What do you know about Amatar?'

'Gently, my boy. Everything in good time.'

A buzzer was sounding insistently in the room. 'Just now,' said Iovve, 'the ship is locking on at the Station. We have about two minutes to pack and get out. And let's hope we don't run into anybody whom the fact of our continuing existence might startle or distress. So why don't we just get everything together and walk out through the freight port.'

Andrek was defeated again. His arms dropped from Iovve. Very soon, he thought, we are going to have a long talk, about many things. He looked about the room. 'What'll we do about Raq? Take her along?'

'Out of the question, dear boy. Have you observed her condition recently?'

'Condition?' Andrek went over to the fold in the porthole drape, which Raq had selected as 'home'.

'Not too close,' Iovve called out.

Standing about a yard away, Andrek could make out the little silken ball, nearly complete. Raq stopped work on it and covered it with her body as his shadow fell on her.

'Great bouncing Alean eyeballs!' said Adrek softly. 'It's an egg-sac! She's a mother!'

'Or soon will be. I think, my boy, we'd better give our god-fatherly blessings from a safe distance. There's nothing like motherhood to foul up a conditioned recognition reflex.'

'But – the ship's crew.... If we leave her here, they'll be bitten.'

'Yes, won't they!' agreed Iovve gleefully. 'Sorry we won't be here to watch the fun. But we can't move her. The alternative is to kill her here and now.'

'We can't do that.' Andrek clenched his teeth. 'All right. Goodbye, Raq, and thanks.'

Cases in hand, they sneaked down back corridors to the freight elevators.

*Xerol*'s flank was sealed into the docking locks of the Node Station at several points. Officers, crew, and passengers used the forward tubes. Fuel and water lines were intermediate. The Freight Room was aft.

Holding to the hand rails, Andrek and Iovve floated over, around, and through stacks of metal boxes, mostly bound with metal straps to the floor, walls, and ceiling of the Freight Room, propelling themselves from time to time by gentle nudges of toes and fingertips. As they approached the great doorway opening into the Station, the clutter and congestion grew. They encountered several of the crew, working with cargo, but hurried past without challenge. They had a bad moment when the last exit seemed hopelessly blocked by the flow of goods on a conveyor belt running *into* the ship. But they waited a few seconds and then sailed over the belt on to the Station dock.

That area also was cluttered with stacks of boxes, trunks, and even furniture.

'Doesn't it strike you as odd,' said Andrek curiously, 'that everything is going *in* to the ship, and nothing is coming *out*? And look at *that*.' He pointed to a huge roll of carpetry being hoisted out towards the ship's loading conveyor. 'Are they dismantling the whole Station and shipping it back to Goris-Kard?'

'Nonsense, my boy. Quite a bit of staff turnover at a lonely outpost like this. In addition to the Arbiters' Chambers, the Station maintains co-operative facilities for scientists from all the twelve galaxies. There's always a stream of new staff coming in, old staff leaving. And of course, they take their baggage with them.'

'I suppose so,' said Andrek. He looked around doubtfully.

*Xerol* was not the only ship tied up at the Station docks. To *Xerol*'s rear was another, larger craft. Andrek could not make out the strange letters on her loading tubes. Iovve saw him peering at it, and whispered, '*Varez*, from Andromeda.' And up ahead was still another ship. Her loading tubes were active, too. In fact, cases, crates, trunks, and even people were moving up the tubes of both ships. But nothing, and no one, seemed to be coming out.

Many of these people were obviously non-hominid. Several had more than two legs, and some even wore transparent helmets, evidently to carry with them their own strange atmospheres.

Iovve took him by the arm. 'Now then, counsellor, I believe we can take this hall to the lobby.'

The corridor echoed eerily with the clanging of their magnetized shoe soles as they moved deeper into the Station.

'Ah, yes,' said Iovve. 'Here we are.'

Andrek looked about him, puzzled. Something was strange, wrong. A slight difference in the tint of paint along the edges of the corridor floor told him that not long ago – perhaps yesterday – a carpet had lain there. The phone boxes in the corridor walls were empty; as were the wall clamps for the portable fire extinguishers. He started to ask Iovve about it, but the other grasped his arm and pointed ahead.

They were just outside the main lobby. It was crowded, and through the shifting mass of people, on the other side of the room, was the registration desk. And there, three officers of *Xerol* leaned across the counter, deep in conversation with the clerk.

Andrek and Iovve shrank back into the dimness of the hallway.

As they watched, the three officers left the clerk and began circulating slowly through the lobby, looking covertly but carefully at the faces of the occupants.

'I think they are wearing slug-guns,' said Andrek nervously. 'Suppose they come out here?'

'I don't think they will. But suppose they do? The Station is a big place, with lots of places to hide. Just now, they are merely suspicious. Huntyr didn't check in with the captain on docking. He's missing. Vang's missing. And Hasard. They're worried, but they don't know anything for sure. Certainly, they

128

don't know that we are alive. The thing that puzzles them is, why didn't Huntyr leave the ship through the passenger tubes? You see, they don't really know whom they're looking for. I think their concern is primarily Huntyr, not us.'

'I hope you're right. Anyhow, they've stopped.'

The three officers had met at the main lobby entrance. They took one last look around, then left, headed for the passenger tubes.

'Now,' said Iovve, 'let's test an ancient axiom of Ritornel: be grateful for the unwitting gifts of others.'

'I don't recall that one,' muttered Andrek.

'Naturally; the younger generation is not well informed in religious matters. This way, my boy.'

They walked over to the registration desk. The clerk looked up at them.

Iovve said, 'I believe we have reservations. Huntyr and party.'

'Oh yes, of course. Are you Mr. Huntyr?'

'No, *that's* Mr. Huntyr.' Iovve nodded at Andrek. 'I'm Brother Vang.'

'How many in your party, Mr. Huntyr?'

'Three,' said Andrek. 'Mr. Hasard will be over from the ship in a few minutes.'

'Very good. Here are your keys. Second level. Shall I put your luggage in the auto-tube, to go directly to your rooms?'

'Never mind,' said Andrek. 'We'll carry them. Also, I have been asked to give you a message from Mr. Andrek, of *Xerol*.'

'Yes?'

'He is staying aboard ship, and will not be needing his reservation.'

'That's a coincidence. Captain Forgaz was just here with the same information. And he was inquiring about you, Mr. Huntyr.'

'Sorry I missed him,' said Andrek. 'I'll call him from my room.'

'As you wish. Are you returning in *Xerol*?'

'No,' broke in Iovve. 'We're going on. We already have reservations on ... ah ... *Varez*.'

'*Varez*? To Andromeda? But she's leaving soon. You can board her now. You won't have time —'

'She's delayed,' said Iovve smoothly. 'Engine trouble.'

'Oh. If you say so.' The clerk shrugged politely. 'The rate is twenty gamma per room, payable in advance.'

Andrek placed some bills on the desk, then he and Iovve

turned away and headed for the inner level.

Just as they entered the corridor from the lobby, Andrek stopped and looked back. On the other side of the registration desk the clerk was putting on a heavy outer jacket. He zipped up the fasteners, then reached for a hat on the hat rack.

'Why are you stopping?' hissed Iovve.

'I think the clerk is about to leave – for good, I mean,' said Andrek wonderingly.

'And what's wrong with that? There's certainly no need for someone to be there twenty-four hours a day. Come on.'

'Just a minute,' said Andrek. As he watched, the clerk put several ledgers, a small locked box, and three valises, one after another, into the auto-chute marked 'Ship: *Xerol*'. Then he came around to the front of the desk, pulled down a metal grille, and walked away towards the corridor leading to *Xerol*'s passenger tubes. Andrek's eye came back to the grille over the registration counter. A small sign in the centre read 'Closed'.

Andrek turned back to Iovve, started to ask him a question, then decided it would be futile. One thing was now clear. The Station was closing. And Iovve did not want him to know that it was closing. But why should it close? There had to be a reason. He would have to find out.

When they reached their rooms, Andrek said, 'I want to talk to you after you unpack.' He unlocked the door to his own room and went inside. It was, as he had predicted, carpetless. But around the edges of the floor was an outline of where a carpet had been – and recently. Overhead, one dim fluor was left burning amid six empty sockets. The entertainment centre was identifiable by a gaping hole in the wall and a few dangling wires. There was not even a waste basket. Except for the bunk bed and one towel in the washroom, the room had been stripped.

Something cold and heavy began to grow in the bottom of Andrek's stomach.

There was only one explanation. And on a subconscious level, he must have suspected it all along, even when he had not wanted to think about it consciously. Again, he had the frustrating feeling that he saw only a part of a much larger drama. But at least it would readily explain that part: namely, how Iovve expected to die.

He went next door and knocked. Iovve let him in.

Andrek said grimly: 'The Station is stripped down to its bare operating essentials. Everyone here has already moved out or is preparing to move out. Why? What's going on here?'

Iovve peered at Andrek, as though attempting to assess how much the advocate knew and how much he had merely guessed. 'Really?' he said. 'How observant of you. I hadn't noticed. Perhaps their assignments are completed. Perhaps the League is finally closing the Station. It could be any one of a number of things.'

Andrek smiled at him wickedly. His voice was deceptively quiet. 'Iovve, my very dubious friend, you undoubtedly have extraordinary skills in many fields. For these, you have my undying admiration and respect.' The tones became even softer, more reflective, tinged with faint regret. 'In one area, however, you are a bumbling fool. You just don't know how to tell a convincing lie.'

'I — What? I'm not on your witness stand, Don Andrek!'

But now, in a sudden, shattering change of pace, the advocate's voice thundered out: '*A QUAKE IS COMING, ISN'T IT?*'

Iovve stared at Andrek in amazement. 'By my beard! You are a wonder.'

'Just answer the question.'

'Well, if you put it that way, yes. A quake is coming.'

'And you didn't tell me. Why?'

'Because you never asked!' Iovve lifted his gloved hands in a gesture of helpless innocence.

'*When* is it coming?'

'Well, my boy, obviously not within the next few minutes.' He looked at his watch. 'When is your hearing with the Arbiters?'

It was futile ... hopeless. He had tried, and he had failed. It was like dealing with some elemental force of nature, that knew only its own blind destiny, and held no negotiations with mortals, except to bend them to its own primeval force and design. Iovve was like a tide, a flood, a storm. Iovve was like (he thought wryly) a space quake.

A quake was coming, and Iovve was simply not going to discuss it. The game would have to be played on Iovve's terms.

Andrek said, 'My hearing with the Arbiters? I don't know. Soon. I'll have to find out from the clerk.'

'That's easy. The Arbiters' Chambers are right down the hall. Suppose we check in with the clerk and then take a peek into the Seismographic room. We might find out when the quake is coming.'

Andrek shrugged his shoulders.

Iovve looked at him with reproach. 'Your distrust stabs me in the heart.'

You seem to have survived, thought Andrek. 'Come on,' he said.

'I'll just take this along,' said Iovve, picking up his medical case.

'What for?' Andrek knew the question was wasted breath even before he asked it.

'I may need it down in Seismographic,' said the pilgrim vaguely.

Together they walked down to the Arbitration Chambers.

The Arbiters' Clerk took Andrek's name with mild surprise. 'The Terror Case, isn't it?' He riffled through his papers. 'Here we are. Just as I thought. Routine show-cause.' He peered up at Andrek. 'Actually, counsellor, no need for you to be here. No one is going to show cause. You can take the next ship out, if you like.'

'I'll stay for the hearing,' said Andrek. 'When is it scheduled?'

'In an hour or so. It's the last thing on the docket. As soon as the Arbiters collect, I'll give you a call. What's your room number?'

'We'll be in Seismographic,' interposed Iovve.

'Indeed?' The Clerk frowned. 'I thought it was closed down – locked up.'

'It is,' said Iovve. 'But that's where Don Andrek will be. It's just a few steps away. We can be back here very quickly.'

'All right. Go ahead. I'll call you there. You probably have about half an hour.'

Holding the medical kit with one hand, Iovve dragged Andrek out of the room with the other.

## 10 : The Right Key, and Beyond

A few minutes later they stood in front of a door. In its centre was a simple legend, in the twelve official languages of the Cluster. Andrek could read only the Ingliz: 'Seismographic Room – Authorized Personnel Only'.

The door panel was completely smooth except for one rather small hole in the centre. Andrek took this to be the keyhole. He watched as Iovve pushed tentatively on the panel with his shoulder. Nothing budged a micron. It now occurred to Andrek that Iovve had no key. But would that be a real problem? He recalled the pilgrim's entrance into Huntyr's office. But of course this was no mere commercial lock. If Iovve were able to open this door, Andrek wanted to watch him do it. He wanted to study Iovve's technique. It would be an opportunity to learn something about the man.

Iovve bent down and peered into the keyhole. 'Hm. Thermal profile.'

'What do you mean?'

'The key has to have several different temperatures along its length, such as, for example, 20°-10°-300° minus 5°, and so on. Each of the actual key-tooth temperatures has to be accurate to a fraction of a degree, or the profile of the series of thermo-couples inside won't close and complete the electric circuit to pull the bolts.'

Andrek looked at him blankly. Something like this was clearly beyond the simple portable equipment that Iovve might carry concealed under his robes. He had divided feeling about it. In a way, he was disappointed. On the other hand, he was not able to suppress a small malicious feeling of satisfaction in seeing Iovve thwarted.

He said, 'Well, that's that. You don't have that kind of key. You'd need a probe connected to a complete heating and re-frigeration unit, something weighing several hundred kilos. The official key is probably being loaded on *Xerol*, right now.'

'No doubt, my son. On the other hand, let's see what we can do. Stand back, boy.'

Rather dubiously, Andrek did as he was asked.

In a rapid movement, so quick that Andrek could see very little, Iovve ripped off the glove from his right hand. And then his actions were completely hidden by the loose folds on his robes. From the stance of his shoulders and right arm, Andrek guessed that the pilgrim was holding his bare hand, or possibly only the index finger, to the keyhole. At one point, when Iovve stood back a few centimetres, Andrek thought he caught the odour of hot metal. Then the other pressed in again, and then there came a smooth metallic rumbling, as of heavy rods sliding, and then the door stood ajar.

Iovve pushed in. 'Now, that wasn't too difficult, was it?'

Andrek noted that the glove was back. Mildly awed, he followed the pilgrim inside.

He looked around curiously.

The Seismographic Room was in the very centre of the Station. Whether by deliberate functional design, or designer's caprice (Andrek could not surmise which), the room had the shape of a dodecahedron. Ten of the pentagonal faces of the polyhedron were clustered with instruments. One, evidently the 'floor', had only a big work table and a few chairs. Directly above this was the 'ceiling', bare except for an over-sized clock in its centre.

'This room,' said Iovve, 'has been called the Eardrum of the Universe. Actually, the term is somewhat grandiose. It does however collect, integrate, and transmit Node weather data to each of the twelve sponsoring galaxies, along with proton density, ursecta activity, space temblors, meteorites, the works. At the moment, and from now on to the instant of the quake, it transmits automatically. As you have so cleverly deduced, my boy, a quake is certainly coming, and that is why all the normal operating staff have already shipped out.'

Andrek stared at him bitterly. 'And that's why everything of value has been dismantled. The station will be left here, stripped, simply to broadcast the quake. Why didn't you say so?'

Iovve lifted his arms piously. 'I was thinking only of you, my son. I didn't want to make you nervous. You have an important hearing shortly, you know.'

How could my forthcoming hearing be of any possible concern to you, thought Andrek. You're up to something. What it is, I don't know. But somehow it involves me. How? No use to ask. And how close is Iovve to the end of his pilgrimage? And is he entirely sane? But these, like all the other questions, are futile. The time has come to part. I'll have to start making plans. How do I get out of here? How do I get back to Goris-Kard without getting killed? And when I get there, what do I do about Omere? And Amatar? Everything depends on getting away from Iovve. Will I be able to do that? What does this treacherous creature want of me? I think I will tell him now, exactly what I think of him.

'You are either mad,' said Andrek flatly, 'or you are a scoundrel.'

'Or both?'

'Or both. And right after the hearing, I'm getting out.'

'On *Xerol*?'

'Of course not. But there are other ships. We saw a couple when we landed. I'll stow away on one of those.'

'Do as you wish, my boy.' Iovve met Andrek's angry eyes calmly. 'Meanwhile, excuse me a moment.' The pilgrim craned his head upwards and studied the clock for several seconds. Then without a word he clacked over to a bank of instruments at the far panel and peered at them closely. Shaking his head, he broke contact with the floor and floated up to the clock. He opened the clock face and moved the red hand around in a near semicircle.

'What are you doing?' demanded Andrek suspiciously.

'Merely correcting the setting,' Iovve called back cheerily. 'Be with you in a moment.'

'What was the red hand?'

'Sort of a special indicator – just a scientific gimmick.'

'It has something to do with the quake, doesn't it?'

'Why yes, I guess you could say that.'

'It tells you when the quake is coming,' persisted Andrek coldly. 'You know, and you don't want me to know.'

'Really, my boy, I'm not on your witness stand. Your suspicions cut me to the quick. Yes, it does predict the time of the quake.'

'When is it due?'

'When? Not immediately. Surely, you can see that. You haven't even had your session with the Arbiters yet. I hope, my son, that you can take comfort from the fact that right here at the Station is a collection of the best judicial minds of the Twelve Galaxies. Their mere presence here should reassure you. And why? The reason is simple. These judges acknowledge a sacred duty to their respective governments, sworn under solemn oath, to protect and preserve their laws and legal systems. And to preserve the law, they must first preserve themselves. Hence, the faithful performance of their sworn duty requires first, and above all, a most delicate, watchful, and continuing regard for their own skins. Accept my assurance that they would never violate so sublime an obligation by a callous disregard for an oncoming space quake.'

Andrek laughed, despite himself.

The intercom sounded. 'Don Andrek, calling Don Andrek.'

The advocate grimaced and stepped over to the phone panel. He flipped the communications switch. 'Andrek here.'

The clerk's face appeared on the screen. 'Don Andrek, the Arbiters will convene in a few minutes.'

'Thank you. I'll be right up.' He flipped the switch over and turned back to Iovve. 'The quake,' he said quietly. '*When?*'

The pilgrim drew himself up to his full height and stared back at Andrek. 'James, Don Andrek, it is not my intent that you shall die in the quake. In fact, let me remind you that I have saved your life three times, and instead of plying me with foolish questions, you should be expressing your gratitude. You owe me a debt. Will you concede that you are in my debt?'

Ah! Now it was finally coming out. Iovve might be both a liar and a scheming scoundrel; yet he schemed with method. The moment was now at hand that would explain why Iovve had saved his life that time in Huntyr's office, and the reason for Raq, and the journey, as bodyguard, with him on *Xerol*. But he did not intend to make it easier for Iovve.

'I will concede it, *arguendo*,' he said warily.

'A curse on your legal niceties,' barked Iovve. 'But for me, you'd be dead thrice over!'

Andrek was equally harsh. 'Did you save my life three times for a price?'

The pilgrim shot a searching glance at him. Andrek got the sudden impression that he had said exactly what the other had expected him to say, that the trap had been baited, and he had walked into it. So now the question of the price of his life was up for discussion; he himself had just put it on the agenda. Well, then, what was his price? He was genuinely curious. Iovve's demand might also answer several other questions. So he waited.

Iovve's voice was now soft, almost sorrowful.

'Ah, my son, what an ungrateful, mercenary attitude! By my beard! You seek only to be rid of me, and to be freed from your obligation. Well, then, out of my boundless affection for you, and yielding to your insistence, I suppose I might be able to think up some little task that you could perform, so as to relieve you of this debt, which you feel so burdensome, and so to put

136

matters in complete balance between us.'

Andrek smiled sardonically. 'And what is this little task?'

'Just this. Save Terror. Persuade the Arbiters to leave the planet here at the Node, untouched, unharmed.'

Andrek stared at the pilgrim in amazement. Well, there it was. Payment for his debt. Save Terror! Was it for this that Iovve had brought him to the ends of the universe? Save Terror? Whatever for? Who had need of such a bleak, desolate, devastated ball of rock and frozen seas? Well, then, what *had* he expected? He did not know. But certainly not this. This was impossible. 'By the blind eyes of Alea! What are you thinking of? The Great House has sent me here to make sure Terror is destroyed, not saved. The Arbiters are sitting here for that purpose. It is all over.'

'Not at all, my boy, not at all. You disappoint me. You are seeing events only in terms of black and white. A binary response unworthy of an illustrious Don. So let us consider the matter. Terror is under a "show-cause" order, which means that the planet has this one last chance to show cause why it should not be destroyed. In fact, you are here for the purpose of opposing any such plea, in the remote event it is made. Right?'

'Quite right,' said Andrek. He laughed in sputtering unbelief. 'So now, you think I can save Terror simply by reversing the position of the Home Galaxy?'

'If done persuasively – yes. Especially considering the circumstances.'

'What circumstances,' said Andrek suspiciously.

Iovve lifted his gloved hands vaguely. 'Oh, you know. These condemnation proceedings are boring, routine.... The Arbiters want to get it over with and get home. Some of them have probably already gone.'

Probably to beat the quake, thought Andrek. He said: 'If I reversed position on a case like this, I could never return to Goris-Kard. In fact, I wouldn't be safe anywhere on the Home Galaxy. I'd be a hunted man the rest of my life.'

'You already are.'

They looked at each other. Unhappily, Iovve was quite correct. Nothing that he did here in the case of The Twelve Galaxies vs. Terror would have the slightest effect on his death sentence. He could condemn Terror; he could attempt to save Terror; he could ignore Terror. It would be all the same: Oberon would still search him out and kill him.

Andrek lifted his shoulders wearily. 'You're right, of course. I can't go back. I am hunted. And I don't even know why. Curious, isn't it? As far as the Arbiters are aware, I'm a fully accredited representative of the Home Galaxy; yet, personally, I'm under a worse interdiction than Terror.'

'Then you'll do it?'

'Not so fast. You haven't explained *why* you want Terror saved.'

'I can't tell you everything, not just yet. But I *can* say this: it is needful that Terror go into the Deep.'

'And how will saving Terror put her into the Deep?'

'It won't. At any rate, not directly. But at least it would hold her here at the Node until the quake comes. And eventually a quake must come. If Terror is still here, the quake will crack her into the Deep. It's just a question of waiting.'

Now they were finally getting somewhere. He felt he had the pilgrim off balance. Andrek bored in. 'The thing that you have carefully *not* explained,' he said, 'is why it is needful that Terror go into the Deep.'

'True. I haven't explained that. But if you take the case – and save the planet, then I'll tell you.'

Should he settle for this? Perhaps he'd have to. He should know by now he couldn't force Iovve to talk when Iovve didn't want to talk. Still, he had caught a glimpse of a fantastic cosmic scheme. Terror in the Deep! If it were madness, it was a breathtaking madness, and he wanted to know more about it. He temporized. 'Even if I were successful, the reprieve would be only temporary. The Great House would discover the "error" and ask for a rehearing. And they'd get it.'

'That would take weeks. By then, Terror will be in the Deep.'

Andrek stared in hard surmise at the other. Iovve was quite right. All that was necessary was to have the planet waiting here when the quake struck. For this, a week's delay in the proceedings would be just as effective as a complete and final reprieve. But now he felt his bargaining position was strengthened. He would try once more. He said, 'This gets us back to my original question: when is the quake due?'

But Iovve was not to be swayed.

'Not right away. Plenty of time to save Terror. In fact, that may be a factor operating in our favour. The Arbiters may consider that leaving Terror to the quake is about the same as destroying her by explosives.'

The visor buzzed. It was the Arbiters' Clerk. 'Don Andrek, are you coming?'

'Thank you, right away.' He arose slowly and picked up the Terror dossier.

'Well?' said Iovve, rising with him.

'I haven't decided. Even if I agreed, what arguments would I have? We have only a few minutes – I'd need weeks, perhaps even months, to prepare a competent presentation.' Even with Poroth on the Board, he knew he could expect nothing. The most he might expect from Poroth was that the great jurist would not lean over backwards to avoid deciding in favour of an ex-pupil.

'I don't think so. I believe you have sufficient elasticity of intellect to reverse yourself and present a well-organized analysis of the opposition, all in a matter of minutes. To be a good advocate you have to have this facility; you have to know the case for the opposition as well as your own. I think you are a very good advocate.'

'Let us get one thing straight.' Andrek spoke slowly, carefully. 'Are you telling me that you *selected* me just to do this for you? That you got me out of trouble, that time in Huntyr's office, and then on the ship, just so I could be here and take this case for you?'

'You might say that,' admitted Iovve.

His eyes met Andrek's without wavering. The advocate knew that Iovve now spoke the truth. He had been brought here for the sole purpose of saving Terror, so that Terror might go into the Deep. The whole thing, from start to finish, was insanity on a scale so vast that it made his flesh creep. And he had a sickening conviction that he had merely scratched the surface, that there was more to come. Much, much more. He found himself toying with the idea of running from the room, up the corridor, and back out to *Xerol*. But that would surpass even Iovve's lunacy. He had to keep calm, get a grip of himself. Somehow, there had to be a way out. Meanwhile, he would have to humour his weird companion.

He put his hand on the chamber portal. 'I suppose,' he said quietly, 'that there's a great deal more, and that you'll give me the whole story eventually?' (After it's too late to do anything about it, he added to himself.)

'Yes, dear boy, as you have guessed, there *is* more. So, in the Terror matter, how will you plead?'

'Come along,' said Andrek non-committally.

Iovve followed him meekly out of the room and up to the corridor to the Arbiters' Chambers.

> *Planet, planet, flaming hell,*
> *(Wasn't Alea, or Ritornel?)*
> *What titanic hand of fate*
> *Drew thee to the waiting quake?*
>
> *And in the Deep's eternal night,*
> *What strange chance, or what design,*
> *(Or what monumental mind?)*
> *Shall set thee once again aright?*
>                         – Rimor, Quatrains

As they entered the room the Clerk greeted them in a whisper and checked off Andrek's name on the roster. They were barely in time.

'Remember,' hissed Iovve, 'save Terror!'

'Be quiet!' whispered Andrek. His mind was churning. He had not the faintest idea what he would do. He felt infected by Iovve's madness. Nothing made any sense. His chest was heaving, his pulse was wild. His mouth was like leather, and he was very thirsty. At this moment he doubted his competence to petition the Court for a glass of water.

The robed Arbiters had apparently just finished filing in and taking their seats. Poroth was there, in the centre chair, but was bent over, whispering to a brother Arbiter, whom Andrek recognized as Karbol, of Andromeda, and did not immediately notice Andrek. The sight of this good man was a sharp nostalgic blast: the smell of ancient desks and new books ... the sound of young voices ... wind in the courtyard trees ... back when he had only one concern, to find Omere, and no one was trying to kill him. Andrek gave a hurried glance at the other Arbiters. There were three other hominids, whom he identified from descriptions and biographies in his files as Telechrys, of the Greater Ellipse, Rokon, of the Lesser Ellipse, and Lyph, of the Blue Spiral. These, with Poroth and Karbol, were the hominids, hard, cold, absolutely logical. And then the three non-hominids, Wreeth, Maichec, and Werebel, aloof, elegant, their scaled faces and tentacled arms drowned in alien clothing.

Altogether, there were only eight. Four empty great-chairs. As he realized this, Andrek was suddenly back at his last recital, at the Academy before Poroth's final practice court, and in this instant his petition crystallized, exquisitely ordered, perfect.

The Clerk arose and began to chant. 'Arise, all! Intergalactic Arbiters are now in session. Draw nigh and give your attention. Be seated.'

As he took his seat at counsel's table, Andrek looked about him. Iovve sat behind him, in the first row. The room was practically empty. He looked up. The Clerk was reading from the Docket.

'The sole case is Twelve Galaxies vs. The Planet Terror.' He sat down.

Chief Arbiter Poroth studied the file in front of him. He spoke in slow, careful Ingliz. 'This is a post-conviction proceeding, a routine show-cause.' He looked about the room, and now noticed Andrek for the first time. There was a barely perceptible pause as he gave the advocate a friendly nod of recognition. He then continued. 'I shall sign the destruct order, entered by this Court by due proceedings previously had, and the crew will proceed forthwith, unless anyone now present shall show cause as to why this should not be done.' He picked up the stylus. 'Very well, then.'

This, thought Andrek, is madness. I am going to regret it the rest of my very short life. How startled Poroth is going to be! The Chief Arbiter would probably puzzle over this reversal for years. Andrek doubted that he would ever see Poroth again to explain it to him, or that Poroth would really understand if he did. It was too bad. Somehow, it would help if he could get Poroth away, as he used to on the old Academy quadrangle, and explain everything, and get the advice of his old friend.

He arose. 'My lords, I am James, Don Andrek, accredited Advocate of the House of the Delfieri, of the Polyspiral Galaxy, sometimes called the Home Galaxy.' His voice was, he thought, surprisingly strong and clear. Behind him, he heard Iovve shifting restlessly.

The stylus hung in mid-air. The Chief Arbiter nodded gravely. 'The Court recognizes Don Andrek.'

He was enthralled by a fine madness. How would it be now if he told Poroth, in dry legal terms, that in the past three days sundry attempts had been made to murder him, and that as a matter of self defence and simple survival, he had killed three men, all without the slightest benefit or consent of duly constituted authority, and that he was now a hunted criminal. But no. The native goodness of his boyhood mentor might break through the thick cast of law and precedent, and Poroth might impulsively attempt to help Andrek, at great peril to himself. The advocate was bound to silence. He hoped that Poroth would not invite him to chambers after the hearing.

'My government,' said Andrek slowly, 'hereby withdraws its earlier recommendation for destruction of the Planet Terror. Further, we now enter a plea that the planet be preserved, and we move that the Court so order.' So now it was done; he had accepted – nay, embraced – Iovve's insanity. And for the life of him, he did not know why.

For a moment Poroth stared at him, dumbfounded. Then there was a hurried stirring at the bench as the Arbiters leaned forward.

And now he knew that the past was over, closed, irretrievable. At this moment, he was a stranger even to himself. An entire career had collapsed beneath him, and with it everything supporting and leading to that career, including the Academy, and above all, Poroth. He should be feeling an immense sense of loss. But he was numb, anaesthetized. Of the things he should be feeling, he felt nothing, save only the distant ring of voices in vanished classrooms, and the smell of smoke from piles of leaves burning in the Academy courtyard. Whatever else you may think of me, Dean Poroth, when you return to Goris-Kard and learn everything, at least think back on this moment, with a measure of pride, and know that you taught me well.

Hail, old friend! And farewell! Andrek knew he would never see him again. One by one, all the doors of his past had closed. This was the last, and the best. And he himself had closed it, and locked it, and thrown away the key. Somewhere in all of this there was divinity : for only the gods could have conceived an irony so sublime.

The Clerk and Recorder, he noted, had turned and were staring at him.

'Will the Court instruct the Recorder to enter the withdrawal of the original plea, together with my motion as stated,' he continued smoothly, 'so that this Honourable Court may duly consider the same.'

'So ordered,' rumbled the Chief Arbiter. But he was plainly puzzled. 'Don Andrek, this turn of events is indeed a surprise. I think you must appreciate that it is highly irregular for the party complainant to withdraw the plea in a case such as this, and that the irregularity is further compounded when the don accredited for the plaintiff appears here as advocate for the defendant.'

'Granted, my lord,' said Andrek. He smiled crookedly. 'Yet, I have it on the highest authority, that no turn of events should surprise a truly skilled advocate, nor – I would assume – a truly great judge; and certainly not the eight here sitting as the supreme judicial body of the Twelve Galaxies. In any event, the irregularity, if such there be, will be somewhat mitigated if the Court decides to grant my motion – as I am sure will be the case.'

Wreeth spoke up in a thin reedy whistle. 'Don Andrek, do you realize that you are now proposing to save from destruction a planet that stands proven guilty of starting a nuclear war over a hundred years ago – a war that destroyed every living thing in nearly one-third of your own galaxy – and which was duly condemned for destruction by the Intergalactic Convention for the Control of War.'

'I so understand, your honour. May I plead my motion?'

'Approach the bench, Don Andrek.'

The advocate left his seat and walked up to the rostrum.

'Now, Mr. Andrek,' said Poroth, 'since we must adjourn within the hour, we will ask that you be brief.' Something like a smile flickered around the edges of his mouth.

'I do not propose to waste the Court's time,' said Andrek. 'On the other hand, I do not propose to omit any points vital to a proper disposition of my motion.'

'Proceed.' Poroth leaned back in his chair.

'My petition is founded on three premises,' said Andrek coolly. 'First: procedurally, this honourable Court, as it now sits, is without jurisdiction. Second: substantively, on the merits, Terror ought not to be destroyed. Third: I plea for a thirty-day continuance. I will explain each basis in detail.'

Poroth had now settled thoughtfully back into his great cushioned chair, and was tapping his fingertips together, exactly as he used to, years ago at the Academy, when he was listening to an A-plus brief. Except that now the great man's mouth twitched intermittently. 'Continue,' he murmured.

'The Court,' said Andrek, 'has no jurisdiction because the Court now sitting does not constitute a quorum. The Articles of the Intergalactic Arbitration Convention require three-fourths of the Court be present in disputed matters affecting a planet. The matter is certainly in dispute, yet there are only eight members of the Court present. Nine are required.'

'It is true that four of our brothers have already left,' said Poroth. 'Under the circumstances, I had to give my consent.' He smiled faintly. 'Anything further.'

'Yes, your honour. My motion is further based on the preposition that no witnesses are present who can testify, of their own knowledge, that the planet under interdiction is in fact Terror. It is basic procedure that the accused is entitled to be confronted by his accusers.'

'What!' burst out Rokon. 'Do you deny the planet is Terror?'

'I neither confirm nor deny, your honour.' Andrek's voice was chill, correct. 'I merely point out that nowhere in the record is the requisite identification of the accused planet. For all this Court can know, Terror is presently orbiting its own sun.'

'You well know there are no witnesses,' grumbled Rokon. 'But how could you complain of that? If perchance it is not Terror that we destroy, then your client is saved. Such mistake would place Terror forever beyond the jurisdiction of this Court, by reason of double jeopardy.'

'Certainly, your honour,' said Andrek blandly. 'As to *that*, I speak not so much for my client, but rather as amicus curiae, a friend of the Court. I merely urge the Court that the matter of identification be beyond dispute, to avoid any future embarassment to the Court.'

'And the point of disputed identification is now of course of record,' said Wreeth. His strange features relaxed into something that looked oddly like a smile. 'Proceed, counsellor, to the merits of your case.'

'Thank you, your honour. At the outset, so as not to burden the record, I will concede a number of points. As its name implies, Terror was a planet that generated fear ... hatred ... loathing. The Court may take judicial notice of the fact that the greed of its people was inexhaustible. During the forty centuries of its interstellar and intergalactic culture, its trading, colonizing, and military ships went everywhere – and seized everything they could carry away. By a certain viewpoint, they ravaged a goodly part of the Home Galaxy. Words to describe these people spring easily to the tongue. They were bullies, cheats; they were treacherous and corrupt. They were degenerates, abominable wretches. They were cruel, obscene, and cowards. Looking back on this vanished race, we see them now as utterly evil.'

He paused sombrely. 'And came the revolt, the Horror. They lost the great nuke war ... everything they had ... all their far-flung colonies ... and finally their own planet. Not a living thing there survived. And this is how *we* remember them.'

Andrek looked at the intent faces leaning down at him. 'But I can assure the Court, they did not think of *themselves* in this way. They did not call their planet by our name. No, not "Terror". That is history's oversimplifying corruption of the real name, which is, as you probably know, "Terra". It meant "The Land". And to them that land was loveliness incarnate. They fought among themselves for it, on the land, and on the seas, and they fought to the death. The names of their battles have come down to us ... Thermopylae ... The Alamo ... Tobruk ... Juneau. But so much for their origins. We turn now to their early years in space.

'Within a century of their discovery of the nuclear drive, they had planted colonies on the planets of Centauri and Procyon. And they came singing. In another three hundred years, they had developed the overdrive, and they penetrated the heart of their – and my – galaxy. They colonized my home planet of Goris-Kard. I am one of their distant descendants. For another thousand years, they spread their marvellous science, literature, music, art, laws, and architecture throughout our Home Galaxy. And still the Horror lay ahead. But it was coming, for it was inevitable. Terra's colonies became rich, powerful, opulent. They made contact with the Magellanic Clouds, then with Andromeda. They grew restive under the yoke of the Mother Planet. There were minor revolts – ruthlessly suppressed by Terra. And then came the alliances, the regroupings. And then the Horror broke. We all know this history. What we seem to forget is that most of us in this room trace our ancestry, by varied mutations, back to Terra, and the intergalactic Ingliz we now speak is but a variant of that ancient mother tongue. We exist here today – in this very room – because Terra existed, and her sons, sitting as this Court, must now decide whether she shall finally cease to exist.'

Andrek stood silent for a moment. It was time to come to an end. He could go on forever, but that would simply annoy the Arbiters. He would have to put together a sharp, pithy summary.

'What, then, is our Terran heritage? We cannot begin to count it. We grant much is memorable evil. Yet, if it is beyond forgetting, it is because it cannot be separated from the good. For Terra has handed down to us a mixture of good and evil, of rapine and laughter, of beauty and tears: the passions that distinguish us from the beasts. And her greatest heritage of all, and the one she most needs at this hour, when there is none to defend her, is mercy.'

'There seems to be *one* left to defend her,' observed Poroth. His voice was reserved, dry, but his eyes were twinkling. He looked at his chrono. 'I trust that completes your summation, Don Andrek. Owing to the lateness of the hour, my brothers and I will now confer and give you a bench decision.'

Andrek bowed and returned to his seat. He twisted around and looked at Iovve curiously. The pilgrim seemed lost in thought, hardly aware the presentation was over. Andrek sighed and stuffed his papers back into his brief case. He still wondered why he had undertaken the defence. The last hope of returning to any planet in the Home Galaxy was now certainly gone. In fact, sanctuary would probably be denied him in most of the other eleven galaxies. What was left to him now? He did not know. Perhaps he could take the robe of Alea or Ritornel and hide away in a remote monastery. Yet, in a way, he was glad he had done it. For he had, in this action, for the first and only time in his life, evaded the cynical paradox of advocacy: the undertaking to damage or destroy persons who are strangers for the benefit of other strangers, while yet standing ready to turn on an erstwhile client, rending him for the pay of still another stranger. This paradox, too, he mused, is part of my Terran heritage.

He started. Chief Arbiter Poroth was addressing him. He arose and approached the bench.

The Chief Arbiter cleared his throat. 'The Recorder will enter the following bench ruling on the motion offered by Don Andrek on behalf of the party Terror, in the case of the Twelve Galaxies vs. Terror, wherein the Court is petitioned to order the preservation of the planet defendant: The petition is denied.'

Andrek's face fell. He had done his best, for his profession, and for Iovve, and he had lost. Yet, after all, aside from Iovve's insane scheme, why should it matter? The planet was dead. No one would ever want to live on it again, in or out of the Deep.

He suddenly realized the Chief Arbiter was not through.

'This Court,' continued Poroth, 'is convened by and under the joint authority of our Twelve Galaxies. We are sworn to keep the peace, and to punish those who would arouse enmity, internally or externally. In the ancient traditions of each of our Twelve Galaxies runs a prophecy of the "Omega" – the final, ultimate destruction of everything. Terror brought us very close to this, and we should never forget it. Under our laws, we are required to destroy planets found guilty of initiating nuclear warfare. The record has clearly established that the defendant Terror is such a planet. In fact, at this moment, the destruct crew is awaiting our order to detonate massive charges already placed in the planet core that will literally atomize it. Yet, doubt has been suggested as to two vital points, to wit, whether we have a quorum, and also whether the planet in question is actually Terror. It is our discretion to resolve these doubts either way – for destruction, or against. But we will do neither. We do, however, suspend and stay these proceedings, including any action in respect of the defendant planet, for a period of thirty days, at which time this Court shall reconvene and further consider the matter – if the case is then still before us. So ordered.'

The Arbiters arose slowly, and the Clerk began to chant. 'All rise, all rise. This honourable Court stands adjourned.'

Andrek walked back to Iovve. Through the thick brown bristles of his beard, the pilgrim seemed to be smiling.

'Does that satisfy you?' asked Andrek bluntly.

'Yes, of course, dear boy. Ritornel has spoken!'

'Then, my friend, you can start explaining ... *everything*.'

'And so I will, as soon as we get back to the Seismographic Room.'

Andrek merely shrugged. He did not believe it. Nor did he care very much any more. Furthermore, at the first opportune moment he planned to part company with Iovve.

When they got back to the Seismographic Room, Iovve stole a look at the great clock overhead, and then, as though to forestall Andrek, pointed to the chairs, and sat down. 'Shall we start with Amatar?' he asked.

Andrek started. 'Amatar?' If Iovve were really going to talk about Amatar, he would stay awhile. He took a chair and leaned forward. 'Yes. I want very much to hear about Amatar.'

'You know about Oberon's near-fatal injuries, when his ship was caught in the last quake here, eighteen years ago.'

'Huntyr was telling us.'

'Regardless of his motives, Huntyr spoke truly.' Iovve watched Andrek through narrowed eyes. 'And he mentioned – the Master Surgeon.'

'Yes. The man who destroyed my brother.'

'And the – one – who created Amatar.'

'Create —!' Andrek gripped the arms of his chair. 'What are you saying!'

'You have heard of the practice of parthenogenesis, whereby a single hominid cell is taken from the living body, then developed first into a blastula, which is just a microscopic bubble with a single cavity, then a fully organized gastrula, then finally, after some months, a recognizable hominid foetus?'

'I have heard of it. It was used after the Horror, long ago, when so many monster mutations endangered natural propagation. Today it's just a medical curiosity.'

'Quite so. But not entirely obsolete. In fact, eighteen years ago, when Oberon lay dying in the hospital wing of the Great House, his uncle, the old Regent, called the Master Surgeon and told him to start the neccessary tissue cultures. They hoped that one would succeed, to make an infant Oberon, and preserve the Delfieri line. So the Master Surgeon made the cultures, dozens of them, all from living fragments of costal bone that he was still picking out of Oberon's chest. Bone fragments made the best tissue cultures, since bone marrow is the best source of blood cells, erythrocytes, leukocytes, and thromboctyes.'

'But Oberon did not die,' interposed Andrek.

'No. Oberon did not die. By then, the Master Surgeon had completed that tour de force known as Rimor.'

'Omere,' said Andrek tonelessly.

'Yes, in a manner of speaking, Omere, your brother. And listening to Omere, Oberon decided to live.'

'So the cultures were thrown out.'

'It wasn't that simple. When the Master Surgeon reported to the Regent that his nephew would live, the old man instructed the Master Surgeon to destroy the cultures, to avoid problems in the Delfieri succession. But Oberon had other plans. Out of a sense of perversity and boredom, and a desire to inconvenience the Master Surgeon, this arrogant youth had commanded that the vats be moved into his room. And there the cultures died, one by one, until only two were left. And so it was Oberon himself who first noticed, during the ensuing weeks, the strangeness of these last two growths. For neither was quite what it should have been. In particular, Oberon demanded tests for the second of these. Only then did he discover the impossibility.'

'Discover what?' demanded Andrek.

'The impossibility.'

Andrek gritted his teeth. He knew by now he could not accelerate Iovve's informative process. 'Go ahead.'

'Of course. But progress involves a slight detour. Let me digress a moment.'

'By all means.'

'Now don't pout, my boy. I'm explaining this as fast as I can.'

Andrek groaned inaudibly.

'Sex,' continued Iovve, 'is determined by the cell chromosomes. If the cell contains an x chromosome and a y chromosome, the cell is male; cell reproduction – mitosis – will give only more male cells. If the cell contains only x chromosomes, it will be female, and mitosis will give only female cells. The costal bone cells were all male. Subsequent sampling proved that. Yet, mitosis gave only cells containing two x chromosomes: in a word, all female cells. The callus growing in the second vat was a female foetus.'

Andrek did not understand immediately. For one lone moment he could only stare at the pilgrim in uncomprehending wonder. And then something seemed to explode inside his head. His lips formed a single word: 'Amatar!'

'Yes,' said Iovve. 'Amatar, the Motherless One.'

The advocate was stunned. It was not possible to grasp this. He loved Amatar. He hated Oberon. Oberon would kill him. Amatar had saved his life. They were as different as night and

149

day, as black and white; and yet they were the same. Amatar was Oberon.

Iovve watched quizzically the conflicting emotions at play on the advocate's pale features. Finally Andrek looked up at him. 'I think I understand, now. And the other culture was – Kedrys?'

'Yes.'

'How is it explained?'

'The mutations were probably caused by radiation. There was considerable cosmic radiation still bathing Goris-Kard from the recent space quake. Safeguards had been taken, of course. When the cultures were started, our side of the planet faced away from the direction of the Node, and the culture room was encased in a metre of lead. And finally, of course, each culture was started and kept in a lead-lined flask. And yet it is known that two bursts of cosmic radiation passed entirely through the body of the planet, a metre of lead, and finally into the respective two cultures, and precisely in the right gene, and at the right molecular area in the DNA. No other rays entered the chamber: just these two. A milli-micron one way or the other, and there would be no Amatar, and no Kedrys. With Kedrys the problem is even more difficult. There has to be practically a gamma shower to modify the genes sufficiently to unite avian, hominid, and equine characteristics. Is this chance? In the final plot, does Alea conspire with Ritornel, and is the greatest design helpless without luck? I do not know. One might argue that such chance is ultra-astronomical, that this is too much even for the goddess.'

These philosophical meanderings were wasted on the advocate. He rather suspected that the pilgrim was trying to take flight from the single issue remaining. He would not be diverted.

'Iovve,' he said quietly. 'Who are *you*?'

Iovve shrugged his shoulders. 'You may now rightly ask, and I must answer,' he said simply. 'And since I have nearly completed my pilgrimage, and will soon be dead, you know that I speak the truth. The ancient Terran jurists had a word for this.'

'Deathbed confession,' said Andrek. 'It has a presumption of veracity. So let's assume, for the purpose of argument, that you are finally going to tell me the truth. Will it be the whole truth?'

'I'll try,' promised the pilgrim.

Andrek snorted. 'Whether you actually do or don't, at least it should be entertaining just to watch you *try*. So, go ahead.'

'And so I shall, my dear boy. And I shall begin with the beginning, which is to say, myself. My origins are best understood when viewed in perspective against yours. Your great Home Galaxy is a poly-spiral, which means of course that it is mature, since many billions of years are required to condense into the disc shape and to fling out the balancing spiral arms. The stars, consequently, are nearly all second-generation.'

'Second-generation?' queried Andrek.

'Yes. They are condensed from clouds of hydrogen and cosmic dust containing all the known elements. Such dust is the product of ancient stellar explosions. Let me explain this in steps, so you can understand the vast gulf that separates our two cultures.'

'Please do,' said Andrek. At least this cleared up one point: Iovve was not hominid; he was not even a native of the Home Galaxy. Andrek had rather suspected as much.

Iovve continued. 'A galaxy is born as the titanic amorphous masses of hydrogen at the node condense slowly into stars. These first stars will all be red giants. Tremendous heat and pressures develop, and the hydrogen is fused to helium. Other nuclear reactions take place to make carbon, neon, oxygen.... In fact, all the elements up to and including iron are formed in this first stage, within the body of the red giants. Elements higher than iron cannot be formed in this way, since this method of element formation requires the release of energy, and elements higher than iron cannot release energy in this way. So now, when all the fuel is used up, the red giant explodes – a supernova. The elements it has created are blown into space. The explosion harms nothing, because the red giants do not have planets. And actually, the explosion is beneficial, since the dispersed matter can now mix with more hydrogen, and finally again condense, not only into suns, but also into planets. The sun will this time enter a new stage of element formation. It will again convert hydrogen into helium, but now it will do it differently, more economically. Since it now has plenty of carbon (and in fact, all the elements up through and including iron), it produces heat and energy by the carbon cycle. The carbon cycle is curious in that it makes copious quantities of protons. These protons strike the nuclei of the atoms in this new sun, until, by a process of simple nuclear addition, *all* of the ninety-two stable elements are made. When that sun eventually consumes all its nuclear fuel, and finally explodes, it will of course offer a complete system of elements to that sector of the galaxy. By then, the galaxy will be fairly mature; it will be a spiral, like your Home Galaxy. But that's another story. It's really that planet that I want to talk about, the one condensed from the dust of the red giant's explosion. That planet is really quite a primitive thing. I know. I was born there. Our periodic table stopped with element number twenty-six: iron. You may think that this meant we had at least a well-developed ferrous metallurgy, with hearths, reducing ovens, foundries, rolling mills, and the end products, such as machines made of steel, steel manufactures, steel architecture. But I tell you we had none of this. When the Terrans came, there was only one piece of metallic iron on the face of the whole planet – and that was a small meteorite in a museum. Yet, it could not have been otherwise.

'Consider history in a secondary planet – one like Terra, that starts its history with *all* the ninety-two elements. It first goes through a stone age. (As we did.) Then it discovers copper, and next that excellent copper–tin alloy, bronze. So it then enters into a bronze age. But more than this, it enters into metallurgy. It acquires the skills in metallurgy that it must have before it can have an iron age. So you see, having neither copper nor tin, my people could not have a bronze age, and if no bronze age, no iron age. And the lack of heavy metals had other consequences. Without gold or silver for coins, we had little trade or commerce. Again, our lack of copper denied us the electrical sciences. And since we had no uranium, nuclear power was of course unthinkable. And needless to say, we had no means of interplanetary flight. We did not even have heavier-than-air machines.'

The pilgrim stopped, and seemed to stare through Andrek, and beyond, into flickering scenes of his own far distant planet and youth.

'Go on!' said Andrek tensely. 'You said the Terrans came. Did they colonize your planet?'

Iovve shook his head. 'Our planet seemed desolate to them – not worth their attention, except as a refuelling base. And our peculiar introverted speciality, forced on us by simple lack of other occupations, was not at first apparent to the Terrans. Later, this happy skill took us as honoured guests throughout the Twelve Galaxies.'

'And what was this – skill?' asked Andrek.

'We were physicians and surgeons. The profession was probably inevitable for us. For when a culture is denied technology, it becomes introspective. It turns inward. It occupies itself with its own body, and with the responses of its body. What we had

152

missed in the hardware sciences we more than made up in the science of the mind and body. And when we were finally exposed to other cultures, our prime interest in bodies continued, and was extended to the life forms of our new neighbours. In this manner, most of us left our home planet, to market our one great skill. Yet, we communicated with each other, and we were a cohesive body. Some of us had strange adventures. Ah, the things I could tell you.'

By the Beard of the Founder, thought Andrek, I believe you could! He said, 'I understand now why you belong to the Iatric Order of Ritornel.' He fancied Iovve nearly smiled. 'Continue, then,' said Andrek curtly.

'When the Terran Wars broke out – The Horror – as you suvivors so aptly call it, I called my brothers to one last convention. It was clear to us then, that Terra must eventually be destroyed, and probably a good part of the Home Galaxy with her. We decided what we must do, to give civilization another chance, a return, as it were. I suggested a simple code-word for the operation: *Ritornel*.'

'What?'

'Yes, Ritornel. Does this astound you? I can see that it might, for Ritornel today bears little resemblance to my original concept. Yet, we were the original missionary physicians of Ritornel. Wherever we went, we carried the Prophesy: a virgin, not of mother born, to renew life, on a new world, and thus to complete the Ring. In the course of the centuries, I regret to say, Ritornel has changed drastically. Miracles, martyrs, and myths can ruin a perfectly good religion. When the supernatural flies in the window, logic stumbles out of the door. Today I would not be admitted to any but the lowest circles of the Temple. And of course, in some of the chapters, I would not be admitted at all.'

'Iovve,' said Andrek quietly, 'please listen to me a moment. You have referred to participation in events that took place centuries ago, well before the Horror. No – let me finish.... And just now you have, in effect, told me that you are the Founder of Ritornel. Now, listening to this objectively, won't you grant that some scepticism is justified?'

'James, my dear innocent, you need not believe a word of what I have told you. Nevertheless, I do hope my simple story has not completely exhausted your credulity, for I have not finished.'

Was it possible? mused Andrek. Could he prove it was impossible? And in any case, what difference did it make? For the time being, he'd reserve judgment. 'So you founded Ritornel,' he said non-committally. 'Then what?'

'We took counsel. Midway in the course of The Horror, we decided what to do. We would select an optimum specimen of the best culture known to us. This specimen would actually consist of a male and female of the species, and we would place this couple in suitable surroundings, quite inaccessible, and completely isolated from all other life systems. There, in peace, a new race would be propagated, and in time would dominate the universe. In the beginning, there were many of us, seeking this new couple. But now my brothers are dead. I am the last. Truly, Ritornel is no longer Ritornel. But it doesn't matter. My mission is done. The Ring of Ritornel will soon be complete.'

'And this preservation of the species, this is the true purpose of Ritornel? This is the Ring?'

'The same.'

'But I still don't see the symbolism. Ritornel means "return". What are we returning to?'

'We return to life. Or rather, civilization, after nearly dying, shall return, preserved by and through the selected couple. You may liken it to an ancient Terran oak forest. Every tree may die; yet, if but one acorn be saved, the forest may yet again live. Or again, it is like the preservation of a bacterial culture. If but one cell be preserved, the entire culture can return to life, assuming, of course, that the proper nutrient medium is available. So, first of all, we needed the proper medium within which our male and female specimens could preserve their species. This, of course, had to be a planet. Obviously, it should be a planet of a mature star system – one containing all the elements, not a primitive one, like mine. As The Horror progressed, several candidates became available. For several reasons, we selected Terra. The main argument was that she was completely desolate, and was being hauled to the Node to be destroyed. Our planet *had* to be taken to the Node, for reasons that you will soon see.'

'I see one thing very clearly,' said Andrek thoughtfully. 'I see that you have made an utter fool of me. I thought you were my friend. Your only interest in me was to make that speech before the Arbiters, to save Terra, so that Terra could become the planet of Ritornel.'

Iovve's leathery features twisted into a smile. 'You are too modest, Don Andrek. My interest in you does not end with your famous speech to the Arbiters, legal landmark though it be.

154

Oh, indeed not.'

'All right,' said Andrek. 'Get on with it. I've done your work for you. Here's Terra at the Node – as far as possible from civilization. Is this what you meant by preservation in isolation?'

'Not exactly. For that, we need one thing more.'

'The quake?'

'Yes. As I have already mentioned to you, the quake will take Terra into the Deep.'

'How about your couple,' said Andrek. 'Your male and female specimens, the ancestors of the new race? How do you select them? And then how do you get *them* into the Deep?'

'Very perceptive questions, dear boy. First, let us address ourselves to the rationale of selection. Suppose that you had the task of selecting this seed ... spore ... cell ... this ancestral couple, to become the progenitors of the surviving race. There are hundreds of strong contenders – ranging from the water people that dominate the Hydraid Galaxy, to the chitinous denizens of the arid worlds of the Spereld suns. All are intelligent, cultured, prolific, technically advanced. And all – though they do not yet realize it – are doomed by Omega. Which one will be given the chance to try again?'

'No problem there,' said Andrek. 'The selector owes a duty to his own race to select it.'

'Wrong, my boy. It is quite natural for the votaries to reconstruct the gods anthropomorphically, in their own image. However, when the "gods" create, they should be more imaginative.'

'You talk in riddles, old one.'

'Only because you are naïve, uninformed, and difficult to instruct.'

Andrek laughed. 'Instruct me.'

'Listen, then, and be instructed. We of Ritornel decided very early that mere technical competence in our prospective couple was not enough. We looked for other qualities – racial features that deserved immortality. And our search was successful. We found the characteristics we sought: in the hominid.'

'What characteristics are you talking about?'

'Several. Do you realize that, of the twelve basic cultures, only the hominid dreams? That only the hominid sees visions, and mourns, and has a sense of tragedy? That only the hominid believes firmly in things he cannot see? That only the hominid sings for pure useless pleasure, and laughs, and writes poetry?'

'Really? That's quite curious. I had not thought about it.'

'Well, then, I suggest you give it some thought. What is the hominid, that strangers should prefer him above all other life forms? He is cold and logical: yet he laughs and sings. He is cruel, and he has the lust of the male goat: yet he weeps, and is acquainted with grief. You described him well to the Arbiters. Verily, he is beyond knowing. Perhaps this helped our choice.'

'Very well, then,' said Andrek, 'the Founder of Ritornel selects what is to him an alien couple, two hominids, for deposit in the Deep. And right away your scheme is doomed to failure. For even if you were able to get Terra and your male and female into the Deep, they would never come out again. They'd all be lost forever. Nothing except space has ever come out of the Deep.'

'You are wrong.' The pilgrim reached into his robes and drew out a pendant Ritornellian ring, which he unfastened. 'Catch,' he said, tossing it to Andrek.

The advocate caught it and examined it, at first casually, then more closely. There was something very strange about it. For one thing, the Ritornellian series, from 1 to 12, then back again to 1, was *inside* the ring, whereas in all rings he had ever seen before, the series was outside. Nor was that all. He studied the digits carefully, turning the ring slowly in his fingers. All the numbers were backwards. He looked up at Iovve. 'What are you trying to tell me?'

'It is anti-matter,' said the other calmly.

Andrek gasped and let the ring fly from his hands. It ricocheted against a wall, then floated free, gleaming at him.

'Don't worry,' said Iovve. 'It has been passivated. And in any case, the ursecta would not let it annihilate, here at the Node.'

'But – it must weigh a good twenty grams! There's not a Klein circlet in any of the twelve galaxies with power capable of converting an object that size to anti-matter!'

'True. Not in any of the twelve. But there is one *between* the galaxies.'

'You mean *here*? At the Node?'

'Exactly. Into the Deep, and out again – a perfect Klein. Reverses polarity of the individual atoms, and of course turns everything inside-out and backwards, including the numbers.'

'The numbers!' Andrek jumped up and seized the ring again. 'Of course! This thing *has* been in the Deep! But why doesn't it annihilate on contact with my hand – or even with the molecules of the air?'

'As I said, it has been passivated. It has a surface layer of neutrons that almost completely precludes contact with normal matter. The few molecules that do make contact are harmless. I'm sure you know the theory. The addition of neutrons prevents the approach of particles of opposite charge. The number of neutrons to be added depends upon the structure of a given atom. Calcium is the highest "stable". There you have twenty protons in the nucleus, and you need only twenty neutrons to prevent the approach of the negative shell electrons. For higher atomic numbers you need proportionately more neutrons. For example, the bismuth, you need 126 neutrons to neutralize 83 protons in the nucleus. And thereafter, the addition of neutrons doesn't completely stabilize, and the atoms are radioactive. And that is why an anti-matter body normally glows in the dark. It ionizes the air about it, like a neon lamp. Outside the Node, away from the ursecta, the ring would have a blue glow.'

Andrek looked over at Iovve. He remembered now the curious impression he had experienced on several past occasions ... that encounter in Huntyr's office, and later in the dim-lit cabin in *Xerol*, when the pilgrim's face had been bathed in a pale blue glow. Andrek looked at the ring, then back again at Iovve. His mouth slowly opened wide. The hair began to stand up on the back of his neck. 'You —' he gurgled. 'The Deep —?'

Iovve nodded gravely. 'I have been in the Deep. My body is anti-matter.'

Andrek's heart seemed to dissolve within him. It was impossible, unimaginable. Yet it was true. And this meant everything Iovve had told him was true. He felt as though he were standing on the edge of a bottomless chasm, leaning into the blackness, and beginning to fall. He jerked up straight, and fought off a feeling of dizziness.

'How can this be!' he cried.

'It was part of the plan of Ritornel,' said Iovve. 'We were weak, nearly defenceless. To accomplish Ritornel, we needed immense power, power that would permit us to cope with the armed might of the Twelve Galaxies, and even more important, power sufficient to transmit our selected hominid specimens from normal space into the Deep. We were aware of the work on creation of anti-matter by sending a tiny amount of metal down a Klein circuit, and we knew that tremendous power could be developed at the normal matter/anti-matter interface. Our theorists then determined that the topology of the Node epicentre at quake time was exactly identical to that of a Klein circuit. In theory, at least, any object at the epicentre will be sucked back into the Deep by the quake. So far, so good. It's simple to get a thing into the Deep. To get it out again is quite another matter. Obviously, we needed a diplon, a double quake. The first part would put me in the Deep, the second would bring me out again, into normal space, as anti-matter.'

'And there you would annihilate,' interposed Andrek. 'Except, of course, you very obviously didn't. Why didn't you?'

'My colleagues prepared my body. There were certain surgical procedures, necessary to adapt the dermal nerve endings, and to permit control of the anti-matter/normal matter interface.'

'According to history,' said Andrek heavily, 'the last diplon was over five hundred years ago.'

'Yes, that was the one. The Horror had just begun. I remember every detail. The Node Station was not quite so large or elaborate then, as now, but it was otherwise the same. They left it here, at epicentre, on automatic, to broadcast quake data. There was a chair in the centre of the Seismographic Room. I sat in it, waiting for the quake, the same as now.'

Andrek bent forward, fascinated. 'What was the quake like, when it came?'

158

'Rather a big jolt. The Station simply disintegrated. I'm still amazed that I wasn't killed. And then I was in the Deep.'

'And what was it like, in the Deep.'

'For a man unskilled in the ways of patience, the Deep can be a torture. For a very old creature, such as myself, it was – endurable. Still, it would have been better if I had had a companion. A person in the Deep is a disembodied spirit. He can touch nothing. There is nothing there to touch. Yet, he can imagine he touches. He cannot hear or sense his own voice, because he has neither ears nor throat nor voice.'

'But even if someone had accompanied you into the Deep, you would not have been able to communicate with him,' observed Andrek.

'We weren't sure. Our studies showed that there very well might be a type of rudimentary telepathic communication.'

'Then finally,' said Andrek, 'you emerged from the Deep. And you were anti-matter, possessing fantastic powers?'

'Yes. A long time ago.'

'And you still possess these powers?'

'Yes – and no. Because of the ursecta, there can be no nuclear power of any type at the Node. I have been powerless, ever since we entered the Node area.'

'Your force-field, back on *Xerol* – that really emanated from your own body, didn't it?'

'Yes. That was just an extension of my anti-matter/normal matter epidermal juncture. It's good over a distance of several hundred yards. It permits passage through any adverse shield, too, I might add, because the anti-matter field radiates in vibrations exactly perpendicular to normal electromagnetic radiation. You probably remember this from Kedrys' lecture.'

'Yes, I remember. I also remember that fairy-tale you gave me about plugging your force-field apparatus in to the wall-current, back on *Xerol*.'

Iovve smiled. 'I very nearly tripped up on that one, didn't I? Fortunately, you plugged it in just in time.'

Andrek smiled grimly. 'No, I didn't. But no matter. And I gather then, back on the *Xerol*, when I first found you, you weren't really drugged?'

'Again, yes and no. I was paralysed. No doubt of that. Except for my eye muscles, my nervous system was completely occupied in dealing with the alien normal matter circulating in my bloodstream. It was touch and go there for several hours. I very nearly annihilated. Your antidote reacted with the drug to in-

159

crease its vapour pressure, so that I could finally void it through my lungs and dermis. To be anti-matter isn't to be omnipotent; far from it.'

'Can you be killed?' said Andrek curiously.

'Yes, but only if I am willing to die. With a little care, there's no force within the Twelve that can do me any real harm. Small amounts of nuclear energy I simply convert to protons at my dermal surface. Energy large enough to tear my body apart I avoid by "fading" part way back into the Deep. But I avoid these foolish contests. The best defence is to hide what I am. It avoids all sorts of problems.'

'Suppose I had not been able to persuade the Arbiters to stay the destruction of Terra? What would you have done?'

'Probably nothing. I am powerless here at the Node. It would mean that Ritornel has failed. Five centuries of planning would have been wasted. All my colleagues are now dead. No one would be left to help me. But we need not speculate. Terra is here, ready to enter the Deep, when the quake comes.'

'And now,' said Andrek, 'we come to the one remaining, vital question. Your hominids – male and female. Have you selected them, as individuals, I mean?'

'Of course, Don Andrek. Did you not know?'

'What do you mean?' stammered Andrek. '*Who?*'

'Why Amatar, and you, of course.'

*No thing can freely enter here, nor leave.* – Andrek, in the Deep.

The blood began to leave Andrek's face. 'No!'

'Oh yes! Why do you think we are here! Why do you think I've been telling you all this?' Iovve looked over at Andrek in real concern. 'Don't you understand? It's really quite simple. You will go into the Deep, with the first quake of the diplon. You will come out again with the second quake, and you will then be anti-matter. As anti-matter, you could not possibly marry Amatar. The only solution is for you to use your new powers to take Amatar back with you into the Deep, find Terra, and someday emerge to found a new race, a new universe.'

'Iovve,' said Andrek, shaking his head slowly, 'thanks for the honour. But no thanks. I don't want to be the father of a new race. I'm not the progenitive type. Nor have I any interest in the preservation of civilization. Let civilization take care of itself. And in particular, I have no interest in going into the Deep. From your very brief description, I'm certain I wouldn't like it there. Get yourself another specimen.'

Iovve studied Andrek for a long time before speaking. At last he said, 'Is that your final word?' There was something in his voice that was beyond sadness.

'Yes. I'm very sorry, Iovve, to have it end this way. Stay if you like, but I'm getting out now, while I can.'

'How will you leave?'

'There are three or four couriers waiting to take those Arbiters home. We probably wouldn't even have to stowaway. They'd have to take us as distress cases.'

'They are all gone. All ships are gone. We are alone in the Station.'

Andrek's eyes widened. 'Impossible!'

'Call the desk.'

'That wouldn't mean anything. You saw the clerk leave.' Andrek strode over to the door and opened it. There was no sound in the corridor. The muted background noise of the Station was gone. Absolute silence reigned. 'Oh, no!' he groaned. Leaving the door open, he clacked off down the corridor, across the dim-lit lobby, to the other side of the Station, where the couriers had docked on either side of *Xerol*. His breath hung in frozen clouds around him. The heat had been turned off. And it was becoming harder to breathe. Probably the pressure system had been disconnected, too. And now he saw the loading platform, where only hours before he and Iovve had made their ill-fated entrance to this cursed place.

*Xerol* was gone. He had expected that. He looked up and down the platform wildly. There was nothing. The docks were empty. All tubes were closed. There was no motion anywhere.

His head jerked. There was a sound at one of the loading tubes, so high-pitched as to be barely audible. Rather like a whistle, he thought. He moved quickly up the loading ramp to the outer wall. There, he located the whistle. It was a tiny leak in the valve sealing the loading tube, and air rushing from the Station into the vacuum of space was making a hissing sound. The Station was bleeding to death. His arms drooped. Slowly, he turned and retraced his steps.

It made no sense. He could have got away, yet Iovve had treacherously, cruelly, diabolically detained him until all the ships had gone. The Station would be at the epicentre of the quake. Nothing in it could possibly escape. His body, dead or alive, must soon enter the Deep.

He opened the door to the Seismographic Room and stepped inside.

The pilgrim was sitting where he had left him. But now he was motionless, statuesque. Andrek realized that Iovve had now deliberately slipped into his death trance. His life-mission had failed, and his pilgrimage was at an end.

Only – it was not so. Andrek now knew that he was going into the Deep, willy-nilly, and then out again. And when he came out, he would annihilate – unless certain vital surgery were done to his nervous system.

He struck the pilgrim lightly on the cheek. 'Iovve, wake up!'

But the other continued to stare off into some unknown world, immobile, unhearing.

Andrek slapped him – hard.

Iovve groaned, then turned his head slowly towards the advocate. But his eyes were vacant, nearly dead.

Andrek felt along the sides of the seated figure. It was just as he suspected. He began to struggle with the grey robe, and finally got it off over Iovve's head. Some sort of corset was bound over the chest. Andrek unbuckled it hastily and threw it aside. He sucked in his breath. Folded across Iovve's chest were two

162

extra pairs of arms!

In order to merge inconspicuously into the bimanual society of the Home Galaxy, the pilgrim had bound up the four extra arms that would instantly declare his arachnid origins.

As Andrek began to flex and massage the arms, he examined them closely. The whole assemblage was remarkable. The 'elbow' and 'wrist' were bulbous joints which apparently gave a play of several complete revolutions to the hands. And such hands! Each held six fingers, in opposing tiplets. Andrek surmised that this digital structure must have been very useful to Iovve's spider-like ancestors for clambering about their giant webs. In deft rapid motions he stripped the gloves from Iovve's 'normal' hands. As he had suspected, they were similarly contrived. And probably somewhere on Iovve's body was a vestigal spinneret. Small wonder Iovve had held such an exquisite rapport with Raq! Andrek suppressed a shiver and proceeded grimly with his task.

The pilgrim was still weaving his web in the best tradition of his forbears, but with improvements. Being invisible, it was deadlier. And it was a paradoxical web: to save his own life, he, Andrek, the trapped insect, had to awaken the spider.

His attention was drawn again to Iovve's hands. One finger on each was beginning to glow in a rhythmic pattern, corresponding roughly (Andrek guessed) to Iovve's heart beat. As the glow grew brighter, the pulsations levelled out. Iovve's hands had built-in illumination!

And then Andek noticed that one of the fingers was changing shape. It was, in fact, assuming several shapes in succession. First, it grew out into a long thin rod. Then the rod curled into a full loop, and finally the tip became blade-like. Andrek touched the edge of the blade and instantly jerked his finger away and stuck it in his mouth. The knife edge was not only microtome sharp: it was alive. It cut simply by contact, without pressure or motion. And evidently any part of it could be heated – or frozen – at will. This would explain its use as a key to enter the Seismographic Room. In surgery it worked by the light of its opposing finger, while (Andrek imagined) the other fingers of the same hand held hemostats, clamps, and sponges.

And there were six of these remarkable hands! Small wonder that Iovve, physician and surgeon, could pick any lock in the Twelve Galaxies!

He stood back and glared at the pilgrim. Surgeon of Ritornel indeed! And what are you now? Space cabbage!

There was a great deal to be done, and very little time. He had to awaken Iovve, and Iovve must then make certain subtle but basic changes in his, Andrek's, body. If Iovve had come out of the Deep, as anti-matter, without being annihilated, so could Andrek. The friar-surgeon knew how.

But Iovve, apparently determined to bring his long pilgrimage to an end, could not be aroused.

There was one last thing to try.

Andrek found Iovve's medical kit and opened it with trembling fingers. He flipped back to the drug section. Quirinal. Here it is. He jabbed the syringe needle into the rubber stopper and filled the syringe. Two cc.

He came over and shook Oovve.

'Wha —?'

Good! This was some kind of contact. He spoke loudly. 'Quirinal, Iovve!'

'Quir —' muttered the pilgrim.

'Klein circlets,' said Andrek grimly. 'Activate them, the Klein circlets in your body – *now*, or you'll annihilate.'

Iovve blinked owlishly. 'Klein —?'

Andrek screamed at him. 'Iovve! Concentrate! To your system, this is anti-matter. If you're not careful, we're both dead. You'll have to *convert* it to anti-matter quirinal, drop by drop, as it enters your blood stream. Can you do that?'

'Drop by drop.'

'Concentrate, Iovve! Here it comes!'

The pilgrim gasped as the needle jammed into his arm. 'Easy. Awake now. Slowly, slowly. All right, I have it under control. A little faster. Good. Faster still. Stay with it. So you've come to your senses. Good boy. Stay with it. It's working rapidly, quite rapidly. All the rest, now. That's it.'

Andrek's face was wet when he pulled the needle out. He looked at Iovve quizzically.

A change was coming over the pilgrim. His six arms, in opposing pairs, began a strange rhythmic pattern, flexing, unflexing. The fingers were locking, unlocking, as though long strangers to each other. He now stared coldly at Andrek. 'Strip.'

Andrek's heart leaped. 'Of course.'

Iovve jerked his head towards the table. 'Over there. I'll have to stretch you out.'

'Are you going to use an anaesthetic?'

'You might call it that. But don't bother me with your silly questions.'

'Sorry.'

'And don't be humble. You don't know enough to be humble. I'll explain as I work.'

Andrek exhaled heavily, and was silent.

Iovve said, 'A man made of anti-matter has two basic problems. He must avoid contact with normal matter, and he must develop a vastly different metabolism. If he eats an apple – or even breathes – he annihilates. If his nervous system is not drastically modified, he can be safe only while asphyxiating in free fall in a vacuum. So – what must be done to him? It would be fairly simple if we could passivate his entire skin – his available topological surface, and leave it at that. But that would solve only part of the problem. He would then be *too* well protected against contact with normal matter. Some contact is necessary, because his new metabolism is going to be powered by the energy generated at the controlled juncture of his skin with the world of normal matter. In his former world of carbohydrates, proteins, and vitamins, he could sum up his metabolism requirements in terms of fifteen hundred to two thousand calories a day. He still can – but now he converts mass, generally from the dead cells of his epidermis, into the same number of calories, by the ancient energy/mass equation. In a word, our anti-matter man annihilates, but he does it slowly, almost imperceptibly, a few million atoms at a time. He has, if he so will, a half-life of several hundred thousand years.'

Andrek exhaled in slow wonder. 'But how is this accomplished?'

'Surgery. To passivate the skin, we have to make the positron shells around atoms of anti-matter repel the negative electron shells that surround normal atoms. This in itself is not too difficult. It's the same principle that keeps the negative electron in stable orbits around the positive nucleus, in an atom of normal matter, without spiralling inward and annihilating the nucleus. And what is it that keeps the electron from spiralling inward and combining with the nucleus? Simply the fact that it moves in acceptable orbits. It's the same with the anti-matter/ normal matter juncture. Any approaching normal atom is forced into an inert pattern, at the will of the anti-matter man.

'It becomes tricky,' continued Iovve, 'when we have to let a minute number of atoms react – from time to time, and completely at the will and order of our anti-matter man – to provide his daily energy requirements. This requires accurate *voluntary* control of his dermal cells – which normally are involuntary. The change has to be made in his medulla, obviously before he becomes anti-matter. And changes have to be made in the alveoli of his lungs. He will no longer need air as a source of oxygen; yet, if he is to be able to communicate vocally in a normal-matter world, he will need to be able to draw air of normal matter into anti-matter lungs and blow it back out again through an anti-matter voice box. Again, anatomical alteration is required.

'And now we come to the final step. I have to go into your brain. In a word, my boy, you'll have to be completely rewired. It won't hurt – there are no pain sensory endings in the brain, but after it's over, I want you to remain very quiet. Otherwise you might jar loose some of your new circuitry. And of course, for all this, I'll have to put you to sleep.'

Andrek started under the straps.

'No choice,' said Iovve, anticipating his question. 'However, if this works at all, you'll come out of it before the quake hits. And of course if the operation is a failure, you will never know it. So, relax!'

Andrek was perspiring profusely, and his thoughts were chaotic. There was one last thing about Iovve that he had almost grasped, the name that Huntyr had been trying to pronounce as he died. But it kept eluding him, possibly because it was too horrible to accept. Iovve was ... was ...

At this moment he observed, with blank amazement, that several of the surgeon's fingers had apparently passed *through* his skull, as though it were empty space, and were busily involved deep in his cranium.

And then he knew the final identity of Iovve. These hands, which, by his invitation – nay, by his demand – were now in his own brain, were the very hands that had created Amatar and Kedrys.

As he floated out into darkness, he knew. And it was beyond irony. These hands had destroyed his brother.

Iovve was the Master Surgeon.

*The Deep is the Beginning and the End, at once the womb and the coffin of time and space, the well-spring of life and death, the mother of nodes. I was cast into the Deep from the die cup of Alea, and Ritornel is lost in the far eons. I wait, and I think.* – Andrek, in the Deep.

He saw the clock, straight ahead. Gradually, it came into focus, and he recognized it. It had a red hand, and a black hand. It was the quake clock, in the Seismographic Room. The black hand was oddly close to the red hand. He was becoming rapidly orientated. He was still on his back on Iovve's improvised operating table. His head hurt. He put his fingertips gingerly to his forehead, and felt bandages there.

At this sign of life, Iovve stepped over. 'How do you feel?'

'I don't know,' said Andrek thickly. 'Was the operation a success?'

'Yes, I think so.'

Andrek studied the pilgrim morosely. Should he denounce the Master Surgeon for what he had done to Omere? Should he take his vengeance now, within the short time remaining before the quake? He closed his eyes and breathed heavily. It wasn't that simple. This strange creature had given life, long ago, to Amatar, and, just now, to him. And in any case the great overriding immensity of the quake was about to exact its own vengeance.

He said:

'When is the quake due? Or is that still a secret?'

'No, there's no reason for it to be a secret any more. It is due very soon. Within the hour.'

Andrek was now almost indifferent. 'I imagine you're right. But would you mind explaining how you know?'

'By the frequency of the temblors – the harbingers of the quake.'

'But according to the instruments, there hasn't been a temblor in days,' demurred Andrek.

Iovve smiled. 'Of course. Let me explain. For hundreds of years the instruments have recorded each temblor, as well as each quake. There is a time, before a quake, when the temblors come faster and faster, and their vibrations higher and higher. It's like —' He looked about the room. 'Here, let me show you.' Iovve picked up a wooden lath and flexed it several times. 'This will do nicely. Now, we need a stethoscope.' He picked the instrument out of his medical kit and handed it to Andrek. Andrek sat up on the table and inserted the stethoscope plugs in his ears.

Iovve came over to the table and bent the lath into a quarter circle. 'Put the stethoscope bell here, at the centre of the arc, and listen carefully. But when I say "stop", remove the bell instantly. Do you understand?'

Andrek nodded.

'So.' Iovve continued to bend the lath. 'Do you hear anything?'

'Clicks. A lot of them. Faster. Going up the scale.'

Iovve watched him closely, then suddenly was motionless. The lath was nearly a semi-circle. 'And now?'

Andrek looked at him blankly. 'No sound. Nothing.'

'Stop!'

Andrek jerked the stethoscope away.

The lath broke in half with a loud crack.

Andrek stared mutely at the other.

'Don't you see the analogy?' said Iovve gravely. 'The lath loses elasticity just before the break. The component fibres disintegrate, slip, and slide. For a brief interval there is no further audible evidence of stress. Then, at the break area, the structure collapses altogether. It is the same with the quake. The long silence is the prelude, the last thing before the great break.'

Andrek sat down heavily. 'And that was why everyone was in such a hurry to leave. They all knew the exact moment, didn't they.' It was not really a question.

'Yes.'

'I suppose the period of silence is fairly precise, then,' said Andrek.

'To the minute,' said Iovve calmly. He leaned forward. 'If we might go on to other matters, there is something which, until now, I have not been able to discuss with you. Your brother. You know now, of course, that I am the Master Surgeon.'

'I know,' said Andrek bleakly. 'And I remember where I first saw you. It was when I was a boy. I came to get Omere at a bar. The Winged Kentaur. I met you there. It was you, even though you wore a hood over your face. But I remember the eyes, the blue lights.'

'Yes. It was only a couple of days later that Huntyr brought Omere in to surgery.'

'And there you did an evil thing,' said Andrek quietly. 'I am very glad you are about to die.'

Iovve shrugged. 'I have lived too long to be greatly concerned with good and evil. These are concepts peculiar to the hominid ethos, and alien to me. I had known the sex of the blastula that became Amatar almost from the first, even before the Regent demanded that Omere be converted into Rimor. If I had refused the Regent, I would have been banished from the Great House, and I would not have been able to follow the growth of the girl-foetus. And that was unthinkable, for this was the Sign. I had waited for it for centuries. I had to stay. But completely aside from this, I think it might be fairly argued that I did a great service for your brother.'

'How so?'

'From a combination of dissolute living and a lung disease, he was slowly dying. I saved his life.'

'By killing him?'

'That depends on the definition of existence. Certain portions of his cerebrum survive in the computer. By his own view, he lives.'

'But you did not get his consent. You did not give him a choice. He might have preferred to die.'

'True. He did want to die. But under the circumstances his wishes were irrelevant.'

'Then it was murder.'

'Was it? He disappears as Omere; he reappears as Rimor.'

'No. The Omere that disappeared is not the Rimor that reappears. Where is Omere's heart? His arms? How can he smile? His body is dead.'

'He is not dead. He is immortal.'

'He was slain by immortality.'

Iovve sighed. 'You are so involved emotionally that you cannot reason. But perhaps your feelings reason for you. And perhaps, if I were hominid, I too would feel one of your strange hominid emotions. Which one, I'm not sure. Regret, is that the one—? No matter. I would like to point out a possibility to you. What remains of Omere can, I think, be saved, but the price is high, for the human ego is a most fragile thing. Would you be willing to accept into your mind that of another? Could either survive? At minimum, it would mean the loss of your own identity as James Andrek, and this, of course, might be impossible for you or any other hominid. Yet, I mention it.'

Andrek understood nothing of this.

Iovve peered at him, speculating. 'You hominids are sometimes beyond comprehension. At the moment, Don Andrek, you rail silently, helplessly, against your fate. And yet you are to serve as the doorway to the future. It is I who have opened this future to you; yet, next to Oberon, it is I whom you hate most. Perhaps you can find some small comfort in this, that the instant I die, you will be reborn.'

Andrek let his breath out slowly. What could he say? There was nothing to say. 'How long, now?' he asked softly.

'Very soon. In seconds. Watch the ceiling clock. When the red hand coincides with the black. . . .'

Andrek flicked a glance upwards at the time-disc and made a quick estimate. About thirty seconds. It was curious. He had watched Iovve setting that clock, foretelling this climax, now bare seconds away. If he had only realized this in time, he could have escaped. But now he felt nothing, not even anger at himself for being a fool. He murmured under his breath. 'Omere, I am so sorry.'

Iovve looked up. 'You said . . .?'

But Andrek could not have replied, even had he willed, for he sat on the edge of the table in paralysed awe, watching a luminous blue circle form about the head of the Founder of Ritornel.

The halo grew rapidly, and soon completely enveloped the pilgrim. It throbbed with a strange iridescence.

And thus, thought Andrek, does the quake announce its coming, by the gift of transfiguration to him who has made the journey, and kept the faith, albeit, only his own faith. (But what other kind is there?)

The developing quake was drawing away the ursecta. Iovve was becoming nuclear again.

Omega had found the pilgrim.

In one instant the deadly quiet suddenly deepened, and then in the next the entire universe seemed to explode within Andrek.

He was seized, his body spread-eagled by the titanic embrace of space-time, and instantly he was cracked like a whip. All this was done to him in the briefest instant, amid a convulsive monstrosity of movement, but without pain.

And then it was over, and he was alone, floating in blackness. He could not see his hands in front of his face, and when he attempted to touch his cheeks with his fingertips, he made no contact. Shaken, he tried to find his chest. It was futile. He clenched his jaws in anxiety, only to realize he had no teeth, jaws, skeleton, or body. He had no sensory perception whatever. He could not call out, because he had no vocal chords.

He was a tiny speck of intellect floating aimlessly in eternity, existing only (he thought wildly) because he remembered that he was once a human being, once ensconced in a responsive three-dimensional universe that had once acknowledged his existence.

The tides of time closed over him.

He was adrift in the Deep.

*It is not possible to explain complete solitude. No one can know who has not been in the Deep. While I was there, several things finally became clear. And some did not. If ever I escaped from the Deep, my first concern would be Omere. I did not know what to do about Amatar. It was unthinkable to take her back into this place of gloom and non-existence. No, there would be no Ritornel. It pleased me a little to think that Iovve's great plan would be thwarted. On the other hand, if I ever did emerge from the Deep, I would be anti-matter, and I could never marry Amatar.*

*Meanwhile, the Deep had to be endured.*

*In the beginning, it was not unpleasant. To be the only thing in the Universe is to be the Universe. And to be able to remember everything, second by second, whenever one likes, can be very gratifying. And so I remembered my tenth birthday. My brother's poetry premiere in the Great Theatre of Goris-Kard. My first day at the Academy. Poroth. An evening with Amatar. And then comes the terrible part. When I am halfway through, I remember that it isn't the first time I have remembered. No, not the first ... nor the second ... nor the hundredth. And after the memories, come the meanings, the symbolisms, the variations. And when I remember that these are repeating, the hallucinations begin.*

*But it had to go on. Because of the fear. Fear that if I ever stopped thinking altogether, I could not begin again, and I would cease to exist. For what would there be to start me again? No one else was there with me. No stimulus existed in that place, nothing to awaken me, nothing to provide continuity, saving only the remembrance of my last thought. But this could not go on, not this way. If this be eternity, yet let there be order in it. So I repeated all the memories of my life. Every day of that life, every hour, and every minute ... everything that I could remember ... right up to the quake. To each completed recollection of my life, I gave a number. And when I remembered my life all over again, I gave it the next higher number. And then the next higher. Again, and again. In this way I repeated my life to the number of eight hundred and forty-six thousand, nine hundred and four. And then I seemed to remember that I had done all this before, and that once the number had exceeded one million before I had forgotten everything and begun again. And even as I was preparing to start once more, the second quake of the diplon came. – Andrek in the Deep.*

At the ninth hour of the fourth day after his departure from the Great House, Andrek appeared within the Music Room.

The manner of his coming was never subsequently explained by the Guard. No one had seen him enter. No shield line was touched. No force was used. It was as though he had somehow materialized from nowhere.

Andrek's eyes swept the little auditorium. The place was silent, empty. As his gaze came back to the console, a voice came from the overhead speakers.

'Who's there?'

'Hello, Omere. It's Jim – I'm back.'

There was a moment of silence. Then the voice again, believing and unbelieving: 'Jim-boy! You made it! They didn't kill you!'

The effect of this simple question on Andrek was astonishing, even to him. He had not heard his brother's voice in eighteen years, and not since boyhood had he heard this term of affection from his brother. And now this greeting came from a near-inanimate thing of printed circuits and transistors, with just enough bits and pieces of the original Omerean cerebrum to cast doubt on the identity of the whole assembly. Without volition, a low anguished moan arose in Andrek's throat, a sound so despairing that it made his own hair stand on end. He choked it off abruptly.

'Jamie? What did you say?' asked the console.

Andrek got control of his voice. 'Yes, I made it. They tried to kill me. But I got away.'

'But Jamie, you can't stay here. If they find you, they'll kill you on sight.'

'I'm going to stay.'

'You're – going – to stay?' The voice was hoarse, wondering.

'Yes.'

'Well, then, Jim-boy . . .?'

'Still here, Omere.'

'I can hardly hear you. Can you turn up the volume a little?' The voice held a hysterical edge.

'Of course. Which knob?'

'The black one, lower right, clockwise, about six turns.'

Andrek's hand was on the knob, and turning, when an urgent voice burst from the doorway.

'Jim! Stop! That's the oxygen line for the neural plasma! You'll kill him!'

Andrek jerked, then hurriedly reversed the knob. 'Thank you, Amatar.'

The girl entered the room and walked towards Andrek. She then noticed the pale blue radiation surrounding the man. Her eyes widened, and she looked at him questioningly.

'No closer, Amatar,' said Andrek gently. 'We cannot touch – my control is not yet good enough.'

'Jim-boy!' hissed the console. 'You *have* to turn the knob! I *want* you to turn it. It will kill me. I know that. I want it to kill me. You don't know what it's been like. Eighteen years. The brain of a man in the body of a computer. Utter hell. You still have time. A flick of the wrist. You are my own brother. You have to do this for me! If I had knees, I'd be on them in front of you now!'

'Omere, no!' pleaded Amatar.

'Quickly, Jim-boy! I hear guards coming. *The knob!*'

There was the trample of boots in the corridor. Two men in uniform stopped in the doorway behind Amatar, who blocked the doorway. A full patrol, led by a lieutenant, joined them within seconds. Looking through the doorway, he saw Andrek. The officer's hand started towards his biem holster; but then he changed his mind. 'Mistress Amatar,' he called out, 'the sergeant will escort you back to your apartment.'

'No,' said the girl flatly.

The young man sighed. 'Very well.' He pressed a little black plate at the side of his throat and seemed to talk into the air. 'Captain Vorial? Lieutenant Clevin. Sir, the patrol is here with me, just outside the Music Room. James Andrek is inside. The Mistress Amatar is blocking entry. Sir? Yes, sir, it's impossible if you say so, sir. Nevertheless, it's either Don Andrek or his twin. Yes, sir, I will hold.'

'Jamie!' cried the console. 'What's going on?'

'I don't really know,' said Andrek, 'but I think the patrol officer has just notified Security that I am here. We should have all sorts of important visitors within a few minutes.'

The console spoke incisively. 'Then you can still make it. Turn the knob, Jim-boy.'

Andrek did not move. He continued to study the console in silence, as though he were penetrating the ornate casing by some supernatural vision and examining the interior.

Suddenly, from the corridor there was the sound of more voices and running feet.

Andrek looked up. The patrol broke its circle, and Oberon stood at the doorway.

The Magister gave one hard look at Andrek; his body seemed to jerk. He hesitated a moment, then stepped into the room. He was breathing heavily. 'Amatar,' he said, 'come with me.' He put a hand on her arm.

The console shrieked. 'It's Oberon! Jim-boy, kill me ... kill me ... *kill me*!' The room burst with wild animal cries that bounded in and out of insane laughter and horrid weeping. 'You didn't do it! You moron! Idiot! Ass! Curse you forever! You are no longer my brother! I spit on you!' The voice died away in a racking wail.

Andrek's face convulsed momentarily in shuddering, massive pain, and then was immobile.

Oberon pulled the girl back through the doorway by brute force. His head snapped towards Lieutenant Clevin. The officer and two guards ran into the room. The men reached out to seize Andrek's arms.

The advocate's body tensed briefly at the contact, and the blue glow was seen for an instant to spread forward and envelope the bodies of the two guards, who then – vanished.

The lieutenant jumped back, cat-like, and drew his biem.

'Don't shoot!' screamed Amatar.

'Kill him!' cried Oberon.

A pale green pencil of light flicked out from the lieutenant's biem. Andrek's chest glowed red for a fraction of a second, but otherwise nothing happened. The advocate watched the officer almost curiously.

Oberon barked: 'He has some kind of body shield. No matter. The room is now isolated with our counter-shield. And the captain is bringing up heavy equipment.'

The lieutenant backed away from Andrek, then bumped into something at the doorway. 'Magister,' he said urgently to Oberon, 'lift the field and let me out.'

'I cannot do that. Andrek might escape.'

Andrek laughed. 'Go ahead, Lieutenant. Here, I'll hold your field open for you.'

The officer stared at the advocate, then tentatively thrust his arm at the doorway. It went through. He lost no time jumping into the corridor.

Oberon was a brave man, but he was not a fool. He started down the corridor, pulling Amatar along behind him. He was stopped by an unseen force; he knew immediately that he had run into some sort of mass field. But it was unlike any he had ever known before – because it was moving, forcing him and Amatar back to the doorway. Yet, it seemed to have no effect on the guards.

Andrek nodded to them both almost apologetically as they were forced into the room. 'The carrier matrix is selective, keyed to your individual electro-encephalograms.'

The Magister was pale. 'Your electronic trickery cannot save you. You have used violent force on my person. How can you possibly escape the consequences?'

'Sire,' said Andrek gravely, 'you do not understand. No force on Goris-Kard, save possibly Kedrys, can now hurt me. But even Kedrys knows that if I am to be destroyed, it must be by annihilation, and that all of Goris-Kard will go with me. However, with you and Amatar in the same room with me, I anticipate no further attempts on my life.'

The console spoke. 'Jamie...?'

'Yes, Omere.'

'What you just said ... would you explain it?'

'Of course. My whole body is anti-matter. I can control the space-time juncture, where my body contacts normal matter here. The consequences are quite remarkable.'

Oberon's mouth trembled. 'I assume then, that there is no practicable way of killing you?'

'I believe that is correct,' said Andrek.

'Don't bother us, Magister,' snarled the console. 'Jamie, does this mean you have made the Klein circuit? That you have been in the Deep?'

'I have been in the Deep,' said Andrek sombrely.

'Alea's Sightless Eyeballs! Then you understand what it is like to be stuck in this – box. And you *can* blow this thing. Nobody can stop you. I'm sorry I talked that way to you, Jimboy. Forgive me.'

'No problem, Omere. But first we must decide the fate of the man who had our father killed in cold blood, and who has done this to you, and who has tried very hard to kill me. What do you recommend?'

'What father would want, I don't know. I know very little about his death. You'll explain it to me some time. For myself, I'm not sure, either. Oh, I have thought about a proper

176

punishment, long and often. It's just that I don't know what it ought to be. If there were only some way to do to him what he has done to me: some way to take away his body, but leave his mind, and keep him that way for a few million years. But who can do it? Where is that other rat, the Master Surgeon?'

'Dead.'

'Pity. I hope it was something painful. Then there's no good answer for Oberon. You'll just have to kill him.'

Amatar gasped. 'No!'

Andrek turned to the girl. 'I will not kill him. Yet, I must punish him, and his punishment shall reflect in some measure what he has done to my father, and to Omere. It is but just.' He addressed Oberon. 'My father would have given his life, for you, or for the service, or for the state, within or beyond his duty. No one needed to ask him. And yet, you did not let him give it. In a moment of pique, you took it. He was entitled to a better death. It is within my power to cause you never again to take a human life, and this I do.'

'What do you mean?' whispered the girl.

'I shall send him into the Deep.' He faced Oberon. 'In a few billion years, these twelve galaxies will be cold and dead, and I long dead with them. A new galaxy will be born at the Node, with many warming suns. Terra shall circle one. Let your hope be this, that you can endure the Deep to find Terra again, and your own sunrise.'

On the girl's face, horror mingled with awe.

'You mean – take him to the Node?'

'No; that is not necessary. The Deep is everywhere. A very thin boundary separates us from it. This boundary is weakest at the Node, where the Deep frequently breaks through to flood the Node with new space. However, by the expenditure of energy, and with some knowledge of space-time, we can break into the Deep from any time-point in the visible continuum.'

'I do not understand,' said Amatar. She continued sadly. 'Yet, I believe you can do what you say. And so, it must come. And I have one favour to ask of you. You must do it for me, in remembrance of what might have been between us.'

'What is that?' said Andrek uneasily.

'My father cannot survive in the Deep, alone. Send me with him.'

Oberon stared at the girl, his usually immobile features in turmoil. Clearly, he grasped the enormity of the fate proposed for him, and he foresaw the solitude of drifting alone on the wastes of eternity, with madness denied him. And yet, clearly he must forbid Amatar to share this journey without end. His vocal chords, diaphragm, and tongue tensed and gathered to pronounce his decision, and his brow knotted with the effort to speak. But he could not speak.

Andrek watched Amatar's pallor deepen.

She dropped to her knees before him. 'I beg you to permit me to go with him,' she said quietly.

'You do not have to go,' said Andrek sadly. 'He has not asked that you go. And the Andreks are too greatly in your debt to permit it.'

'I must go with him.'

'But *why*?' demanded Andrek in despair.

'In all my life I have done nothing, accomplished nothing. And now I have an opportunity to be useful to one I love greatly. You concede you are in my debt. Then pay the debt. Send me into the Deep with Oberon.'

'Hold on!' cried the console. 'Jamie, you can't do that to Amatar! We love her!'

The girl was firm. 'Omere will not need me any more. For life, or death, he has you, Jim. And you know what it is to be alone in the Deep. Oberon my father cannot endure there without human contact. You see, dear friend, I do not reproach you. I plead with you.'

Andrek breathed heavily. 'I would not harm you, Amatar; yet, Oberon must go. If you will go with him, if this is what you really want . . .' His face contorted in indecision. It was ironic. All his new fantastic power, the power that had destroyed him as a human being and which could, with little effort, destroy everyone in this room – this power availed him nothing. It was torment. His brother's wish was first, but if he followed through on that, then Amatar would insist on losing her human existence to follow Oberon into the Deep. She would be on his conscience forever – and he knew he would live nearly that long. This, then, was the cruel stupidity of vengeance. The effects could never be confined exclusively to the guilty. And he realized now how impossible decisions are made. The decision-maker seizes on chance, and hardens his heart to abide by the consequences.

As if in answer to his thought, a flash of golden light caught his eyes, and he turned and saw the Alean die sitting on the table by the console.

Amatar's eyes followed his glance.

178

'Omere,' said Andrek, 'there's a die here, with the "2" facing up. Do you know anything about it?'

'Sure. It belongs to Oberon. Before you left for the Node, Amatar made him roll it, trying to get a favourable number for you. But it came out "2", the sign of the diplon. The worst. It stuck in a crack in the table. Vang insisted that the time would come when it would be rolled again. So they left it there.'

'I submit,' said Oberon, 'that Vang spoke truly, and that the time is now at hand. We must cast again, so that we may know the final word of the goddess.' His chin lifted proudly. 'Yet, I do not plead for intercession.'

Andrek studied Amatar. 'We will roll the die. But understand: Oberon your father goes into the Deep. The die merely determines whether you accompany him.'

'I understand,' the girl said calmly. 'May I cast?'

'On one condition.'

'Which is?'

'That you unscrew the clasp, so that it is mechanically feasible for the die to show a "2". "Two" is an unfavourable number, and would count against your request to accompany Oberon.'

Amatar picked up the jewel, unscrewed the clasp, and dropped the die in the cup. She rolled it out.

'Three,' muttered Oberon. 'The number of pentagons intersecting at an apex. Favourable to Alea, and therefore to Amatar, and to her wish to accompany me.'

Andrek frowned at the Magister. There was something sickening about the man. How could a number be interpreted as favourable, when it would send Amatar into the Deep? But then, in a sudden insight, he understood the man's unreasoning terror of total isolation. Eighteen years ago this man had hunted the krith and risked the quake; Oberon had animal courage. But he lacked (and knew he lacked) the monolithic mental integrity that he would need when imprisoned within his own mind, with no human contact, for eternity. Perhaps, thought Andrek, each of us has his breaking point, beyond which we are helpless cowards, and in our unseeing fear drag those we love to death with us. I understand; yet I do not forgive.

He would have to adjust the rules a little.

'One throw cannot determine,' he said flatly. 'A majority is required. The die must be rolled again.' He nodded to Amatar.

The girl cast the die again.

'A four,' said Andrek quickly. 'A number unfavourable to Alea, and to Amatar.'

'One for, one against,' said Oberon. 'She must cast again.'

Andrek nodded to the girl.

The next was a five.

'The number of sides in a pentagon face of the die,' said Oberon. 'Most favourable, you will agree.'

'And that's two favourable out of three,' said Amatar.

'Don't let her talk you out of it, Jim-boy,' said the console. 'Figure something out!'

'There is a question,' said Andrek coolly, 'as to whether we should combine the original two throws with these three. As I recall, Oberon, your first throw with this die, eighteen years ago, just before your accident, was a "1". And the second, four days ago, was a "2". Both are unfavourable numbers. The combination of the first two throws with these three would give three unfavourable out of a total of five. We shall combine. And having combined, to remove all doubt, we must continue.'

Oberon glared at him, and sputtered, ' This is unheard of ! '

Amatar simply glanced at him, then cast again. 'Six – favourable – the number of pentagon faces in one-half of the die.'

'Yes,' agreed Andrek smoothly, 'but now, since we have combined, the contest stands at three to three.'

'By *your* rules,' said Oberon acidly, 'the casing will never come to an end. When she rolls again, even if it is favourable, you will think up some reason why it is not.'

Andrek was imperturbable. 'Perhaps. Once more, Amatar.'

A seven.

'Unfavourable,' said Andrek. 'And you have only three out of seven. You lose, Amatar. I therefore deny your request to accompany Oberon into the Deep.'

'You are wrong, dear friend,' said the girl quietly. 'I am winning. Have you noted the sequence? One-two-three-four-five-six-seven. The next will be "8". We are going around the Ring of Ritornel. The god Ritornel rolls the Alean die!'

Andrek snatched the die from her, studied it in momentary disbelief. 'Impossible! Ritornel is a hoax, a fantasy! There is no god of Ritornel!' He rolled it on the table.

'Eight!' whispered Amatar.

Andrek cast again – on the floor.

'Nine!' cried Oberon.

And again.

'Ten!'

Again.

The console sang out. 'Don't tell me! Eleven!'

'Yes,' clipped Andrek. 'It was eleven.' He handed the die to Oberon. 'Cast, Magister!'

Oberon of the Delfieri rolled the die on the table.

Twelve.

After that they passed it around.

Eleven.

Ten.

Nine.

Andrek stopped. It was even as Iovve had predicted. When you create a religion, you must expect that the faithful will take it away from you, and finally, that the imagined gods will become real, and seize you. But then, if the Ring were real, how could the god himself be false? And had all of this really happened before? In each of a myriad past, long dead galaxies, had an Andrek paused in wonder, as he was doing now, to speculate: 'It seems indeed to be the pattern of Ritornel. But if the god is speaking to us, what is he saying?'

'He says "return ... repeat..."' said Amatar.

'How can that be? Neither you nor Oberon have been in the Deep before. This is meaningless.'

'Then it can harm nothing to continue,' said Amatar firmly. She cast the die again.

Eight.

Seven.

Six. Five. Four. Three. Two.

'There is no Alea ... no chance,' intoned the girl, as though hypnotized. 'Everything that is done, has already been done. All that ever has been, shall be again. All that will live hereafter, is dead in the past. So that, James, Don Andrek, however strange and marvellous your powers, nothing that you now do is by your will; you are but the tool of Ritornel, to accomplish that which has already been accomplished, so that the pattern will begin again.'

Andrek laughed shortly. 'If that is true, and I greatly doubt it, it makes absolutely no difference what I shall now choose. Whether you go with Oberon, or not, you seem to think it is done by the will of Ritornel, and not by your will, or mine, and that it is all predestined. Believe this if you like. I will have none of it.' He paused. His eyes caressed the girl's face moodily. 'I would like to decide, by knowing what is best for you. But I do not know what is best for you. I know only what you want. And that, I think I must give you, because now, we can never have one another. You can go into the Deep with Oberon. This is my decision. If this is also the will of Ritornel, so be it.'

'Don't forget *me*,' said the console hesitantly.

'I shall not, Omere. I now attend to you. I want you to relax, and to listen to my voice, and to my thoughts. Save for you and me, motion in this continuum now will cease. You and I are entering a different time plane, because what we are about to do will take many hours. Let sleep descend, so that I can examine thoroughly your neural systems, and understand their operation.' He continued gently. 'In your original cortex were some ten billion nerve cells. But the Master Surgeon did not transfer all of these to the console. Most of the gross motor areas were left behind. You have neither arms nor legs, nor in fact muscles of any kind. Yet your memories are intact – some three hundred billion billion bits of information stored away as twists and alterations in the amino-acid protein chains of your individual neural cells. These are highly proliferated in your convolution of Broca – for motor speech and music, and in the temporal lobe, for visual registry and storage of memory images of words, and in the second frontal convolution for writing; in your parietal and occipital lobes for visual imagery. The circuits take much time to memorize, but I have nearly eternity. Sleep, Omere!'

Andrek straightened slowly, eyes closed.

The full time had passed; the transference, the superimposition of Omere's cerebral networks upon his own cortex was finished. And even though the juncture of minds had been paced and orderly, the real meaning of it finally now began to hit him. He paused to get his breath.

Omere's thought spoke to him: 'I know that I am now in your body. Am I you, or are you me, or – who's who?'

'The question is irrelevant. We are together.'

'Open our eyes, then, Jim-boy. I would like to see Amatar.'

Andrek turned towards the girl.

'And may I borrow your larynx?' said the part of him that was Omere.

'It is yours.'

'Amatar,' said Omere-James, 'how lovely you are.'

'It is the voice of Omere!' she said, wondering. She whirled towards the console. 'How —?'

'My brother and I share this body,' said James-Omere. 'Rimor-Omere sleeps. He will never waken.' He raised his arm towards the console. 'When at night I go to bed, I put three bullets in my head....'

The sharp cracks of three successive explosions shattered the room.

The face of the console fell away, red liquid flowed down the sides. There was a crackle of sparks, and then black smoke billowed out of the casing.

James-Omere winced and clenched his teeth. 'Is it suicide?' he thought. 'Or is it murder. Or mutilation? Or nothing, since there is no corpus delecti?'

'Your legal mind is getting us all befuddled,' thought Omere-James. 'Why give a name to what had to be done?'

There was a sudden commotion in the corridor.

'It is Kedrys,' said Amatar simply.

They looked out through the doorway. The pegasus-kentaur, assisted by Phaera, the Ritornellian priestess, had rolled up a strange assembly of apparatus, dominated in the centre by a massive metallic cone. Phaera adjusted the wheeled platform until the cone pointed squarely at the doorway.

Once, James-Omere caught Kedrys' eyes. A strange smile flickered briefly about the youthful mouth as the two looked at each other. Then Kedrys returned to the levers and knobs of the machine. He seemed in his element, completely poised and confident.

The part of Andrek that was Omere whispered mentally to the part that was James: 'He seems pretty sure of himself. Can he break through?'

'Yes. But I don't think he will. Wait, I think he wants to parley.'

Kedrys called through the doorway. 'Don Andrek!'

'Yes, Kedrys.'

'Let me in, or I'll destroy your field – and you!'

'Do you know what I am, Kedrys?'

'I know. I've analysed your field. You're anti-matter. But I can still kill you.'

'I know you can. And when I annihilate, Amatar dies. And you. And all of Goris-Kard. Do you want that?'

'No. Of course not. But neither do you. So I think you must listen to me, Don Andrek.'

'I will listen to you. But I promise nothing.'

'This machine, Don Andrek, drew you here from the Deep. When the second quake of the diplon cast you out of the Deep, you were brought here, to the Great House. But for me, you might have reappeared in some other galaxy, and centuries away.'

'I know this. Why did you do it, Kedrys?'

'Not for you, Don Andrek. I did it for Amatar and me. The thing that must happen next is our destiny.'

'I do not understand.'

'Let me in.'

'Yes, come in.' Andrek released the shield, and the youth trotted in. He stood by Amatar and folded one great wing around her. He spoke solemnly. 'We came from the same body, she and I, and we are more than brother and sister. Our destinies are inseparable. We began together, and we must continue together. From the beginning, I have known this hour would come. I accept it. Whither she goes, I will go. And now, Don Andrek, your ring is finished. But Amatar and I will seek Terra, in Time, and in the Deep. If we find it, our ring begins. And no hominid that ever existed, not even you, Don Andrek, could possibly imagine the Ring of the Kentaurs.'

James-Omere groaned inaudibly, with a final realization of

the complicated, impersonal futility of revenge and punishment. So now he must imprison yet another innocent with the guilty. And yet none of this could undo the wrongs that Oberon had heaped upon the Andreks. Punishing Oberon now could not be of any possible benefit to anyone, now or in the future. But, great injuries had been done, and he knew time and space could not rest until he had flailed out in vengeance. So he must proceed. To the end of our days, he thought bitterly, we are animals, devouring, and being devoured, and taking our revenge against those who would destroy us, and nothing beyond this is imaginable to our primitive understanding. So be it.

He said: 'All that you say may be true. And any future that you may have may be indeed beyond my imagining. Yet, we are concerned here and now with a very present problem. You propose to go into the Deep with Amatar. I do not ask this of you; yet I am glad that you are willing to go with her. Perhaps with your help she can survive. But it is only for her sake that I permit you to join these two. I do not care what happens to Oberon. And so, Kedrys, I give her into your keeping.' He concluded heavily. 'It would be best if the three of you joined hands.'

Amatar gave Oberon one hand and Kedrys the other.

Cold sweat was gathering on Oberon's face. It dripped from his brow through his eyelashes, and he blinked. 'This is a senseless evil, James, Don Andrek, but get on with it.'

Yes, thought James-Omere. Perhaps it is senseless, and perhaps I am evil. I do not know. And you may be innocent, as the hawk is innocent, and the krith, who slay for survival. Perhaps retaliation cannot alter you, or deter others like you. Nevertheless, I judge you guilty, and condemn you, together with the truly innocent. And if I am skilled in this art, it is because you instructed me!

'We are ready,' said the girl calmly.

Amatar! thought James-Omere. Oh, Amatar.

He raised both arms, and the pale blue radiance flowed out from him and enveloped the little group. They were gone, and it was done.

Andrek stared numbly at the emptiness of the room. He wanted to scream. Instead, he moaned in desolation. 'Oh, purify me!'

Even as the thought formed, he was aware of a novel process at work within his brain. It was a rapid thing, a bombardment of words and groups of words, cadences, concepts.

> *'I'd never hoped to see your face*
> *Even through another's eyes . . .'*

(*He* held you in his arms, Amatar. And now I'm mixed up inside him.)

Music was breaking through with the poetry. First a melody, then counterpoint, and then individual instruments, a voice, tenor, and finally a chorus. And then, as the James part of James-Omere was bound enthralled, the orchestration faded, and yielded to the final lines.

> *'We'll remember that embrace*
> *When you're adrift in sunless skies*
> *O Amatar, farewell!'*

It was over in seconds; but no sound had passed Andrek's lips.

'Thank you, Omere,' thought James Andrek.

'Do not fear for her,' said Omere. 'Kedrys can cope with the Deep. Truly, I think he planned it this way.' There was a pause, then the strange introspection continued. 'What now?'

Idly, Andrek bent over and picked up the golden die. 'We have one more throw, don't we? And suppose it comes out "1", to complete the whole Ring of Ritornel? What would it all mean? That all this has happened before, and that (behold!) there is no new thing under the sun? Should we find out?' He looked through the doorway at Lieutenant Clevin and the Priestess Phaera.

The lieutenant's mouth was open wide, and his face glistened with sweat. His world had collapsed in front of his eyes, and he was numb with awe and fright. Phaera, perhaps better protected by the fatalism and foreknowledge of her faith, looked broodingly through the doorway into the blue-radiant eyes of Andrek. To herself she murmured: 'Who shall foresee the will of Ritornel? And if Ritornel chooses to complete the Ring by uniting saint and chimera, who shall say that he is not altogether wise and just?'

'A girl! A female woman!' breathed Omere-James.

'Not for you, my lusty friend,' reproved James-Omere. 'Remember, we're anti-matter. And have you forgotten Amatar so soon?'

'No, Jim-boy. Not so soon. And not ever.' Andrek's mind began to sing again. It started in a low key, and gathered volume and cadence. 'The great mythbook, whence cometh all things ... whence pegasus, and whence kentaur, and all the fabled wonders. Yes, Amatar, we remember! Can Adan beguile thee from the thunder of the racing hoof, or from the beating of great wings, and visions beyond our farthest seeing? O motherless children, and all that follow thee, enter now into enchantment!'

He paused. 'No, we'll never forget. But life goes on. And after being cooped up in that hell-box for eighteen years, I can at least *think*.'

And now the singing began again in Andrek's head. Poets ... proctors ... singers ... shysters ... ladies ... loves. It's a big universe, little brother. Somewhere, there's an anti-matter galaxy, and anti-matter girls awaiting. Maybe it *has* all happened before. But it hasn't happened to *us*.

He tossed the die carelessly over his shoulder and burst into song.

> '*A barrister-bard from Goris-Kard*
> *Set forth in search of a dame.*
> He *liked them wild,* he *liked them tame.*
> *Both liked —*'

Lieutenant Clevin and Phaera listened in vain for the end.
The Music Room was empty.

*No man is so fleet that he can outstrip his fate, nor strong
enough to seize another's. –* A Rede of Ritornel.

*No destiny is certain; that which is given, is taken away.
That which was to be, will not be. –* An Axiom of Alea.

Phaera rushed into the room and scooped up the die.

The lieutenant cried out in alarm.

She called back. 'It's safe, Clevin. Come on in.' She looked at
the die, and then she smiled.

'Was it a "1"?' demanded the lieutenant. 'Is the Ring complete?'

Phaera covered the die with her hand, and looked up serenely.
'In our ancient racial consciousness, going all the way back
(some say) to our Terran ancestors, there is a myth of creation,
where Ritornel took the first man from the Deep, and then
created woman from his body, even as Amatar drew life from
the rib of Oberon. So if I say to you, it was a "1", you will say
that it was inevitable, because the great Ring must be repeated,
as is foreordained.'

The lieutenant had by now recovered much of his reason, and
some of his courage. 'Since Amatar came from the body of
Oberon, the cycle is now repeated, as it was in the beginning,' he
said. 'For it is not events that determine Ritornel, but Ritornel
that determines events. To complete the Ring, it had to be a
"1". Therefore it was a "1". There was no other possibility.'

Phaera laughed at him wickedly. 'There was a second possibility.'

The lieutenant's eyebrows arched. 'What do you mean? I see
only Oberon and Amatar. What is the other alternative?'

'Kedrys and Amatar.'

The lieutenant's face showed his shock. 'But that's insane. It's
even . . . *bestial*!'

A sensual smile played around the mouth of the priestess. She
appeared to consider the problem. 'All men are bestial. But
Kedrys is not a man. Yet, in a sense, you're right. Admittedly,
even now, *she* is not nearly *his* equal, either mentally or physically. But when Kedrys reaches full maturity, and faces the fact
that Amatar is the only female on the planet Terra, he may be

inclined to overlook her deficiencies.'

For a long, silent moment the lieutenant did not seem to understand. Then he came to life abruptly. 'The die!' he cried. 'It will tell! If the Ring is complete, and Oberon and Amatar are the next ancestral couple, the die will show a "1". But if it's to be Kedrys and Amatar, then the Ring is broken, and it would be some other number. What *was* the number?'

Phaera laughed in great glee and tossed the golden jewel to him. 'Number? There are Twelve. Take your choice.' She sauntered past him towards the corridor. 'I only wish I could be there to see the children!'

# Other Panthers For Your Enjoyment

## Science Fiction and Fantasy

☐ H. P. Lovecraft         **AT THE MOUNTAINS OF MADNESS**    25p

A great collection of sinister and uncanny tales for connoisseurs of terror.

☐ H. P. Lovecraft         **THE CASE OF CHARLES DEXTER WARD**    25p

A short macabre novel by the 20th century's undisputed master of horror.

☐ Keith Roberts         **PAVANE**    30p

An alternative universe in which 20th century England is still under the grimly reactionary rule of the Roman Church. 'His blend of telling detail, gripping story line and pure exalted fantasy is little short of miraculous' – *Tribune*. 'Brilliant' – *SF Review*

☐ Roger Zelazny         **LORD OF LIGHT**    40p

'A triumph' said the *Magazine of Fantasy and Science Fiction*. 'A rare work of SF imagination' added the *Sunday Telegraph*. And the final accolade – the Hugo Award. In an era yet to come and a planet far distant from this one a group of way-out men and women, backed by a powerful technology that makes ours look primitive, take over the role of the ancient Hindu pantheon.

☐ Roger Zelazny         **THE DREAM MASTER** 25p

A mind-stretching story of a lonely voyager's nightmare journey into the infinity of inner space. By a master of contemporary SF.

☐ John Blackburn         **CHILDREN OF THE NIGHT**    30p

A pothole on the Yorkshire moors and an ancient race emerging from it to once more – after eons of time – take its 'rightful' place on Earth's surface – 'rightfully' meaning that humans go to the wall. One of the eeriest thrillers published in years. John Blackburn is streets ahead of all his competitors in this field.

Obtainable from all booksellers and newsagents. If you have any difficulty please send purchase price plus 7p postage per book to Panther Cash Sales, P.O. Box 11, Falmouth, Cornwall.

---

I enclose a cheque/postal order for titles ticked above plus 7p. a book to cover postage and packing.

Name_____

Address_____